ESCAPE TO PARADISE ISLAND

TRISH OLLMAN

DEDICATION

This book is dedicated to my wonderful husband Ian Ollman who always knows exactly what to do. Also to my darling granddaughter Jade Ollman, who I love to the moon and back.

Books by Trish Ollman:

'Escape to Paradise Island' – A Novel

'A Girl from Birkenhead' – An Autobiography

'Dear Alice' – Wartime Letters from a Soldier to his Wife.

All available on Amazon and KDP

ABOUT THE AUTHOR

Trish Ollman has been married to Ian since she was 16, and had 2 children by aged 17. She spent the first 21 years of her life in Birkenhead, Merseyside, UK and emigrated to Australia when she was 21 and had 2 more children. Trish and Ian now live in Canberra, Australia.

CHAPTER 1

PARADISE ISLAND

Imagine if you will, a Tropical Paradise so beautiful, you may never want to leave. Surrounded by the bluest of blue Ocean, with a backdrop of souring mountains, palm trees, and the singing of native birds and wildlife. Thatched chalets, some lining the shoreline, others set in amongst the rainforest, and all with little suntrap balconies for sunbathing or just relaxing. The air invades the senses of the nose with the large, colourful frangipanis, fragrant smelling lilies, and the luscious scents of honeysuckle and jasmine and other tropical flowers that invade the Island Resort. A week here will cost you as much as going to Bali or Fiji for the week, but the Island is known locally as 'The Love Island' because of its beauty and tranquility. You can partake in everything it has to offer, or do nothing at all. It also doesn't allow children under the age of eighteen, which makes this the perfect place to either come and renew your love, or to just find it. Welcome to Paradise Island.

Situated 27 kilometres east of Mackay, in the Northern Tropics of Queensland, Australia, Paradise Island is visited by over twenty thousand people a year. Having couples or singles each week on the Island can make for a different mix every time. Most visitors arrive at Mackay, the nearest mainland point, by plane, although those more ambitious take their car and leave it in the long stay car park at Mackay Airport. From Mackay, there are two modes of transport to Paradise Island: by boat, or, for a fair bit extra, by helicopter. Once on the Island, you are escorted to a Reception building and given your chalet number and key, along with a comprehensive list of all of the Island's activities, meal times and rules, admittedly though, these are very few. Once you get to your chalet, and maybe you are one of the lucky ones with a chalet that looks out directly onto the beachfront, you can unpack and read the information pack given to you at the Reception. The long list of activities often surprises most. Things as diverse as Archery, Cocktail Making and Tasting, Karaoke, Scrapbooking Classes, Craft, a 9-hole Golf Course, 2 swimming pools, one fresh water, and the other salt. Mountain walks, Candlelit Dinners, a Moonlight Champagne Cruise (always popular), Snorkelling, Jet Skis, Canoeing, Speed Boating, a small Gym and a Beauty Parlour. Each evening in the Entertainment Lounge, there is a different show, maybe a singer or a Group, and dancing. There are even fun and games such as Trivia Nights, and different Card Games. What about winning or losing a few dollars in the Casino, or catch one of the latest movies in the Island's own luxurious cinema?

Most of the women can't resist a visit to the Beauty Salon, with its Spa and Sauna. There is also a small infinity pool and lots of soft and comfy lounges on which to relax. There are enormous white robes, fluffy white towels and comfy slippers for the Guests' comfort, and in the changing rooms are baskets of many varied and expensive toiletries and perfumes, where the women, and the occasional male, can pamper themselves. Panpipe music drifts through the air and it is a place few want to leave. However, if all of this is too much for you, just grab yourself a beach chair or your towel, and lounge on the sand or by one of the pools. Most guests never know where to start. Soon it's time for lunch. The large restaurant is situated high up on the first floor of a big modern glass and steel building, with an open side looking out onto the Ocean. Perched on the balcony are many tropical birds of all colours; blues, reds, greens, and purples, all chirping away and waiting for their opportunity to flit across to a just vacated table and pick at the leftovers. Lunch here is a 'Help Yourself' affair. The tables are bare, polished wood, with small vases of tropical flowers in the centre of each. There are soups, cold meats, potato salad, prawns, oysters, green salad, and different breads, followed by cheesecake, chocolate brownies, rich chocolate cake and French meringues. Naturally tea and coffee are in abundance. Wine is also available, by the bottle or the glass, Red or White, House or Speciality.

Then it's back to the chalet to put on your swimmers, with a sarong or sundress for the ladies, and board shorts, or occasionally Speedos or Budgie Smugglers, for the more confident men. A lot of times, sunscreen is forgotten in the rush to get out and start your countdown of activities, and there's many a sunburnt body by the end of the day. Many guests, hot and bothered from the journey from wherever they've originated from, and the humidity that is the hallmark of North Queensland, head straight for one of the pools or the beach. Books are taken out, beach towels in all colours are laid out on the sun lounges or hammocks, then, to the swish and sway of the palm trees and other vegetation, you can relax. But wait! Why relax when there is so much to do. The men might want to have a go at Archery, while the women may head straight to the Craft Project class at 2pm. You might make a mental note that the Snorkelling Lesson is on at 4.30pm at the Snorkel Hut on the beach, and arrange to meet up for that, or, as do most of the older visitors, stay on your sunbed with your book, only to break off every hour or so to have a quick dip in the pool or the Ocean, a few steps away. Snorkelling starts at 6pm. That is when the tide is low and the fish plentiful, and most people are game for what is often their first experience. With snorkelling mask and large black flippers on, they straddle to the water's edge and go in, mostly to chest height. Some people's first sighting of fish swimming so close to their legs and feet is too much, and they rush out laughing and screaming, but most people love it. This is what holidaying is all about. And what better place to do it all than at Paradise Island.

Back to the chalet for a quick shower and a change into evening dress, then it's up to the Restaurant for that candlelit dinner. This time waiters serve it up in smart black and white uniforms. The satin white walls shimmer under a dozen small chandeliers, sending shadows hiding in corners around the room. Covering the tables now are fine, pure white linen tablecloths. A candle, inside a cut-glass container, flickers across the dim, mood lit room. The menus, printed on parchment in Italic gold writing, seem to offer an endless and varied selection, but it doesn't matter what you chose. You've got seven nights here, so plenty of time to enjoy all of what's on offer. There are three courses from a top renowned chef, with wines to go with them. Choose from Giant

ESCAPE TO PARADISE ISLAND

Balmain Bugs, Prawns, Barramundi, Lobster, Scotch Fillet or T-bone Steak, with all the accompaniments. Choosing what to have, and your wine to go with it, is the hardest thing you'll do all day.

Afterwards, you can retire to the Piano Bar or the Games Lounge to wait for the nights' entertainment to begin, or just relax and sample some of the Island's specialist cocktails. For entertainment, there is something different on each night. The Entertainments Manager, Theo, will make sure everything goes to plan. For those who like a late night, it's back to the cocktail bar for some cocktails you've never even heard of, with the promise of a Cocktail Making class the next day and maybe spend some dollars at the Casino. Finally, tired out from your first day on Paradise Island, you make your way back with a slow, leisurely walk in the balmy, fragrant warm evening air, accompanied by the sounds of the cicadas, and scurrying small creatures, to your chalet, and retire for the night. Sound good? Get yourself here then. Welcome to Paradise Island.

CHAPTER 2

BIANCA

Bianca unlocked the door to the 2 year olds Room in the Child Care Centre, where she worked as Room Leader. She looked at the calm space before her. All the toys neatly in their place, with the books stacked correctly on the tiny bookshelves. Within half an hour or so, it would be mayhem, but for now it was calm. The calm before the storm, she thought. She walked into the little kitchenette that ran off the room and made herself a cup of coffee, then went and sat on one of the tiny chairs that were dotted around the room with their little matching tables. Thoughts of her upcoming wedding crowded her mind. In just 3 weeks' time, she and Joel were getting married, but so far, she had only been able to come up with 8 guests on her side and 6 on Joel's. She'd asked her Room Assistant, Taylor, to be her Matron of Honour, so that was sorted, but she had no other family to speak of and very few friends, as she'd only been in Brisbane for a few months. Bianca had been brought up in Canberra, had gone to a Catholic School and failed miserably at her final exams. She did however, go on to do a Diploma in Childcare as she'd always loved children and, when the opportunity arose, had found herself a job at a Child Care Centre on the other side of the City. After finishing school, her life had been good. She had not made close friends in school and she rarely went out, but she was happy.

It had taken her 2 years to get her Diploma in Early Childhood, and during that time she'd shared an apartment with Penny, one of her only friends. They had a good system going between them: one night Bianca would cook while Penny tidied around and the following night they'd swap. Weekends, neither girl did anything, living on take-a-ways when they had the money, or toast with beans or eggs when they didn't.

Bianca dated a few boys, but all were casual and nothing serious ever came from them. Luckily, once she'd got her Diploma, she'd found the job at the Chile Care Centre easily enough. She enjoyed her work there and was eventually made Room Leader. But then disaster struck. Her Mum had died. 10 months earlier she had been diagnosed with bowel cancer and had refused chemotherapy, saying she'd lived a happy life and didn't want to go through 12 months of worse sickness in order to live another few years. Bianca and her father and sister had been furious with her, but in the end, it had been her Mum's decision. As if that wasn't bad enough, her Dad had, within 6 months of her Mum's death, married a horrible woman, Brenda, who Bianca had hated at first sight. And the feeling was mutual. Bianca thought that Brenda had only married her Dad as he had his own house, his own teeth, and a bit of money! Soon a rift between Bianca and her Dad had developed and she hadn't spoken to him in over a year.

She decided that a move to a different part of Australia might be good for her so, after some research and enquiries into jobs and accommodation, she had decided that Brisbane would be a good place to live.

She gave her Notice in at work and packed up what few belongings she had, and moved up there. Bianca had found another job easily enough. Then, after only a month of her moving there, she'd met Joel. After only a short courtship, he'd asked her to marry him and she'd said yes. However, Bianca found that Joel expected her to make all the arrangements for the wedding and seemed to have no interest in doing anything himself. Naturally, she'd sent her father and Brenda an invitation to the wedding but they sent back a polite refusal, saying they had another prior engagement. Bianca, hurt, had vowed never to speak to her Dad again. Her only sibling, Taleah, had been living in London for the last 18 months and couldn't get the time off work, nor afford the airfare to come home for the wedding, and Bianca was really going to miss her sister as Bridesmaid.

Joel was in a similar, although very different situation to Bianca. He was a loner with only a few work mates to invite to the wedding. His family had been torn apart by an alcoholic mother and a father who had sexually abused him and his sister for years when they were children. It had started when Joel was 9 and his sister, Jacqui, had been just 7. One night, after he'd witnessed his mother passed out, drunk, on the lounge, his father had come into his bedroom. They'd talked a bit about footy, and his dad had asked him how he was going at school. Joel found this quite disturbing as his dad had never before come into his room and asked him any questions about how he was going. Without any warning, Joel's dad had put his hand under Joel's quilt and grabbed his penis.

"Got a nice little todger on you there son." He'd grabbed Joel's hand. "Here, feel mine. See how big and hard it is. When you're a man that's what yours will be like. I'll show you what we men like hey." The nine-year-old Joel then had to go through unspeakable things and felt powerless to stop it. And so, it had begun. For years Joel had had at least two weekly visits into his bedroom from his dad. After the first time, Joel, although something told him that this was wrong, found that he didn't have the courage to tell his dad to stop. A few months later, he'd found his sister lying on her bed crying.

"What's up Jacqui?" he'd asked her.

"I'm hurting."

"Where are you hurting?" Joel walked further into his sister's room.

"I'm hurting down there," 7-year-old Jacqui had pointed to her private parts so Joel knew immediately what she was talking about. Joel didn't know what to do, but he knew that what his dad was doing was wrong, to them both, so he decided to do the only thing he could think of, and that was to go and tell his mum. He'd gone to the kitchen to find her, but she was so drunk she could hardly stand. Joel tried to tell her, but his mother wouldn't believe a word he said and slurred at him to stop lying. So, Joel had stopped talking about it and it was never spoken of again, until at the age of 17, he finally found the courage to leave home, taking Jacqui with him.

For a few nights, they'd stayed with one of his only friends from school, and Joel had started looking for a job. Once he'd found one as a hospital porter, he and Jacqui moved into a one-bedroom apartment. But life for Jacqui was too hard after the years of abuse, and she was soon taking hard drugs to numb the pain. She would go missing for days on end, skipping school, with Joel frantically walking the streets looking for her. Sometimes he'd find her, slumped under a bridge with other users, other times he'd just had to wait for her to make her own way home. Eventually she moved in with another drug taking friend of hers and Joel was left on his own. Somehow, and Joel never knew how, but he and Jacqui had lost touch, and now he didn't know where she was, or if she was even still alive.

Life for Joel was hard, but he'd managed to hold down his job at the hospital. He tried, with some success, to forget what had happened at home but he found himself tongue tied when spoken to, and couldn't find it in himself to be sociable. Most would have called him a loner. One day, at the local supermarket, he'd bumped into Bianca in the meat aisle. Bianca had casually said to him how shocking the price of the meat was these days. Joel had mumbled a reply and somehow, they had continued with their shopping, walking side by side down all of the aisles, with Bianca chatting away to him. Joel, being shy and an introvert, barely said a word. After the checkout, Bianca had asked Joel if he'd like to go to the adjacent Café for a coffee. He'd agreed and so had started a very odd coupling. After a while, Bianca always wondered why Joel never attempted to kiss her when they parted, or hold her hand or show any affection to her. One evening, she decided she'd take the bull by the horns and do it herself. Her kiss was little more than a peck on his lips, but Joel seemed to accept it and it became the norm. 3 months later, Joel got official Notice to move out of his apartment, as the owner wanted to move back in himself, so it seemed a natural progression for Bianca to ask Joel to come and stay at hers. She had a spare room, and, at first, Joel had slept in there. But as time went on, their relationship grew and Joel became slightly more confident and comfortable with Bianca. It seemed that even though they had little in common emotionally, they did get on, liking the same TV shows, the same food, and the same movies.

At night, though, it was a very different matter. Joel had next to no libido and only performed when Bianca got so frustrated that he would do so to avoid a row. Joel couldn't really get a proper erection so he and Bianca had found other ways, all distasteful to Joel, to satisfy her. One night, after another failed attempt, Joel had burst into tears, saying how sorry he was and that he'd try harder in future. It was then that he had told Bianca of his past, of the sexual abuse he'd suffered since he was 9 years old, from his father. Bianca was stunned, but then unbelievably angry. She wanted to go to the Police but Joel had insisted, no, he didn't want it all raked up again, and for her to just leave it. Bianca insisted Joel get counselling and he agreed. That night, he'd turned to her in bed and held her hand. He asked her to be patient with him and to try and understand that he did love her, but because of what had happened to him as a boy, he found it very difficult to be a proper man to her. Bianca, crying, told Joel that she loved him so much and that they could find a way to work through their problems. That's when the normally shy and reluctant Joel asked his beautiful Bianca to marry him.

Now, with only minutes before the children were due to come into the Child Care Centre at the start of the day, some holding shyly onto their mother's hands, others bombarding their way in to get to their favourite toy, Bianca felt a sadness overtake her. She'd always wanted a big wedding but now there were just going to be a few guests there. Now, with the onslaught of tiny children arriving, all thoughts of the wedding were forgotten. After a busy day, Bianca made her way home only to find Joel was, for once, home first. He was sitting on the lounge eating a plate of beans on toast. Deep-rooted anger and frustration stirred in her.

"Couldn't you have made us something decent for dinner? It's always me who makes yours. You could have at least made an effort with something nice. We're getting married in 3 weeks Joel, or have you forgotten? You're really going to have to make more of an effort you know." Bianca slammed into the kitchen and made herself some scrambled eggs. Sitting in front of the TV later, she was still frustrated and angry with Joel. She looked at her watch. 6.30pm, that would make it 7.30am in the morning in London. She felt an overwhelming need to talk to her sister, who she knew would probably be up and getting ready for work. She dialled the number and Taleah answered on the fourth ring.

"Hey Sweets. It's me. I didn't wake you, did I?"

"Bianca? What time is it?" Taleah spoke through her sleep muddled brain.

"Oh, my God. I haven't woken you up have I?

I thought you'd be up and getting ready for work." There was a short pause while Taleah woke up properly. "I've got the day off Bea. What's up?" Bianca let out a huge sigh.

"It's nothing really. I just wish I could kick a bit of life into Joel. He's driving me nuts and we're not even married yet!"

"Are you sure you even want to marry him, Bea? You two seem like chalk and cheese to me in the bedroom department. What makes you think you can live a Happy Ever After life?" Taleah was always quick to admonish her sister. Bianca had told Taleah of their problems in the bedroom and said that Joel kept putting off getting counselling.

"Isn't sex one of the greatest parts of being in love? It can't be much fun if you have to force him all the time. I know he's got issues with his past but that's why you need to insist that he has counselling. You can't go on like this!"

Bianca heard the frustration in her sister's voice and felt a panic in her stomach. Taleah was right, of course. They couldn't go on like this. But what Joel needed was time and understanding. There was no doubt in her mind that she loved him and wanted to be his wife but they had to get this sorted out. Taleah had been right. Sex was a big part of a marriage.

"OK my darling sister. I'll let you get back to sleep and ring you at a more reasonable time at the weekend."

"OK. Speak to you then Bea. And remember, counselling!"

Bianca had bought a mid-calf length, off-white dress with little pearl buttons sewn onto the bodice. Taylor had a beautiful dusky pink dress, which perfectly matched Joel's tie, which he was to wear with the first suit he'd ever owned in his life – he was usually in board shorts and tee shirts when not in his Porters uniform. He'd got one of his colleagues as his best man so everything was organised. They were having a small Reception in a Private Room of the local Club. Then there was the Honeymoon. At first Bianca had thought that a Honeymoon would be a waste of money, something they didn't have a lot of. But when she thought about it, she'd realised it might do Joel good to go somewhere warm and sandy and relaxing. A change of environment, that's what he needed. The following day, she'd seen an advert in a magazine. It showed a glossy picture of a beautiful Island with palm trees and a beautiful sandy beach, with the words,

'COME TO PARADISE ISLAND AND LEAVE YOUR CARES BEHIND. LET LOVE BLOSSOM. NO CHILDREN UNDER 18 ALLOWED. 7 NIGHTS FROM JUST $1,299. ALL MEALS AND ENTERTAINMENT INCLUDED.'

There was a phone number and an email address, but it was the words 'Let Love Blossom' that had caught her eye. Maybe, just maybe, Joel could let go of his inhibitions in such an environment. At least they could try. She dialled the number and booked them a week there and then.

CHAPTER 3

ANNA

Anna opened her eyes and tried to think what day it was. Sunday? Yes, it was Sunday. She'd slept well, thanks to her 2 magic pills she'd taken the night before. Anna had always had problems with not being able to get to sleep. Her mind was always filled with the day's events, or what was happening in her life, or should that be her 'non-life' she thought. A few years ago, her doctor had given her some pills to take at night and, like magic, they worked. At first, they'd made her feel all groggy the next morning, but as time went on that stopped and she was able to wake up and face the day ahead. So today was a Sunday. The thought struck Anna that for her, it was just another day. She'd given up her part time job a few months ago in a moment of dark depression. She had a lot of depression these days. Today, she would, as always, stay at home, while Ken went out to Golf or to the Club, or any of his other usual haunts. Anna looked across at him, still sleeping. For 64, she supposed women would still find him a very attractive man. His hair was not quite grey, apart from at the sides, but his stubble around his chin was darker. He had piecing blue eyes and a long Roman nose. However, Anna now no longer found Ken attractive or even appealing, as she once had. She knew that for at least the last ten years, Ken had been having affairs. There had been give-away signs of him smelling of perfume or cigarette smoke (neither of them smoked) when he came home from long hours away, but in the early days, on more than one occasion, Anna had looked at Ken's phone while he'd been in the shower. She'd seen explicit text messages from different women, all saying pretty much the same thing, telling him how good he was in bed, and also

'Can't wait till we are together again' or 'Promise me that you'll leave her so that we can be together?' They were all the same. After reading the first message years ago, Anna had gone into their bedroom and cried and cried. Then she'd got angry. But for some reason, she'd never confronted Ken. Ever. She was too afraid of losing him, even though she didn't know why.

Life for them both went on as though nothing was wrong. Ken worked as an Insurance Rep and had a pretty easy life. Anna did everything for him, acted as his housekeeper, not his wife. Looking at him now, sleeping, she didn't really know if she still loved him, or if she even found him attractive anymore. She didn't think so. She couldn't remember the last time they'd had sex, and had accepted years ago that she wasn't enough for him. They had so little in common and she knew he didn't find her attractive either. He made that very clear. He had a very high sex drive, where she had almost none. They were lucky to make love once a year and it was always over with very quickly, with a clumsy fumble, then the sex itself when Ken was drunk, and Anna had lay back thinking what to have for dinner the next day. Ken had stopped telling her he loved her many years ago and she never expected it to start happening again any time soon. Ok. Sunday. What could she do today?

Ken had just finished his breakfast. He'd had the same thing every morning for years, 4 Weetbix with milk. He wondered which excuse he would give Anna today. Playing golf with Geoff maybe? Or he could say he was going to Manly for the day with a few mates. Living in Sydney gave him so many places he could say he was going to. It didn't really matter anyway. She never questioned him. That was one of the reasons he stayed with her. He could do whatever he wanted and never get a peep out of her. She made his meals, cleaned the house and made sure his clothes were always ready for him to wear. But, oh, she was a grump. And dowdy. No life in her at all. Ken thought she was too old before her time. She certainly wasn't the woman he'd fallen in love with all those years ago. She made his life easy, that's why he stayed. Plus, she'd really let herself go. She must weigh over 100 kilos at least, he thought. And why didn't she do something with her hair. It was a mixture of brown and steel grey streaks, shoulder length and very thin. He'd told her to get it cut and coloured, like he knew many of his lovers did, but she never did more than go for a trim. Ken had lost count of the number of different women he'd had affairs with over the years. They'd all flattered him, told him how good-looking he was, how good he was in bed. His sexual prowess was his speciality. He could have them screaming for more and he loved it. He loved the power he had over a woman. People say that sex is over rated but to Ken it wasn't.

He had to admit he had a certain type. They had to be no more than 35 – 45 years old. Hair colour didn't matter, but it had to be at least shoulder length so he could grab it and pull it back during sex. A woman also had to have a good-sized pair of tits, as he liked to suck on them like a baby, and massage and tweak the nipple to turn his women on. He wasn't a gentle lover by nature so they had to like a bit of rough as well, and if they wanted something a bit different, well, he would certainly oblige. Today Ken was meeting his current lover, Ruby, in Centennial Park. She was bringing a picnic lunch for them and then they'd go back to her place, where they would shag for the rest of the day. Ruby liked it rough, as did Ken, so they were the perfect match. He'd met her in a bar one night and bought her a drink. At closing time, he'd gone back to her place. At first, he'd been gentle with her but as her lust grew she'd asked him to do things that Anna wouldn't have done in her wildest dreams. She'd wanted it in every conceivable position and she enjoyed every moment, as he knew she would. They'd had sex until the early hours when he'd crept home to find Anna fast asleep on her side of their bed. He'd been going with Ruby now for about a month, and hoped to go with her for many more months to come, as she certainly fulfilled all of his desires. It didn't take him long to make his decision. He'd tell Anna he was going to meet his mates in the Pub at Manly for the day. Yes, that's what he'd do, he thought, as he finished his Weetbix.

Anna had picked up her Crossword Book and was trying to concentrate on it. Ken had long gone to Manly, if indeed that's where he was going, and it was almost lunchtime. Anna and Ken had only one child, Millie, who was 37 and married to Brock. Millie and Brock had Anna's gorgeous little grandson, Milo, who she adored. Millie lived in Moss Vale, about an hour away from her parents, and she visited her mum regularly. A few years ago, in a moment of immense sadness and intimacy, Anna had confided in Millie about her Dad's affairs. At first Millie had wanted to confront him and kept telling her Mum to leave him, but Anna remained adamant that Millie say nothing and let life go on as normal. Millie could hardly look her Dad in the eye, nor barely speak to him for a long time but gradually things had returned back to normal. From then on, Millie was Anna's only ear to listen to. Anna put down the Crossword Book and picked up her phone and dialled Millie's number. When she answered, Anna could hear the baby crying in the background.

"Hi darling. It's only me. I can tell this isn't a good time to talk. I can hear my darling grandson yelling his lungs out." Anna had said as Millie answered, sounding tired.

"Oh, he's been at it for an hour now Mum. He's been fed, nappy changed, I've sang to him, rocked him, nothing seems to be working!"

Anna always had a few tricks up her sleeve for crying babies. "Why don't you put him in the car and drive him round for a bit? That might help."

Millie agreed and said she'd give it a try now. But what was it her Mum had wanted to talk about? Anna, knowing that this was not the right time, said,

"Oh nothing. Just a chat, but we can do it later when Milo has settled."

Anna could hear Millie gathering together Milo's things to take him in the car as Anna had suggested.

"OK Mum. Speak later. Byeee."

Anna, feeling depressed and alone, went into the kitchen to make lunch. Eating her sandwich, she wondered what Ken was actually up to today. Had he really gone to Manly with his mates to the Pub or was he with his latest girlfriend? She told herself she didn't care. But really, she did.

She thought back to when they first met. It had been at a party in the 70s. She'd had a big plastic bag full of vinyl records in her hand when she'd walked into the house where the party was being held. Ken had spotted her immediately and had gone over and offered to carry the bag in for her. Once he'd put the bag down by the record player, he'd offered to go and get her a drink. Shortly, he came back with a glass of white wine for her and a bottle of beer for himself, and a joint in his hand. Anna had never smoked a joint in her life, but under Ken's insistence, she took the joint and drew on it, chocking immediately. The only reaction she'd got from it was a dizzy feeling and, deciding it wasn't for her, and had never tried it again. On that first night, they'd got chatting and found they had a lot in common, especially the modern-day music. They'd both had a fair bit to drink when Ken had invited Anna back to his place. Both being young and inexperienced, their first try at sex had been a bit hit and miss but after a while, Ken had started to work out what Anna liked. And he himself was growing in confidence as a lover. A few weeks later, when Anna was gasping and thrusting her hips, Ken would quickly reach over to the bedside table and pick up the small foil packet containing a condom and roll it onto his erection. Ken could come quickly if he wanted to, so with just a few quick thrusts both of them would come almost together. They had soon become a couple, and after a year together, Ken asked Anna to marry him and she'd agreed. She'd found the man of her dreams and couldn't have been happier. For the first few years they had experimented with various sexual positions, but whenever the more boisterous Ken had tried to be rough with her, Anna had always stopped him. That wasn't for her, she'd said. Soon though, the sex had become boring, and infrequent. Anna had grown happy with this arrangement, as she seemed to have lost her sex-drive as she had got older. She and Ken had been together for 40 years now. Two bookends holding up two very different set of books.

She remembered something Millie had said to her a few months ago.

"Mum, why don't you do yourself up a bit. Get your hair done. Buy some new clothes. Paint your nails. Anything. Just do yourself up. Make Dad want you again."

Anna thought of her daughter's words now. She realised she wasn't really happy with the life she had. She was still relatively young at 64. Yes, that's what she'd do. She'd book the hairdressers appointment tomorrow and arrange for Millie to leave Milo with Brock for a few hours and they could go shopping for new clothes together.

Anna felt the first flicker of excitement inside her that she hadn't felt in years. She'd try and get Ken back. She'd try and get some of the romance back. After all, wasn't that why Ken was looking elsewhere for it now, she thought? She remembered the beautiful Advert in this week's 'NOW' magazine and went to fetch it from the coffee table. She found it quickly enough. There was the lovely glossy picture of the most perfect Island imaginable with the words

'COME TO PARADISE ISLAND AND LEAVE YOUR CARES BEHIND AND LET LOVE BLOSSOM. NO CHILDREN UNDER 18. 7 NIGHTS FROM JUST $1,299. ALL MEALS AND ENTERTAINMENT INCLUDED.'

'Let love blossom.' They were the words that caught her eye. At the bottom of the advert there was an email address and a phone number for bookings. Anna decided on a plan. She'd do herself up, get her hair done, buy some new clothes, get a manicure even, and book her and Ken a week there. She'd tell him it was an early birthday surprise. Ken wouldn't know her by the time she'd finished with herself! She sighed happily. For the first time in many years she felt excited! She picked up the phone and booked a week there for them both. She couldn't wait to tell Ken when he got home.

CHAPTER 4

SUE

Sue threw the magazine onto the coffee table in disgust. The headline on the front cover had shouted "Baby Number Three for Kate", but, as always, once you actually read the article it said that a 'source' close to the Royal Couple predicted that Kate probably wouldn't stop at two, and that her having another baby was a distinct possibility! How did the magazines get away with it, thought Sue? It was the same every week. Headline grabbing, she'd had once heard it called. What to do now? Sue hated Sundays. Work took up

ESCAPE TO PARADISE ISLAND

Mondays to Fridays, and Saturdays were shopping, but Sundays, well, what could you do on a Sunday! There was a small street market on each week near her house, but she'd been to it so often, and it was always the same stalls there every week, so it held no attraction for her anymore. She'd looked in the local paper to see if there were any movies on that she might like to see, but nothing caught her eye. If it wasn't warm and fuzzy she didn't want to see it. It was only 2pm. Sue supposed she could make herself an early afternoon tea. She had a nice packet of shortbread and some Earl Grey tea in the kitchen. She got up and went and put the kettle on and got down the biscuits. Sue knew she shouldn't be eating them. She had put on ten kilos in the last year and was starting to hate the way she looked with the extra weight. That was the thing, though, with her. She'd put on ten kilos then take it off again, only to put it back on again. All her adult life she'd gone up and down like this. The problem was she liked her sweets too much. Biscuits, cakes, chocolate, puddings, they all went down well. The kettle boiled and she went about making the tea, still not knowing what to do for the rest of the day.

Sue had grown up in Wollongong on the New

South Wales south east coast, the only child of Norma
and John Bailey. She'd done really well at her private
Catholic School and gone on to Wollongong
University to do a Teaching Degree. She'd always
wanted to teach High School, never Primary School,
as she felt she had a better affinity with the older kids.
Her specialist subject was History. She'd been
interested in it from an early age. After three years at
Uni, Sue had easily found a casual teaching job at a
local State High School. After teaching there for two
years, her position had been made permanent. And
that's where she'd stayed for the last 28 years.
Obviously, she'd got to know all of the other teachers,
but she'd formed no really strong friendships with any
of them. Staff Room gossip never really interested, or
applied, to her. And of course, most of the other
teachers came and went with great regularity. But the
years had flown by. Sue had a good relationship with
all her students and they all loved her lessons. She'd
had a few dates with various men she'd met along the
way but no serious boyfriend, and she'd only had sex
once when they'd both had too much wine. Sex which
had been over within a minute and to which Sue had
felt nothing at all. Over the years, she had tried to fill

her life trying different things. She'd done pottery, gone to writing classes, played tennis, lawn bowls (even though she was the youngest there!) and had even gone to cookery classes and learnt how to make such dishes as Paella and Saltimbocca, something she would never have even attempted learn by herself.

Most of the time, Sue felt no need for a man in her life. She managed very well on her own, could change a fuse and a light bulb and got a Tradesman in for anything else. However, five years ago, a new Math's teacher, Gordon Simpson, had started at the school. For some peculiar reason that Sue couldn't understand, all of a sudden, whenever she saw him, her tummy would have butterflies in it. As she'd never known love, she didn't know if this was what it felt like, but over the months she and Gordon, another loner like herself, had built up quite a rapport. One day, at lunch break, Gordon had asked her if she'd like to go out to a local Chinese Restaurant with him that weekend. Sue had said yes and that was the beginning of their relationship. After an enjoyable meal and two bottles of house wine, a drunken Gordon and Sue had just gravitated to her apartment where, once inside, they had sedately taken each other's clothes off and made love on the floor in the lounge. Sue had only ever had one other sexual encounter before and did not have enough experience to know if Gordon was a good lover or not. As it turned out, he was a 'fumbler'. Even though drunk, Gordon had managed to unzip his fly and take out his small, erect penis. He'd pulled Sue's 'Granny Knickers' down and inserted himself, with much fumbling, into her. After about 30 seconds Gordon had come, shuddering as he released himself. Afterwards they had got into Sue's bed. She felt a strange sense of being unfulfilled and asked Gordon, somewhat sarcastically, if he'd enjoyed their lovemaking. Gordon had told her that he'd been a virgin until he was 30 and had only had a one-night stand in a drunken stupor with a colleague. He also had had no real experience in what lovemaking was all about. Sue found it very odd to be laying in her bed next to another person, even though she'd just experienced the most intimate experience you could with them. Although disappointed with Gordon's lovemaking, Sue realised that it had been his first time and only her second, and that they would both have to just learn along the way.

To say that both were unattractive would be

cruel, but neither would have won a beauty contest. Gordon was tall and lanky, with large horn rimmed glasses and a rather large nose. Sue was short, 5ft 3 inches in fact, overweight and with short mousy brown curly hair. She also wore glasses, the old-fashioned kind, and had thin, pursed lips. After the initial sex, Sue and Gordon had continued with their somewhat unusual pairing, and settled into a routine of having the 30-second sex once a week. It never occurred to Sue to ask Gordon for more. For her that was what sex was all about. It was the man's world. Life at school and at home carried on as normal, and the two of them never told any of their colleagues of their affair. This went on for two years. One day, Gordon suggested they go down to the beach front at Fairy Meadow and take a picnic. Once the food had gone, Gordon hesitantly got down on one knee and asked Sue to marry him. Sue still didn't know how to recognise love or if she was 'in love' with Gordon, but by now he had become a permanent fixture in her life, so she said 'Yes'. The following day, to the amazement of their colleagues, Sue and Gordon announced that they were getting married. Everybody was shocked. They'd had no idea they were together, they'd said. Their marriage was a very quiet affair, as that's what they both wanted. Only Sue's parents and Gordon's dad (his mum had died when he was 16) and a few of the teachers from school were there. Afterwards, they had a reception dinner at the same Chinese Restaurant where they'd had that first meal together. They then went back to Sue's Apartment, where Gordon was to move into that evening.

And so, life for the next 12 years went on at a mundane pace, with neither Sue nor Gordon showing any real love or affection for each other. The sex never changed. Gordon would fumble, put it in, go in and out, and 30 seconds or so later, come with a shudder. Sue, although she felt her insides tighten at the beginning of their sex, had little else to go on and thought that was it for her. She often thought it a marriage of convenience, although they rubbed along OK together. Sue still played tennis while Gordon joined a chess group. Together they went on short breaks away, visiting Sydney, Melbourne, and Brisbane. But all the time there was no spark in the marriage, and after 10 years, they had stopped having sex altogether.

ESCAPE TO PARADISE ISLAND

One day, Sue, who usually drove home from
school with Gordon, went for a 'Girls only' drinks with
some of the other female teachers, telling Gordon that
she would be home by midnight. But by eight she
decided to go home as everybody else seemed to be
getting drunk and acting really stupid, and that was not
Sue at all. Home in front of the TV with a cup of
camomile tea sounded like a much better proposition.
When she got back, she put her key in the lock and
turned it, not noticing the strange car parked in front of
her block of apartments. Once inside, something made
her stop. All the lights were off when they should have
been on, with Gordon home. That in itself should have
made her suspicious. Sue could hear funny noises
coming from the bedroom. Quickly she turned on the
hall light and rushed up to the bedroom and opened the
door, only to find Gordon, completely naked and on all
fours, with an equally naked man lying under him on
the bed. Both looked at Sue with astonishment on their
faces, the strange man trying to cover his erect penis
with his hand. Gordon, whose penis was also erect,
started to speak, but Sue was out of the room like a
shot. Shaking she took the car keys from the hall table
and drove to the nearest Motel. She text Gordon

straight away as soon as she'd checked in.

"I WANT YOU OUT OF THE APARTMENT BY THIS TIME TOMORROW NIGHT. GONE. NEVER, EVER, CONTACT ME AGAIN. BASTARD!"

There was a mini bar in the room and, although not usually a drinker, Sue took out a miniature bottle of whisky and downed the lot.

The Divorce was easy. Gordon didn't contest it and even paid all of Sue's Solicitors fees. As Sue had requested, he'd been gone by the following night and when she'd returned back home there was not a single sign that Gordon had ever lived there. He'd taken everything that he'd ever owned. Sue could barely even walk into the bedroom, the last sight she had seen there was so engraved onto her brain, so she'd spent the next two months sleeping in the other bedroom. The following day she'd put the apartment on the market for sale, and luckily, as it was so immaculate, it had sold in the first month. Had she had any inkling that Gordon had been Bisexual? Sue didn't think so, but they'd grown so far apart that she probably wouldn't have given it a thought anyway, nor would she have known the signs. Afterwards, Gordon had gone to live with his Dad, and Sue went looking for a new apartment. She saw three on that first Saturday, one overlooking the sea and which suited her perfectly. Plus, she could afford it with her share from the sale of her old apartment, along with a small mortgage. She decided to put an offer in on it immediately and it was accepted the same day. Within two months she'd moved in. Sue realised that she and Gordon had never truly been lovers. She'd leaned on him and he on her but that was it. Sue felt an outcast. Fancy been cheated on by your husband and a MAN! Would she have taken it any better if it had been a woman? Maybe. She didn't know. Gordon had given up his job at the school immediately and moved across town to another school. Sue stayed where she was, teaching History as always, getting to know her students again for the school year, then having to get to know a whole new set all over again every new year. She loved her new apartment from the start, even making friends with the elderly couple next door. She started cooking different meals every night, and tried to make something from a different country each time. It became her passion. Sue found that before she knew it two years had passed and she was still single and on her own She still loved her apartment and its wonderful views across the Ocean, cliffs souring in the distance, and the sound of waves crashing if it was really quiet outside. Although happy, Sue felt alone, and though not completely lonely, wished for someone to share her life with again. She wanted someone to talk over the day's events with, to cook for. Outside on her balcony, there was a small table and 2 chairs, and one balmy evening, as she sat outside, drinking her cup of Camomile Tea and reading a magazine, an advert caught her eye. There was a glossy picture of a beautiful Island with the words

"COME TO PARADISE ISLAND AND LEAVE YOUR CARES BEHIND AND LET LOVE BLOSSOM. NO CHILDREN UNDER 18. 7 NIGHTS FROM JUST $1,299. ALL MEALS AND ENTERTAINMENT INCLUDED."

'Let Love Blossom'. Sue liked the sound of that. She would be 50 soon. Would love ever blossom for her? Sue thought she'd like to find out.

"I'll phone and ask for a brochure tomorrow," she told herself.

CHAPTER 5

RACHAEL

Cooking was something Rachael had always been good at, but this way of cooking was completely new to her. She had just started trying out different recipes to see if eliminating certain foods would help her son, Jake, with his Oppositional Defiance Disorder and ADHD. Jake's problems had first appeared when he was four, with him having massive tantrums, beyond the norm for his age. He was nine now and showed no signs of getting any better. Rachael and her husband, Harry, had tried the traditional medicines, along with therapy and counselling, but nothing had ever really worked. Sarah, Rachael's friend, had suggested taking dairy, gluten, grains and red meat out of his diet, as well as reducing his sugar intake (Ha!! Good luck with that one!) as well as increasing his 'good fats'. Rachael thought she'd have to look up 'good fats' later. Tonight, though, she was trying to make a Quorn stir-fry. She'd never even heard of Quorn before, let alone cooked with it and fed it to her poor children. The Recipe said to fry the Quorn for five minutes, then add chopped onion and red pepper (as if the kids would eat that!!) then add coconut cream (wasn't that diary? Gee there was so much she didn't know!!) and coriander. Ummm. Smelt good but deep down Rachael knew that getting the kids to eat it would be like getting Donald Trump to shave his hair off! The front door opened and her two eldest children, Jake, 9, and Sophie, 7 came barging in, heavy backpacks from school on their backs. Rachael and another mum took it in turns to bring the children home from school each week, and this was her week off.

"What's to eat Mum? I'm starving." Jake made his usual war cry.

"I've made you all a fruit platter today kids. We are cutting down our sugar from now on."

"Why?" asked Lily, 3, the youngest, who was sitting on the lounge playing with her dolls.

"Because it's not good for your little bodies my darlings. Now come on, let's eat our fruit platter."

Jake immediately reared up. Rachael felt the pit of her stomach go weak, just like every other time Jake started. He'd been a difficult baby, starting to do the normal things much later than the other children his age, but by the time he was four he had started to have uncontrollable tantrums, swearing (where did he get those words from? Certainly, not from home!) and throwing toys and chairs at the walls. It was like looking at the devil himself when Jake had one of his tantrums. Rachael and Harry had taken him to see Specialist Paediatric Doctor after Doctor, who had tried him on different medications, but none with any success. They'd taken him to counselling for two years, again without success. When he'd finally been diagnosed with ODD and ADHD at the age of 7 they'd breathed a sigh of relief. At least now they knew what the problem was. But how to treat it? They didn't know. Rachael had done a lot of research on the Net but they'd already tried everything. This change of diet was, for her, the last resort.

"I'm not eating stupid fruit," Jake shouted. "I want those chocolate biscuits in the biscuit tin." Rachael, in for yet another shouting match, said,

"No Jake. Today we are having a lovely fruit platter I've made. It's better for you than chocolate biscuits. It's got your favourite strawberries on it!" She felt the tears well up in her eyes at the thought of another fight.

"Mum, Lily's wet her knickers again" Sophie was always quick to tell tales on her younger sister.

Rachael went over and changed Lily and admonished her for not using the toilet.

"You're a big girl now Lily. You should be using the toilet. You're three."

"I'm sorry mummy. I just forgottened," Lily hadn't quite managed to get her words all right yet.

Lily was the quiet one of the family. She played really well on her own during the day when the others were at school but her one major fault was that she wouldn't go to bed at night. Sometimes Rachael and Harry would be up till 11 or 12 trying to get her to stay in her own bed. Often, they gave in and let her go in their bed just for the sake of getting some sleep.

"Come on Mum. I want some biscuits. Can I get the tin?" Jake was demanding.

"I'll say it one more time Jake then you'll go to your room for the rest of the night, but today we are having the fruit platter!" And that was all it took to set Jake off into one of his almighty rages. He started swearing like a trooper, bright red in the face. Throwing anything in sight around the room and at Rachael, punching her in the stomach and trying to bite her. The other two children were used to such exhibitions of Jake's tantrums and just sat watching on the couch. After twenty minutes Jake calmed down and fell, exhausted, onto the lounge. Rachael looked around her, at the mayhem Jake had caused and felt like crying. She wished Harry would hurry up and come home. He travelled a lot with work, selling and installing Computer Software, but was expected back any time now. Rachael wanted him home so that she could have a break.

Rachael had been brought up in Coffs Harbour, a coastal town halfway up the east coast of Australia. She'd hated school and, as a result, had not done well there, and when she'd left, she had persuaded her parents to let her go and live with her Aunty Gwyn in Byron Bay. But Byron Bay had quite a reputation of being an easy place to get drugs and for being a party town. Unfortunately, after only being there for a week, Rachael had given in when another girl at a party she had gone to had offered her some weed. Rachael soon became hooked and had to find a job, and quickly, so that she could afford to buy her precious drug. Thereby started a succession of jobs, waitressing, working behind bars and even in a little store that sold homemade crafts in the village. When she was twenty, Rachael looked at her life and decided she was going nowhere. With a great deal of effort, she stopped smoking weed and decided to move back in with her parents in Coffs Harbour. There, after a few years of working in Cafes and other dead end jobs, Rachael's parents, Noeline and Trevor, had paid a lot of money for her to do a Private Secretarial Course, which she'd amazed herself by enjoying and doing well at. After she'd finished the course, she'd been lucky enough to get a Receptionist job with Baldwin's, the Computer Store in town. Rachael had worked there for two years, and when an opportunity arose, she'd moved up into a vacant Secretarial position, as PA to Harry Summerton, the Business Operations Manager, giving her more money and more responsibility. Harry was a hard but fair man to work for and Rachael soon found herself happy in the job. But at the Annual Christmas Party, where they both got very drunk, Harry had asked Rachael to go out for drinks with him again, and the rest, as they say, is history. Soon, they had fallen in love, became engaged, and had the big fairy tale wedding. The children then came in quick succession. Now, with a hefty mortgage and three kids to feed, life was tough and Harry worked hard to provide for them. Rachael had given up her job when she'd had Jake, and Harry earned enough so that she didn't have to go back to work until the children were older. As Jake had grown and his problems increased, Rachael realised she may never be able to go back to work. It was a sobering thought.

Harry was older than Rachael, ten years older in fact, and had had a different upbringing from

Rachael. He'd been brought up in England with his brother Josh and parents, Jane and Terry, and they'd emigrated to Australia in 1990. Terry was a Surveyor and getting a job in Australia had been easy for him. They'd rented a house in Sydney at first, and had planned to save up and buy one of their own, but somehow it never happened and they continued to rent. Harry did well in his final years at school and went on to become a Sales Executive in a firm that sold Computer Hardware to other businesses. He had loved it all in Sydney, the buzz, the crowds and, especially, the harbour. He had a friend who had a small boat and they spent many a pleasant weekend out on the water, watching the Opera House float by and sailing under one of the most famous bridges in the world. But after five years in Sydney, disaster had struck as Harry's dad had lost his job. The firm he worked for had gone bankrupt. Rather than go on the dole, his dad had decided to accept another job hundreds of kilometres away in Coffs Harbour, and so the family had moved there. Harry had been 22, and at first had planned to stay in Sydney and get a place of his own, but rentals were expensive and hard to find. Finally, his mum had persuaded him to start looking for jobs in Coffs

Harbour and move up there with them. Harry found one soon enough with Baldwin's and made the move up there. Over time, he'd had a number of casual girlfriends and one relationship, which had lasted two years. All of his male friends announced that he would forever be a bachelor but then he'd met and fallen in love with Rachael. They'd met one night at a party. Most people there were smoking weed and, Rachael, who had fought so hard to give it up, was finding it difficult to stay and not give in. Just when she had decided to leave, a really good looking man about her own age, came over and asked her if she'd like a drink.

"Why not?" Rachael thought. "He looks really nice."

When the man came back with their drinks, he'd introduced himself as Harry Summerton, and told her a bit about his life. Rachael was impressed that he had such a good job at Baldwin's Computers, and at such a young age too. Harry was flattered and flirted up a storm with Rachael. She had mentioned to him that she had just completed a Secretarial Course and was looking for work. Harry told her that his company were looking for a Receptionist and Rachael had thanked him and said she'd give them a ring tomorrow. Harry had moved away to talk to some other friends but Rachael secretly hoped she'd see him again. That dream was to come true as the following week, Rachael had applied for, and got, the Receptionist's position at Baldwin's. She saw Harry often, although they never formed a relationship and there was a rumour amongst the staff that Harry was dating a woman older than himself, so all the other girls backed off him. Although friendly, Harry never seemed to flirt with any of the girls at work, and Rachael wondered why he had flirted with her when she'd first met him at the party. It wasn't until the Christmas Party a year later that Rachael found out that Harry was actually now single and when he'd asked her to have drinks with him she'd jumped at the chance!

Now, as if by magic, the front door opened and Harry was home. He looked around the wrecked room and said to Jake

"You been in one of your strops again mister?"

"Hello darling." He kissed Rachael then went and kissed the girls.

"Right Jake. Get this mess cleared up NOW, or else you lose your Xbox for a week!"

Rachael was always amazed that Harry could handle Jake so much better than she could. Jake started to slowly and unenthusiastically pick everything up and put things back in their right places.

"Now can I have a chocolate biscuit 'cos I've picked everything up?" Jake pleaded.

"NO! I'm sick of telling you we are having fruit. That's it Jake. I'm not saying it again."

And with that Rachael went into the kitchen and brought out the platter of apples, bananas and strawberries she'd made earlier.

The following week, Harry had to go up to Brisbane for work and left the house early. Rachael, left alone to do the school run, frantically ran around the house shouting at the two children to get their school bags, picking up odd socks, and packing lunches. Lily was grizzling, which wasn't like her. She was still in her pyjamas and had a wet nappy, but Rachael would dress her once they were back from the school run.

"OK Kids. Let's roll," Rachel shouted. All three children appeared but Jake had his trainers on and not his school shoes.

"Where are your school shoes Jake?"

"Why? I'm allowed to wear these ones if I want to!" Jakes tone of voice made Rachael feel sick with anger.

"No. You can only wear trainers for PE Jake. So, go and get them off and put your school shoes on." Rachael breathed deeply, wondering what would come next.

"You can't fuckin' tell me what to do, you bitch," Jake shouted, then stormed out to the car.

Taking stock of the situation, Rachael thought she had two options. Get Jake back in and have an all-out fight with him, or just let the teachers at school deal with him wearing trainers. She chose the latter and ushered Sophie and a still grizzly Lily into the car. Half an hour later, as she walked back into the house, the phone was ringing. It was Jake's teacher.

"You know the school's policy on uniform Mrs

Summerton. Why is Jake wearing trainers and not the correct school shoes?"

Rachael, having had these types of phone calls from the school regularly, said,

"I'm so sorry Mrs Plainer." (Wasn't flattery and being pleasant the best way to get around a problem?) "You're such a wonderful teacher for Jake, but you know how difficult he can be. He wouldn't put his school shoes on this morning and as we were running late, I just left him. I'm sure you understand."

Mrs Plainer was used to Jake and his mum.

"OK, well if you could try and get him to wear his school shoes tomorrow that would be appreciated. Thanks. Bye."

Rachael put the phone down and surveyed the detritus of breakfast and a morning of having three children in the Summerton house. Her friend, Sarah, was due to come over for a coffee at ten so Rachel thought she'd better go and get the place in order. She remembered Lily who, still grizzling, had gone to lay on the lounge and watch Dora. She went into Lily's bedroom and picked out an outfit for her and the nappy changing gear and went and fixed Lily up. She and Harry had been up with their youngest child until 11pm last night until finally Lily had given in and gone to sleep in her own bed. Having got Lily dressed and with a cup of milk and a biscuit (Oh no, what would Jake say!) Rachael started cleaning the pigsty that was her house. At exactly ten she felt it was clean enough for Sarah's visit. Sarah had moved into the house next door last year and knew of Jake's problems. But she was childless herself and wasn't much practical help, but she was a good listener, and for Rachael to have a good moan to. As was usual, Sarah arrived on the dot of ten. She was a cheerful happy woman, in her mid-thirties, married but without children. She tossed a magazine onto the coffee table.

"Here's this weeks' 'Pure Woman' Rach. Usual crap in it about Kate having her sixteenth baby and Harry marrying a girl from the Scottish Highlands where she's a sheep breeder!"

Rachael, who had just poured the coffee, cut up some banana bread she'd bought yesterday and laid it on a plate. Taking it though into the lounge room she looked at Sarah's immaculate dress, her lovely blonde hair and the lightest touch of makeup, then down at her own dowdy, unkempt appearance.

"I wish I could look like you at this time of the morning Sarah," she said.

"Rach, I haven't got three children to look after. You have!"

It was true and something Sarah didn't like to think about it, as she wasn't in the slightest bit maternal, but felt guilty for not being so. Rachael took a piece of banana bread and said between mouthfuls,

"I don't know what we're going to do about Jake. He just seems to get worse, and I dread to think how he's going to be when his hormones kick in, in a few years! He called me a 'fuckin bitch' this morning. How am I supposed to take that Sairs? I'm sure he's teaching the other two to speak like that as well, although they haven't started to yet, thank God!"

Sarah sipped at her coffee. "Rach, there's got to be someone else you can take him to see. Some Specialist, even if it's in Sydney. There must be Support Groups on Facebook for parents of kids like Jake. Have you looked?"

"No," said Rachael. "I hadn't thought of that, but anyway, what's that going to do to help?"

"I don't know hun but it's worth a try," Sarah was ever the optimist.

Later, as Harry arrived home, Rachael mentioned to him about taking Jake to see a different Specialist, maybe in Sydney. Harry had just said, OK, why not, and that he'd look into it later that evening when the kids were in bed. Loud screeching was coming from Sophie's room. She'd been given a kids Karaoke Machine by her grandparents last Christmas, and it had a microphone attached. As usual, Sophie was singing full pelt. Although only 7 years old she wanted to be a pop star just like Rihanna. Rachael had bought her some temporary pink hair spray and a bright red lipstick for dress ups and Sophie certainly played the part. The only problem was, Sophie couldn't sing. If truth be told, her voice was terrible and the whole house had to put up with her screeching. Rachael felt as though her head would burst but didn't have the heart to tell her. What with Sophie's screeching and Jake starting to whine for some chocolate, Rachael asked Harry to put down his newspaper and "sort the bloody kids out" while she went for a bath. Luckily Lily had gone down for a nap so that was one less to worry about. Rachael picked up the magazine that Sarah had left earlier and took it up to the bath with her. It was while she was reading it, having her much needed soak, that she saw the advertisement; A full colour glossy picture of a beautiful Island in Queensland. The caption read:

"COME TO PARADISE ISLAND AND LEAVE YOUR CARES BEHIND AND LET LOVE BLOSSOM. NO CHILDREN UNDER 18. 7 NIGHTS FROM JUST $1,299. ALL MEALS AND ENTERTAINMENT INCLUDED."

Rachel wondered if she could surprise Harry with a week there for their tenth Anniversary, which was coming up next month? The only problem was, who could they leave the children with? They'd never been away without them before as Jake was too hard for anyone to manage. What about Mum, thought Rachael. I can only ask her! With that thought, a loud voice called out "MUM, hurry up. Dad won't let me have any chocolate biscuits!"

CHAPTER 6

THE ARRIVAL

Anna unfastened her seatbelt. Their Qantas jet had just landed at Mackay Airport. She couldn't believe it. In a couple of hours or so she and Ken would be on Paradise Island. She'd had a hard job convincing Ken to come with her, telling him it was her birthday surprise for him. He'd had so much to take in the last few weeks. His wife was like a different woman. She'd had her hair cut really sort and had blonde highlights. Her nails were a shade of shocking pink and her clothes were different, more modern somehow, he'd thought. He had to admit it was a great improvement on the old Anna, but she still looked old and dowdy to him, and no amount of hair colour or painted nails could alter that. When she'd told him about the surprise early birthday present to some Island in Queensland, his first reaction had been to say 'No Way', but Anna had gone to so much effort lately to make herself look nice that he hadn't the heart to say no. Now as they disembarked from the plane, the warm tropical air hit them. As they made their way into the terminal, Anna gave a smile to herself. Right Ken. Let's see what this week brings!

Sue, who was also on the same flight, as she'd driven to Sydney Airport from Wollongong (there being no large airport in Wollongong), gathered her carry-on bag and her handbag together, and proceeded to wait her turn in the aisle to disembark the plane. While she waited, her mind went over the things she'd done to make sure everything would be OK at home. She'd got the niece of one of the other teachers in her school, Paula, to housesit for her for the week, bought in enough food for her cat, Piper, to be fed, and stocked the fridge and pantry up. She had Pay TV on her television in the lounge room, so there would be plenty for Paula to watch. Her mortgage was due tomorrow but that came out of her bank by Direct Debit so she didn't have to worry about that. During the flight to Mackay, Sue had looked around and seen that everybody else seemed to be a couple or a family. She often felt alone, but at the same time felt that she couldn't live with anybody again. She'd become too set in her ways. Stop, she thought. Isn't this why I've decided to come on this holiday? Maybe there would be someone with whom she might find a 'spark'. Sue had very low expectations for herself, but she had them nonetheless. The queue down the aisle started to move and soon she was making her way into the terminal.

Rachael and Harry had decided to make a journey of it and had driven to Mackay from Coffs Harbour. Sure, it was a long way, but Harry liked to drive, and without the children with them they could put on their favourite 90s music up as loud as they wanted and sing along. Rachael thought how odd it felt without the kids. This was the first time since they'd had Jake that they'd been away on their own together, as usually they had to take the kids with them. Nobody could be expected to have Jake, especially, even though Sophie and Lily were also a handful. A few weeks ago, after much hesitation, Rachael had plucked up the courage to ask her Mum, Noeline, if she and her Dad, Trevor, would have the kids for a week while she and Jack went away to celebrate their tenth Anniversary. Her parents had only ever looked after the kids for a few hours at a time before, and even then, not that often. It wasn't that Noeline didn't love her grandchildren, she did, but they were hard work, especially Jake with all his problems. She was one of those people whose house is always immaculate and she hated it to be otherwise. So, when her grandchildren visited, not only was it usually mayhem but her house got trashed as well. Whenever Racheal and Harry visited with the grandchildren, it took Noeline and Trevor a couple of hours to get everything back to how they liked it. Trevor was much more laid back though than his wife. He didn't care what the house was like. He and Noeline had been married for years and rubbed along together nicely. He loved his grandchildren, although Jake could be quite a handful, especially if he had one of his famous tantrums, but overall Trevor didn't mind them. Only in small doses though, he often told himself! Rachael had chosen her moment carefully. She and her Mum were having an afternoon cup of coffee and had been talking over old times. Rachael thought 'it's now or never' and plucked up the courage to ask.

"Mum, you know it's mine and Harry's tenth Anniversary coming up soon? I thought it would be lovely if we could get away for a week, you know, just the two of us," Rachel's voice held hesitancy. "I know it's a lot to ask, but would you and Dad have the kids for us if we went?"

Noeline was flummoxed. She didn't know what to say. Have the kids for a whole week? No. She couldn't. How could she? She wasn't up to it. But Rachael had put her on the spot. How could she say no? So, it was with great regret that she'd said

"Sure, we'll have them sweetheart. You and Harry go and have a well-earned break."

Now, they were driving up to Mackay to start their holiday, but Rachael was worried sick. How would her parents cope, especially with Jake? She'd tried to bribe him with a new X Box game when they got back if he'd be good for Nanna and Pop, but she wasn't filled with confidence. Driving up, they'd stopped off at a roadside Motel just north of Brisbane for the night, and had now arrived at Mackay. There was a long stay car park not far from the waterfront and Harry parked up, gathered up their luggage and they made the short walk to the terminal, where the ferry would take them to Paradise Island.

Bianca and Joel had also flown to Mackay, but from Brisbane. On the flight, Bianca had had plenty of time to think of ways in which she could tempt Joel into being the passionate romantic she'd always wanted him to be. Their wedding earlier that day had gone off according to Bianca's somewhat low-key plan, with the number of guests being embarrassingly small. However, they'd all had quite a good time and when it came to going to bed, Bianca had thought that the day's events may change Joel's attitude and stir some sort of passion in him, especially as they'd be spending it on Paradise Island for their honeymoon night. Tonight, was their first night as a married couple and Bianca would see if being married had made any difference to Joel and his attitude towards making love. Last week, she'd made an appointment with a Counsellor who specialised in Sex problems. The appointment had been for an hour and, after much persuading and many fights, Joel had agreed to go. But he'd come out after the hour and absolutely refused to say a word of how things had gone to Bianca. They only thing he had said was that it had been a total waste of money and he wasn't going to go back again. Bianca had taken her Maid of Honour, Taylor, into her confidence, having nobody else to talk to. Taylor had suggested that Bianca buy some sexy lingerie and maybe some Girlie Magazines to take with them on their honeymoon to the Island. She also advised Bianca to try and get Joel drunk. That often worked, the wise 22-year-old Taylor had advised, although how she'd know that was beyond Bianca. So, packed away in her suitcase were three totally sexy and very tiny see through, lacy outfits, along with half a dozen Girlie Magazines, and a book for inspiration for herself, *50 Shades of Grey.* Getting Joel drunk should be easy, thought Bianca, as that's what you did on holiday, wasn't it? Bianca was determined that she would give this her best shot. She was going to do everything in her power to make Joel want to have sex with her. Everything. Making their way into the airport terminal at Mackay, Bianca and Joel looked like any other newly married couple. They held hands and Bianca tried her best to look lovingly into Joel's eyes. This was going to be a new start for them. She just hoped Joel would realise it as well, and make the most of their week on what looked like being the perfect place to start their married life.

Those who had flown or driven into Mackay were put into a mini bus and taken to the Ferry Terminal. There were already quite a few people waiting on the jetty. After about 15 minutes a ferry had arrived and they had all got on-board. It was a simple boat, nothing luxurious, just rows of seats and piles of life jackets. Once everyone was seated, the only obvious crew-member ran through the safety drill with them and then they were off. The forty-five-minute ride was exhilarating to some but terrible for others who hadn't banked on being seasick. Soon enough, the boat's engines started to slow down and the Island was in sight. Sue, looking around her, noticed that there was only one other single person on the boat. He was a man, probably in his 70s and with a very dour expression. She was the only one without a partner. There seemed to be lots of young couples and even an older couple, although the man was still very handsome. She wondered if she'd be one of the only singletons on the Island. She hoped not. That would defeat her purpose, although not entirely as she was really looking forward to a relaxing break.

Bianca looked across at Joel. "I think we're here baby. Looks nice, hey?"

Joel just nodded, feeling queasy from the boat ride.

"Let's make this honeymoon really special hey! Let's try really hard?" Bianca's words were more a statement than a question, but there was determination behind her words.

Rachael, still worried, said to Harry "God I hope Jake's behaving himself. I'm sure Mum only agreed to have them because she couldn't say no. I hope the Island has phone signal so that I can check in on them once we get settled." Harry gave a sigh.

"Rach the whole bloody idea of this holiday is for us to have a break from the kids, just for a week. Your Mum will be fine with them. Just relax. If Jake kicks off he kicks off. They have brought up children of their own you know. They've got the Island's landline number in case of emergencies."

Rachael was annoyed that Harry could be so blasé about it. How could she relax!

Anna and Ken had grabbed the seats at the back of the boat. Ken had done this on purpose in order to allow him a better view of the others on board. He tried to size up the women but as far as he could tell, apart from one dowdy middle aged woman, they were all in couples. Oh well, he thought. It wouldn't be the first time he'd seduced a married woman. Anna, feeling the most positive she had in a long time, sat with a smile on her face. Ken was going to fall in love with her all over again, she was sure of it. As the ferry pulled up alongside the jetty, everyone was in relaxed mode and hoped that love would blossom!

CHAPTER 7

THE ISLAND

As they all piled off the ferry, they were greeted by two of the Island's staff, resplendent in their bright blue and black uniforms. Each was greeted with a "Hello. Welcome. Hope you have a great stay." They were all led, crocodile style, to the main Reception building, where, once there, they were given a ticket to put on their luggage and told to leave their bags in the corner. They would be delivered to their chalets by the staff. Each had to sign in, showing their Booking Documents and were given a map and a list of the Island's facilities, along with its Rules and Regulations, although these were few. They were also given a Timetable showing, hour by hour, the daily events that would take place. You didn't have to book, they were told, just turn up. Three couples, including Bianca and Joel, were given 'JUST MARRIED' Badges and they had to pin them onto their tops! There were a few wolf whistles and one guy even said, "Keep the noise down you guys," to everyone's amusement! When they'd received their keys, they all wondered off, their map in hand, to find their respective chalets, where they would unpack, then go and explore the Resort.

Rachael threw her bag on the bed while Harry put his on the luggage rack in the corner. She kicked off her shoes and fell onto the bed.

"I can't believe we're here," she said. "It just doesn't feel right without the children."

Jack sat down on the bed beside her. "Rach, this is why we're here, to forget about the kids. Just for a week. God knows we deserve it."

He was running out of patience with Rachael for carrying on, moaning about the children. When Rachael had plucked up the courage to ask her Mum if she'd have them for the week, she'd heard the hesitation in her Mum's voice as she'd said "Yes, of course we'll have them." Now she was worried sick, especially as to how Jake would behave for his grandparents, and if Lily would go to bed at a normal time. In her heart, she knew that neither was going to happen. Rachael sat up and looked around the chalet. They'd tried to get a waterfront one but there had been none available when she had booked, but the one they had managed to get was surrounded by some beautiful rainforest, and the sound of the birds was quite deafening. The bed was big, very big. The perfectly white feather and down quilt cover and pillowcases were offset by a dark blue coverlet at the bottom of the bed, with the wall behind painted in the same colour. Apart from a large picture on the wall of a beautiful beach scene in an ornate gold frame, everything else was white. They had a bedside table each, with a small white table lamp on it, and there was a white round table and 2 chairs near the large glass door, which opened out onto a small wooden veranda at the back, which also held a wooden table and chairs. Back inside, there was a desk top with a bar fridge underneath, an office chair, a double wardrobe, and a chest of drawers. Natural fibre matting covered the floor, and huge folds of white voile hung from the window next to the sliding door, in front of heavy pull down blinds to keep out the light when required. Jack started to unpack and Rachael went over to join him. He put his arms around her and she immediately felt his hard erection pushing into her groin.

"Later darling," she said. "Let's unpack first."

Bianca kicked off her shoes, took off her 'Just Married' badge and flopped down on the bed. Her dress was ruffled up around her waist, and Joel stood looking at her, a grimace on his face.

"I think this is the time I'm supposed to do something romantic now aren't I, like rip your dress off you and make you scream with passion?"

His voice was full of anxiety and held the sarcasm Bianca was used to. She lifted herself up on one arm and looked at her new husband.

"No, my darling. You aren't supposed to rip

my dress off and make me scream with passion. You're supposed to take it off carefully, hang it up, then take my underwear off slowly, whilst panting with passion yourself!" Bianca's voice was equally sarcastic. "Seriously Joel, this is supposed to be the start of our married life. You should be acting spontaneously and not asking me what you should do. Here, just come and lay beside me. Let's just take it slowly hey, and see how we go. Why don't we just talk about how today's been?"

Joel lay down beside her and Bianca put her head on his chest.

"Let's just have a fabulous week and try and relax and enjoy ourselves hey?"

After they had discussed the days' events, they lay still together. Bianca thought of how passionate her honeymoon night should be and thoughts of what she and Joel should now be doing made her become quite aroused. She looked over at Joel and thought how lovely his face was. He hadn't shaved since this morning and he now had a slight stubble, which Bianca found really attractive. She decided to make a move and give things a try. She had nothing to lose anyway, she thought. She reached down and undid the zip of Joel's pants and took out his flaccid penis and began to stroke it.

"If you're a good boy later on, I've got a surprise for you."

Bianca continued to stroke and pull on Joel's penis. It became slightly erect and this gave Bianca some hope, although Joel did nothing to her in return. She kissed him, on the cheeks and neck at first, then on his lips, biting them gently. Joel stirred slightly and this made Bianca full of hope and anticipation, but he suddenly jumped up and put his penis back into his pants and did up the zip. His face had that look of anger which Bianca was so used to. He scowled at her,

"Let's go and have a walk round. See what's here. It's almost lunch time and I'm starving."

He walked out of the chalet door without a backwards glance at Bianca, who, still laying on the bed, burst into tears. Yet again, Joel had let her down.

Sue unpacked her bag in minutes. She hadn't brought a lot, just a few tops and a skirt, three dresses and a swimsuit and sarong. In her mind's eye, she'd visualised herself in the swimsuit and sarong for most of the day. She'd decided to go completely make up free for the week – not that she ever wore much anyway – so had just brought some moisturiser and sun cream with her other toiletries. Sue also had a Rainforest chalet. She hadn't thought the extra money for a beachfront one had been worth it. Her chalet had a pale blue theme. The cover on the bed was a lovely blue/jade colour with a darker blue coverlet on the bottom. The same paler blue colour was painted on the wall behind the bed. There were little bits of colour, all blues, around the room, with a little pale blue table and two chairs and a lovely painting in a silver frame of a white, sandy beach with palm trees, on the wall. On the white desk, there was some literature telling her about the Island's beginnings as a Luxury Resort, of how a Queensland man had bought the undeveloped Island for a pittance back in the 70s and had only recently, in the last five years, developed it into the Resort it was today. There was a brochure giving her information on some of the native flora and fauna and a warning of looking out for snakes and what to do if you encountered one. Sue was very impressed and, looking around her, was very happy with her new surroundings. She decided to go and sit on the rear veranda, and took a miniature bottle of Vodka and a cut crystal glass from the bar fridge in her room and went outside. There were quite a lot of people walking by, mostly couples or staff members. She did, however, see a youngish man, in his thirties, she thought, striding past from the chalet next door. He had a scowl on his face. Sue wondered if he was alone or with someone, although he was much too young for her. In her mind, she imagined him stopping by to say hello, getting chatting, meeting up with her in the bar for a drink… but then a woman came out of the next chalet shouting "Joel, wait for me, Joel!" She looked like she'd been crying. Oh dear, thought Sue. I wonder what's going on there? I'll have to keep my ears open! She went back inside her chalet and put on her new swimsuit and a sarong. Might as well go and have a look round and see who's here, she thought.

Anna and Ken had managed to get a beachfront chalet. It had cost over $400 more for the week, but Anna thought it was worth it for what she had in mind. She hoped the soothing sounds of the ocean, along with her new look, would make Ken fall in love with her all over again. Their chalet was all wood, a beautiful pale coloured wood which Anna or Ken didn't know the name of. The bed had a bright red cover and a pure white coverlet at the bottom. On the wall was a large picture of a mountain range, set into a dark wooden frame. As well as a small wardrobe, a chest of drawers and a desk with some literature on it with a writing pad and pen, there was a small bar fridge under the desk. Anna looked inside and found a stock of miniature bottles of spirits, two bottles of a high-end beer and some ice. A pair of large glass sliding doors led out onto a covered verandah with a good sized wooden table and four chairs, overlooking the beach and the ocean. Yes, she thought. This was definitely worth the extra money. She thought back to two weeks ago. As she'd promised herself, the day after seeing the advert for the Island, she had gone to the hairdressers and had her mousy hair cut very short and angular, and had a base colour of mahogany and some blonde streaks put in. The stylist had suggested that Anna also get her eyebrows shaped. The difference, when Anna looked in the big mirror in front of her was amazing. She didn't look like the same person. The following day, Anna had arranged to meet her daughter, Millie, to go and look for some new clothes, nothing too modern, she'd told Millie, but something a bit more up to date than what Anna usually wore. They met outside David Jones, the big department store in the City, and spent a good hour inside. They came out carrying three bags, each containing a new, modern top, a pair of black three quarter length pants and a beautiful pale blue dress with a fitted waist. After visiting a few more boutique type shops, and buying Anna two new swimsuits (she wasn't up for a bikini, she'd told Millie!) and a beautiful sarong, they were done. As they were walking to the Taxi Stand, Anna noticed a Nail Salon. "Come on Millie. We might as well go the whole hog!" So, they both had their nails and a pedicure done. Anna came out feeling a million dollars. Now they were finally on the Island and in their chalet. Anna decided to change into her swimsuit and a long white loose fitting cotton shirt and her new sandals. She looked at herself in the full-length mirror and liked what she saw for the first time in many years. Yes, she told herself, Ken would want a bit of this!!

Ken put the last of his shirts onto a coat hanger and closed the wardrobe door. The sound of the waves crashing onto the beach, annoyed him rather than soothed him. They'd passed some chalets in amongst a rainforest on the way here and he'd have much rather had one of those. He looked over at Anna, who was getting dressed. She was putting on some hideous white long blouse. When he'd arrived home two weeks ago and seen her with a new hairstyle, he'd had to try his hardest not to laugh out loud. He thought she looked ridicules. The following day, he'd noticed her nails were painted a bright pink and she had on clothes he'd never seen before. She was probably going through some sort of mid-life crisis he'd thought. Never once did he think that Anna's efforts might have been for him. He'd taken some persuading to leave Ruby behind for a week and go on a money-wasting holiday with his wife. Now, she was suggesting they have a walk around the Island to see what was there. He thought of Ruby, back in Sydney, and felt himself getting hard. He'd seen her the night before they left for the Island, and had gone straight to her apartment without having dinner first. He wouldn't see her for a week and he wanted to give her something to remember him by. Ruby was waiting for him when he'd arrived. She had a bottle of Oyster Bay Sauvignon Blanc in the cooler and two glasses.

"Darling don't go," Ruby had pleaded. "I'm

going to miss you so much."

Ken had poured two small measures of wine into the glasses and they both quaffed them down. Ken wanted to make every moment count tonight.

"I'll only be gone a week. I've got to keep the old girl happy so that we can continue to do this," and with that he grabbed her hand and led her into the bedroom. As usual, their first encounter of the night was frantic. Ken grabbed Ruby by the back of her hair and pulled her face to his. His tongue found its way into her mouth and she responded by meeting it with her own. His hands roamed her body. He lifted her tee shirt up over her shoulders and took off her bra. He continued his kisses and Ruby shuddered and pushed herself closer in to him, feeling his erection trying to free itself. Her nipples were of particular interest to him and he paid them plenty of attention.

"Ken, I'm going to come if you keep that up, slow down," she'd pleaded.   .

But Ken was already building to the height of his passion and ran his hand down, over her flat stomach (why did he suddenly think of Anna's paunchy belly, he wondered?) and unzipped Ruby's jeans. He removed his own jeans but left his shirt on. Ruby looked into his flaming blue eyes and thought how much she was starting to love this man. If only he'd leave his miserable old wife, she thought. Ken, though, was having no more thoughts of Anna.

"That's it baby," Ken's cry was almost manic. "Come on!"

Ruby matched him stroke for stroke and their sex was quick and satisfying. Afterwards, they lay together for a while as they both recovered their breath. Ken rolled over and lay beside her.

"Go and get us another glass of wine love," he said.

Ruby went back into the kitchen for the wine and took it back into bed with them, along with some cheese and crackers. Much later, after another three more similar sex sessions, Ruby had her head-on Ken's shoulders.

"I don't want you to go baby. I'll miss you!"

"I don't want to go either Rubes, but I've promised her now that I would. Anyway, I'll be back before you know it."

Now, thoughts of having to make do with Anna for a whole week made him want to throw up. He put his sunhat on and made his way out of the chalet,

CHAPTER 8

BIANCA

After Joel had walked out on her, Bianca had got up and ran after him in tears. When she'd caught him up, they had walked in silence over to the Golf Course, then to the Archery Range, and over to the salt water swimming pool, with its hammocks and sun lounges. Already the area was almost full. Couples, in the deep green/blue water, were holding each onto each other, kissing and whispering into each other's ears. Women in skimpy bikinis were lounging in hammocks reading, one had her iPod plugged into her ears, eyes closed but feet moving to the rhythm of the music. One young guy pushed another into the deep end of the pool. Everyone was happy and having fun. Bianca had never felt more alone than at that moment. She looked across at Joel who was looking around him disinterestedly.

"Let's go and find the Café and have a coffee before we decide what to do," she suggested and Joel nodded.

They continued their walk towards where they could see the main Reception building was in the distance. Once there, a sign saying 'RESTAURANT' and an arrow pointing east showed them the way. Setting off in that direction they soon came to a small Café, surrounded with bushes of all types of wonderfully smelling flowers, where Bianca knew they would be able to get a coffee from. The Café was called 'Cloud 9', a very apt name for such a beautiful spot, thought Bianca.

"A half strength flat white and a cappuccino please," Bianca ordered from the waitress.

"Certainly. Haven't seen you in here before.

TRISH OLLMAN

You just arrived?" Bianca nodded.

"Hi. Nice to meet you. Hope to see you in here a lot. My name's Sue Wilkinson, but everybody calls me Tiggs. No idea why. It's just a nickname I've had since I was a child."

Bianca picked up 2 sachets of brown sugar and a silver spoon.

"Nice to meet you Sue, sorry, Tiggs. This is my husband Joel. We just got married earlier today."

"Hi Joel. How does it feel to be a married man now?" Tiggs asked, more out of politeness than interest.

Joel cleared his throat. Him, a married man? This was the first time he'd thought of himself as such.

"Fine. Good." He was lost for words and didn't know what was expected of him to say.

Tiggs sensing that things weren't as they should be, said, "Take a seat and I'll bring the coffees over."

Bianca led them to a table in the window, where they

could look out onto the Ocean. It really was lovely here, she thought. To the right was the sea pool, which filled with the seawater that came in at high tide. Again, there were many people sitting around it or laying on beach towels, reading or just sun bathing. Younger people frolicked in the water and everyone was just having a great time. Bianca felt the pit of her stomach tighten. The whole idea of this holiday was to make Joel relax, be happier, and make him lose his inhibitions about making love. So far, even though they'd only been on the Island a few hours, this looked far from happening. Joel was making no effort to make conversation with her or show her any affection at all. It was as though he was somehow blaming Bianca for turning him into a married man, one who now had to perform for his new wife. He seemed to be coming far more withdrawn and not really interested in the lovely surroundings of Paradise Island.

"So, darling, what do you think? It's lovely here. I could live her all year round, I think!" Bianca thought that she had to at least try and open Joel up.

"It's OK. Yeah. It's nice."

"After we've had our coffee, why don't we go

back to the chalet and get into our swimmers and go to the saltwater pool? I like it better than that one over there."

Joel nodded in agreement, and minutes later Tiggs arrived with their coffees.

"Ummm. Just how I like it," Bianca called across to Tiggs. "Thank you."

"Anytime hun. Hope to see you in here every day. I will have learnt your names by the time you leave!" Tiggs joked.

After they'd finished their coffees and said goodbye to Tiggs, Bianca took hold of Joel's hand and they made their way back to their chalet to change. Once inside, Bianca, feeling a sudden rush of love for Joel, couldn't help herself and put her arms around his un-responding neck and kissed him softly on the lips. She pushed her hips up against him but felt nothing. Joel pushed her backwards and she fell back onto the bed.

"Just fuckin' leave me alone for two minutes, can't you? Why does it always have to be about sex with you!" he shouted.

Again, for the second time that day, he stormed out of the chalet. Bianca ran out after him, to try and get him to go back in and at least talk. When she caught up with him, they walked side by side for a while, both saying nothing. Bianca, frustrated and suddenly angry, grabbed hold of Joel's arm and forced him to stop walking.

"Is this how it's going to be? For the whole fucking week, Joel?" Tears streamed down her face. "This is supposed to be our honeymoon. One of the happiest times of our lives. Why are you being like this? Let's at least talk."

Joel frowned, and a panicked look overtook him.

"Look Bea, I'm sorry. Right? It's been a big day. I'm a different man now. I've got responsibilities. I've got a wife. I can't cope with this new me. I don't know what's expected of me now. I just want to spend some time away on my own to think things through."

"Think things through? What fucking things?"

Bianca was livid. They both knew where their problems lay but Joel was just not prepared to at least go to counselling or to have a go and give things a try.

He shrugged off Bianca's hand from his arm.

"Bea just let me go off by myself for a while. I need to sort my head out."

He walked off leaving Bianca once again standing alone trying to hold back the tears, not knowing what to do next to make their situation any better. OK, she thought, if that's how he wants it, he can do what he fucking wants. I'm not going to let him ruin this holiday for me. He can go and sort things out in his fucking head. Furious, she'd gone back to the chalet and gathered her swimming things together then gone to the Pool and found an empty hammock. She took out a book she brought for the holiday, hoping to try new things with Joel, to get him interested in her. It was called 'Fifty Shades of Grey'. She'd heard a lot about the book from friends and about the myriad amount of sex in it, and she thought she might get some inspiration from reading it, although she now realised that it was pointless to even try with Joel. She opened the book up and while she was reading, some creepy, grey haired old sleaze bag of a man had come up to her flirting and trying to make a pass at her. She hoped she wouldn't bump into him again. She might be frustrated with her own sex life but there was no way she wanted it with anyone else but Joel. At dinner that night, Joel had still not returned to the chalet and Bianca was faced with the humiliation of sitting at a table in the restaurant on her own. She had no appetite and just pushed the food around on her plate. Luckily, she didn't see the grey-haired man looking over at her with lust in his eyes. Finally, she decided she wasn't hungry but she'd go for a walk along the beach in the hope of finding Joel. Taking off her sandals, Bianca felt the soft warm sand beneath her feet and walked to the waters' edge. She walked the length of the beach, past couples holding hands, staring into each other's eyes, whispering to each other, she even saw a couple laying in the sand getting rather hot and heavy. She looked up at the gleaming navy blue sky with its full moon, giving everything a honey coloured glow. Stars twinkled, and the soft lapping sounds of the rolling waves made Rachel stand still. This was indeed Paradise. So why did she feel as though her heart had been ripped out?

Joel's intentions were to make his way to the other side of the Island, well away from civilisation. He felt that, once there, he would feel that he was finally in his comfort zone. There was no one to hassle him, no one making demands on him or wanting him to do things he didn't want to do. He spotted a small inlet and decided to make his way down there. Realising he hadn't eaten in hours, Joel spotted a banana tree. The bananas on it weren't ripe but nevertheless Joel took one and ate it, although with difficulty. He'd picked up his water bottle from the table on his way out of the chalet and it was still half full, so he drank a little. Once at the inlet, Joel found a nice sheltered spot and lay down. He looked up at the sky and wondered what Bianca was doing. He had to admit it was very beautiful here. This was the sort of place he could quite easily live, alone, he thought. Joel knew he had problems, real deep seated ones that were affecting his sex life with Bianca, who he loved dearly and wanted to make happy. He'd been trying for the last week or so since he'd seen the Counsellor to work on his breathing and relaxation, that the Counsellor had advised him to do, but with no success. One thing he hadn't told Bianca after his session was that he hadn't been able to tell the Counsellor about his childhood abuse. He'd just murmured to her that he found he didn't really ever want sex and felt that he was being made to perform. The breathing exercises, and the relaxation advice had been given to Joel by the Counsellor on that information alone. When he'd told Bianca that it had been a waste of money, he was telling the truth. It had been. Now, Joel found it difficult, if not impossible, to bring back the memories he had tried for so long to forget. Sometimes, at night, he dreamt of his father's face, inches away from his own, with rancid breath coming from his mouth. He'd then feel the gag as his mouth filled and a chocking sensation, trying with all his might to push his father away, but not even moving him an inch. After these dreams, he'd wake up in a cold sweat, shaking. Luckily Bianca was a sound sleeper and never knew of these night terrors. Sure, he'd told her about the abuse but he'd refused to talk to her about it again, saying he just wanted to move on and forget about it. But he couldn't move on, and tonight was proving that. Whenever Bianca turned to him at night, or pushed up against him in the kitchen, he felt a cold fear running through him. Sometimes he'd resign himself and tell himself to do just do his best and, after much foreplay on Bianca's part, he was able to get a slight erection. Not a big manly erection, but an erection nonetheless. Bianca would start by rubbing Joel's back. That seemed to relax him a little. Then she would give him tiny kisses over his neck and throat, down through his hairless chest then run her fingers through his pubic hair. Often, she had to ask Joel to do the same to her and he did so, but without enthusiasm. As her own lust grew, she'd ask Joel to plant tiny kisses on her body. She would then take Joel's either flaccid or semi erect penis in her hand and begin the rhythmic motions, up, down, up down. Mostly, they were able to get into a rhythm. But slowly, which made Bianca frustrated, then, angry, and they often gave up altogether on many occasions. When they did manage to perform the sex act itself, Bianca would lay almost motionless and bored as Joel reluctantly pounded away for what seemed like an eternity, not kissing or touching her body. Often, he would give up after trying for so long, without success. Knowing that Joel was not enjoying the sex, nor was he making any attempt to turn her on, Rachael would often feel it pointless even to try. In the beginning of their relationship Bianca had shown Joel how to do the sort of things that pleased a woman, things that pleased her, instead of him performing the sex act itself, but as always, he was forever reluctant to even try. Occasionally, on the few times they were successful, Joel made no sound, no groan, just kept his eyes closed and continued to pound away, slowly at first then a little quicker, until after what seemed like an eternity for Bianca, he would come. His body would shudder then slump against hers and they would lie still like that for a few minutes. Afterwards, Joel would always want praise for what he'd just done.

"Did I do it right, honey? Was I OK?" or "Sorry I took so long Bea, but it was OK, wasn't it?"

Bianca always reassured him that it had been great. She could never bring herself to tell him that she wanted more. So much more. She couldn't hurt him, especially as she knew how much effort it must have taken him to do it. Now, looking up at the inky sky, laying in his little alcove, Joel wondered if things would ever get any better for him. Again, he wondered what Bianca was doing. Probably sleeping, he thought. He turned on his side in the foetal position and fell into an exhausted sleep.

Bianca had made her way back along the beach. Joel was probably asleep in bed so their honeymoon night would be ruined, not that she really expected much more anyway. As she walked, Bianca kept running through her head what Joel had told her about being abused as a child. She'd had a wonderful father growing up. He'd played tag with her, Monopoly, cards, taken her to the movies. He was a father every child could wish for. It wasn't until her mother had died and he'd married that awful woman that he'd changed. He became a different man altogether. He was completely downtrodden and uncommunicative. Bianca regretted that she no longer spoke to him. Maybe he could have helped Joel in some way. There wasn't a day went by when Bianca didn't want to go to the Police to report Joel's father for what he had done. But Joel came first and she had to let him be the one to make that decision. Bianca realised that she was sick and tired of always being the one to make the first move, always the first to kiss him, to always be the one to ask for a compliment, or always having to be the one to hold his hand, or initiate sex. She wondered, not for the first time, if Joel's problems could ever be fixed. Would she be able to live her lifetime with a man who had no interest in her sexually at all? Bianca didn't know the answer. All she knew was that she loved him and desperately wanted to help him. She reached their chalet and unlocked the door. The dim bedside lights were switched on and the cover of the bed turned down. Placed on each pillow was a single red rose and a Belgium chocolate. On the table was a small cream embossed card, which said

"Welcome to Paradise Island, Honeymooners. I will be looking after you and your chalet during your stay. Just dial 649 if you need me. Enjoy your Honeymoon. Karen McNulty."

Bianca put the card on the desk and took the roses and chocolates off the pillows. Her stomach was in knots. Joel wasn't here. She hadn't seen him all afternoon or this evening. She then remembered his words. "I want to be on my own." Anger flowed through Bianca like a torrent. Be on your own then you fuckwit. Wherever you are out there I hope you're cold and lonely. Tears streamed down her face. What a great honeymoon night! Bianca got undressed and climbed into the shower. She made the water as hot as she could possibly take it and reached down and ran her fingers over herself, harder and faster. She came almost immediately. "Fuck You Joel," she shouted.

CHAPTER 9

ANNA

Anna and Ken were heading for the beach. They both had their swimmers on and Anna, feeling like a million dollars, even had a bit of a swagger as she walked, sure that Ken's eyes were upon her. Once there, they lay down on beach loungers under an umbrella shade.

"Darling, before you settle, could you go to the bar and get us a drink?" Anna's new-found confidence let her ask. Ken, who could have done with a few stiff drinks himself, agreed, and set off in the direction of the facilities block. He'd had enough of his wife and her 'new look' already and was becoming more repulsed by her every day. Plus, he was missing Ruby and he was missing sex. Looking to his left, he saw in the distance, another pool. There seemed to be a lot of people there so Ken thought he'd go and see what the local talent was like. He only had on his bright blue Speedos and his manhood bulged out proudly. Once at the pool, he noticed that everyone was in couples apart from two young guys who were splashing about in the water. He was just about to turn back towards the bar when he spotted a gorgeous girl, maybe 23, 25, in a red bikini. She had lovely shoulder length wavy brown hair and gorgeous eyes. She was laying, alone, on a sunbed reading, of all things, '*50 Shades of Grey*'. Ken was suddenly alert. Here, he thought, was what he was looking for. He idled over to her.

"Hi. Looks like an interesting book you've got there" his voice was soft and velvety and, he hoped, very flirty.

Bianca looked up and squinted through the sun. Standing beside her was a man with greying hair, probably in his 60's. Surely he wasn't trying to come on to her, was he, she thought?

"Erm, I've only just started it, but yeah. It's supposed to be really good." Ken gave her one of his sincerest smiles.

"I've heard so too. Hey, you want to come for a drink? Your sweating and I bet you need one?" Ken was using all his charm, but Bianca wasn't having any of it. She gave him a filthy look that said 'Piss Off Old Man'.

"No. No thanks. But thank you for asking anyway. I'm waiting for my husband to join me."

Ken, never a one to be so easily given the brush off said,

"Ok. Maybe see you around. Oh, you look lovely by the way!"

Bianca was astounded at the man's flirting but secretly wished Joel could have half this man's confidence. Ken made his way to the bar and got the drinks for himself and Anna, then headed back to her on the beach. He immediately settled down with his book.

"This is nice darling, isn't it?" Anna and her new self was trying her best to make conversation.

But all's she got from Ken was a "hmmm." She'd been trying for the last two weeks to think of new ways she and Ken could fall in love once again, go back to how things were years ago. OK, she could forgive him his affairs. She'd long ago realised that she couldn't give him what he'd wanted in bed, but now she was willing to try. She'd gone to a lot of trouble to make herself look appealing to Ken and she thought he appreciated her new look. Well, he hadn't actually said so, but she'd caught him glancing at her every now and then, and that was a good start, wasn't it? She didn't feel 64. More like 40 now that she'd had her make over, and she was sure that Ken appreciated it.

"I think I'll go in for a paddle Ken. Want to come with me?" she held out her hand to him.

Ken felt sick. She had on a hideous multi coloured swimsuit, ruffled around the waist. Her saggy skin on her arms and legs made her look 70, he thought.

"No thanks. I'm just getting into this book. You go."

Knowing Ken's eyes were probably on her, Anna walked as sexily as she knew how down to the water's edge and slowly made her way into the beautifully warm blue ocean. She stopped once the water was up to her waist. She didn't want to get her hair wet. She wanted Ken to see her at her best all the time. Anna lifted her face to the sun and basked in its warmth for a few moments. Then she realised she hadn't put any sun cream on, so she decided to go and get Ken to put it on for her. The thought of this intimacy gave Anna butterflies for the first time in many years and she rushed out of the water towards her husband.

"Darling, I've forgotten to put sun cream on. Can you put some on for me?" Ken was repulsed at Anna's new simpering voice. Feeling he had no choice, he took the sun cream out of the bag and started to rub it, roughly, onto Anna's shoulders.

"That's nice Ken. Isn't this wonderful? I can't believe we're actually here. I wonder what's for dinner. I'm starving…"

Ken tuned out. He wondered what had come over his usually meek and quiet wife. Yet here she was rabbiting away and boring him shitless. Anna went back into the water for half an hour, enjoying the luxurious feel of its warmth and the small waves washing over her tummy. Walking back up the beach to Ken, she noticed that he was watching her.

"Yes, it's working" she thought. "Look at the way he's looking at me. Tonight's the night my darling!"

On reaching her sun lounge, Anna dried herself off and put on her shirt. Ken hadn't been watching Anna at all. He had been gazing out to sea thinking of Ruby and of what he'd do to her when they got home. Jolted out of his reverie, he realised that Anna was back and blabbering on about how warm the ocean was. He looked at her through squinted eyes and was once again repulsed by her and her new look. He wondered how he was going to get through the next week with her. Anna got her watch out of the bag and saw that it was almost time for dinner.

"Come on Ken. We'd better go back and get changed. It's almost dinner time."

With a sigh, Ken picked up their things and they made their way back to the chalet to shower and dress.

Ken's eyes were scanning the Restaurant. He was looking to see if there was any talent. He and Anna were sitting at a table for two. A short man with dark brown hair and a stubble on his chin, which Anna thought looked rather attractive, came over to them and introduced himself as Theo, the Entertainments Manager. He was immaculately dressed in dinner suit and blue bow tie, which complimented the other staff's uniform. He wished them a happy and relaxed stay on the Island and hoped they would be sure to catch some of the entertainment on offer. For this evening's meal, there was a crisp white tablecloth on the table, and a candle flickering inside a cut-glass holder in the centre. Outside the open balcony, the sun was setting, making beautiful pink and blue swirls intertwining as one mass across the sky. The lighting in the Restaurant was subdued and romantic and Anna thought this was the perfect opportunity to make her move. She edged her sandalled foot up to Ken's leg and ever so slightly rubbed it up and down. Ken, appalled, quickly moved his leg. Maybe he needed time to get used to her new, improved self, she thought, but she'd show him tonight that she was a changed woman. The thought of actually having sex with Ken was something Anna hadn't given much thought to. She'd been so preoccupied with making herself more attractive to him. But somehow, she just knew that Ken was looking at her with new eyes. She knew that after the bottle of wine they'd drink with dinner, he'd be more than ready for her. Ken, still scanning the room, spotted the girl in the red bikini from the pool earlier. He was amazed that she was sitting alone, looking quite sad and just moving her meal around on the plate. He wondered what was wrong. Hadn't she mentioned a husband? He thought to himself that he would seek her out tomorrow and give it another try. When their main course arrived, a steak with king prawns for Ken, and a chicken Caesar salad for Anna, Ken had poured them both a glass of the House Wine and they ate in silence. Every now and again, Ken would look across at Anna and catch her staring at him. This worried him, as back home they barely ever made eye contact. Something made Ken catch his breath. Surely, Anna hadn't gone to all this trouble to improve herself for him, had she? No. Never. What they'd had had died years ago. There was no way of going back to her for him. When he thought about it, he realised that he actually despised her, especially this new version of her. He pushed the thoughts out of his head. It was only for six more days then he'd be back with Ruby, and if Ruby ended up not working out, then there would soon be another one to submit to his charms. When they'd finished dinner, Anna suggested a walk along the beach. She thought it would be a romantic lead in to what she had planned for them that night, but Ken refused, saying it had been a long day and he just wanted to go back to the chalet and get some sleep. Anna, not to be put off, thought to herself, sleep will hopefully be the last thing on your mind tonight my darling! They made their way back to the chalet together in silence, Anna full of nerves and anticipation, and a certainty that she would get what she now wanted from Ken after all these years.

CHAPTER 10

SUE

After she'd unpacked her small amount of clothes and toiletries, Sue had put on a swimsuit and a sarong, sat on her balcony with a drink from her fridge for half an hour then started to walk around the Island to have a look at what was on offer. She soon came to the Island's 9 Hole Golf Course. Sue had never played golf in her life but thought she wouldn't mind giving it a go while she was here. You never know, she thought, I might meet a nice man who could show me how to play. The thought excited Sue and she moved on towards the salt-water pool. Once there, she noticed couples, splashing together, kissing and holding each other in their arms, bobbing up and down in the blue green water. There were sun lounges and hammocks, and Sue picked a particularly shady sun lounger out for later. She'd brought a new book, *'Girl on the Train'* with her, and she was looking forward to starting it. Moving on she found herself at the Reception building. There was a man, probably in his late 40s or early 50s, talking outside to another member of staff. Sue thought he was very good looking. He was of Italian appearance, with thick black hair and a good set of cheekbones and a long Roman nose, was slim and dressed in a white open necked shirt and tight black pants. His shoes looked like they were patent leather, they were so shiny. Sue lingered where she was for a while, watching the man talk. He really was very attractive, she thought. She wondered how she could introduce herself? While she was thinking of ways to do so, the man had finished talking and was walking Sue's way. When he reached her, he said, in a strong Italian accent, (She'd been right about his heritage, she thought!)

"Hello Miss. How are you today?"

Sue, immediately flattered at being called 'Miss', blushed slightly and answered that, although it was a little hot, she had only just arrived and was exploring the Island. The man took Sue's arm and said in that sexy voice of his

"My name is Marcello. I book all the Island's entertainments. I look for Groups, Comediennes, and Artists of all kinds, to entertain beautiful women such as you. Are you alone, or have you come with your husband?" Sue replied that she was alone.

"Please allow me to show you around,"

Marcello took Sue's arm. Slightly flustered, Sue muttered a weak "Thank you. I'm Sue," and allowed Marcello who lead her down a path, which looked like it was heading straight for the mountains and away from the main Resort area.

"I would like to take you to a beautiful place where not many people get to see," said Marcello, his accent giving Sue those unfamiliar butterflies in her stomach again. "This place, it is called 'Bella Aqua', Beautiful Water in my language. Come."

He still held onto Sue's arm, leading her along the path. Soon the path became grass and then rocky ground. Sue was glad she had her sandals on as they continued off the beaten track and through some lush rainforest. After a brisk fifteen-minute walk, Sue, by now quite breathless, looked ahead and saw an opening in the trees.

Marcello said, "Here we are. This is the place. Bella Aqua."

Ahead of them lay a small waterhole, surrounded by lush frangipanis and other colourful shrubs and trees, all ablaze with colour. Parrots and Cockatoos were sitting noisily in the trees, and the sound of frogs and crickets was almost deafening. The water was a clear blue and with the sun shining on it, reflecting shimmering shadows, it looked as inviting as anything Sue had ever seen.

"I swim here most days when I can," Marcello ran his hand over his slightly sweating brow. "Why is such a beautiful woman as you here on your own?" he asked.

"I tried to get a girlfriend to come with me but

she couldn't get time off work," Sue lied. Somehow, she felt ashamed that she hadn't had anybody to come with her. "So, I decided to come on my own anyway."

"Why don't you join me tomorrow, Miss Sue? Come with me for a swim here? You are a very beautiful lady and I'd love your company."

Sue, flustered, as no man had ever spoken to her like this before, answered that she would love to come. It was a magical place and she really liked this lovely Italian man. Marcello said that he'd meet her outside the main Reception building at 11.30am the next day and they made their way back towards the Resort. When they'd arrived back, Marcello had got hold of Sue's hand and raised it to his lips, giving it the tiniest and softest of kisses.

"It has been my pleasure to meet you, Miss Sue. I'll look forward to seeing you in the morning when you and Marcello shall once more meet and swim."

With that he turned and walked into the building leaving Sue astonished at her good fortune at the start of her week on Paradise Island! Inside the Reception building, Marcello was quietly patting himself on the back. He was sure he'd found his obligatory weekly conquest. Marcello had come to Australia from Italy with his parents as Immigrants when he was five, and had quickly lost his accent. But he found the ladies loved it when he put on a really strong Italian accent, when in reality, he was broad Aussie. Sure, this Sue wasn't the type he preferred. She was a bit dowdy and not that attractive, but she was a woman, and to Marcello, who had only one thing planned for Sue, that was enough. When he had first started working as an Entertainments Booker at Paradise Island Resort, he had set himself a challenge of getting at least one new woman every week. There weren't many single women who came to the Island but Marcello always managed to find one who he could charm with his good looks and fake Italian accent. The thing was, Marcello liked sex. Indeed, he couldn't live without it, he was addicted to it. On the odd occasion, he didn't have a woman, he would masturbate two or three times a day. He wondered what sort of lover Sue would make. He'd soon find out, he thought.

The following morning, at exactly 11.30am, he found Sue waiting outside the Reception building, wearing her swimmers and a pink sarong. She had a beach bag in her hand and sunglasses on.

"Good Morning Miss Sue. How are you today? Looking forward to our swim, I hope?"

Marcello gave Sue a small peck on her cheek. This made Sue blush furiously but she said nevertheless "Good morning to you, Marcello. I'm very much looking forward to our swim."

So am I, thought Marcello with a smirk. They once again made their way down to the waterhole. The thought of its blue waters on Sue's once again sweaty body was very inviting.

"You are the only person who I have ever brought to see this wonderful place. It is my hidden secret!" said Marcello.

Sue felt very privileged and attractive, even desirable, that this man had chosen her to be the first person to bring here. When they arrived, Sue watched in awe as Marcello, without any sign of embarrassment, unzipped his pants and slid them off, then giving Sue a smile, unbuttoned his shirt and took it off. He was wearing a pair of tight fitting speedos, which showed his bulging manhood off to perfection, Marcello thought. Sue didn't know where to look, so turned away from him and took off her sarong. She'd chosen a plain black fitted swimsuit, as she thought it would hide her slightly pudgy figure and slim her down. She reached into her bag and pulled out the sun cream. Marcello, spotting this, came over to her.

"Here Miss Sue. Allow me to put the cream on for you."

Sue had no option but to allow Marcello to take the sun cream from her and watch as he squeezed a large dollop of cream onto his hand.

"Turn around Sue." Sue noticed Marcello had dropped the "Miss".

He started to rub the cream into Sue's shoulders and neck, then down her back but as he got further down, Sue noticed a slight change in the movements of his hand. He seemed to more caressing her than rubbing sun cream on her.

"Turn around again now Sue."

It was almost an order and Sue shyly turned around.

Marcello put more cream onto his hand but this time rubbed both of his hands together. He then started to rub Sue's shoulders, then her neck.

"Now, lift you face up Sue," he said, then tenderly rubbed cream into Sue's face. Sue's heart was beating fast and the butterflies in her stomach were working overtime. Surely this man wasn't flirting with her? A good-looking man like this, why would he be bothered with the likes of me, she thought. But Marcello hadn't finished, and added more cream to his hands and started to rub the area in between Sue's large, full breasts. She was mortified with embarrassment and found she couldn't speak, or even move. She looked up to find Marcello looking at her.

"You're very beautiful, you know Miss Sue." Sue noticed the "Miss" was back again. "Come, let's swim." Marcello took her by the hand to the waterhole. "There's only one way in and that's to jump," he said.

"OK. But how do I get out?" Sue wasn't so sure this was a very good idea any more.

"Don't worry Miss Sue. Marcello will get you out. No problem." Oh wow, thought Sue, still seduced by that accent! It made her inside's melt.

"Come, hold my hand and we'll jump in together,"

Marcello had done this many, many times before and confidently grabbed Sue's hand and laughing, pulled her to the edge and launched the two of them into the waterhole. Sue panicked as she went under the water, but then as she emerged to the top she looked around her and got her bearings. Once she'd caught her breath again, Sue saw that it really was quite beautiful, and the water so warm and refreshing. Marcello had also surfaced, and started to splash her.

"I told you it was beautiful, didn't I?" he said.

He swam around the waterhole while Sue just paddled water. After a while she relaxed and took in the beautiful surroundings. The water was clean and clear, the smell from the flowers sublime and the noise from the birds and other wildlife made her think she truly was in paradise.

"It's such a fitting name for the Island, isn't it? Paradise Island," Sue shouted over to Marcello.

He swam up to her and put his arms around her waist, tightening his grip and pulling her close.

"Yes, a beautiful name and a beautiful woman. I am the luckiest man on earth at this moment."

Sue didn't know where to look. Never in her 49 years had a man ever said such a thing to her. Surely this man couldn't be making a play for me, could he, she thought to herself. Not used to such attention, she panicked and pulled herself out of Marcello's embrace and swam to the edge of the waterhole.

"I think I've had enough now, thank you Marcello," Sue needed time to process what had just happened. "Can you help me get out?" She looked over at him.

"Certainly, Miss Sue," and he hauled himself up the bank of the waterhole and, bending, grabbed both of Sue's hands and pulled her out onto the side. Marcello was often used to such behaviour on the first time with all his women. He'd bide his time. Sue might not be looking at him with a lover's eye now but by tonight she would be, Marcello was certain of that. After they had both towelled themselves dry, Marcello told Sue that they must do this again, soon. Although unnerved by the experience, Sue had said that it would be wonderful. They arranged to meet the following day. Now dressed they made their way back to the Resort.

CHAPTER 11

RACHAEL

Rachael and Harry had decided to go directly to the Ocean Pool. Rachael put on her new blue bikini and Harry his Board Shorts. They gathered together books, towels, sunglasses and suntan lotion, taken 2 bottles of water out of the fridge and set off. This was the first time in their ten-year marriage that Rachael hadn't had to pack for the kids. She was still worried sick about how they were behaving, especially Jake, for her parents. Harry had told her that Noeline and

Trevor would be able to deal with Jake for the week and that she should just stop worrying and just enjoy herself.

"Ready Babe?" Harry was heading out the door.

"I'm coming," said Rachael, and they made their way through the rainforest to the Resort's main area.

There were quite a few people at the Ocean Pool. Most were lazing on sun loungers, reading or dozing, but a few were swimming. They found two sun loungers and threw their things on them. Harry grabbed Rachael round the waist and lifted her up, and half walked, half ran to the pool and threw them both in. Rachael spluttered and coughed as she came to the surface and saw Harry laughing. Gee, they hadn't been like this for a while, she thought. It was good to see Harry so happy. They swam and frolicked in the water for a while then got out, and lay on their lounges to dry off.

"Now this is what I call Paradise!" said Harry. "I could do this every day for the rest of my life."

'Yeah, me too" said Rachael, but deep down,

she was really thinking about how her parents would be right now. It was gone four and the kids would be home from school, and Lily would be awake from her afternoon nap. Rachael knew her mother wouldn't be able to cope and the more she thought about it the more panicked she got. She turned to Harry, who was reading his book.

"Oh God, Harry. I'm panicking about how Mum's going with the kids. They'll be home from school now!"

Harry banged down his book onto his knees.

"For God's sake Rach, I'm sick and tired of you going on about the bloody kids. I'm here to relax. Fuck you. I'm going to go and have a round of golf. You stay here and worry some more!" and with that he gathered up his things and walked of.

Rachael felt the tears well up in her eyes. She wondered again why Harry was so laid back about their children, especially Jake, as they were just so difficult to manage. She decided to go to the main Reception building and use the landline there and ring her mum just to make sure everything was OK. She gathered up her things and made her way over. Her dad answered on the fourth ring, but Rachael struggled to hear him over the wailing coming from the background. Oh no! It sounded like Jake. Rachael's heart plummeted.

She shouted "Dad, it's me. Is everything OK?"

Trevor, usually his calm, quiet self, shouted to her,

"Rachael! Is everything alright? Are you there yet?"

"Yes, dad. We're here. Is that Jake screaming? What's wrong? I knew this was a bad idea. Are you and mum OK?" Rachael felt sick in her stomach.

What was she thinking getting her parents to have the kids for a whole week? And this was only day one!

"Rachael, settle down," shouted Trevor. "Jakes having one of his paddy's because mum won't let him take all the blankets off the bed and make a cubby house. And Ruby's crying, I think because she's after a bottle but mum says she's too big for a bottle now." Rachael was nearly in tears listening to the cries in the background.

"Dad, I know she's 3 now but she always has a bottle at this time. Can't you just ask mum to give her one, just until we get home, then I'll try and wean her off it. Please Dad?"

"OK Rach. But you know what your mum's like. Stubborn as a mule, but I'll try."

Trying hard to ignore the crying and screaming, Rachael said again

"Please try Dad. It must be hard enough for her to be away from me for the first time. If she could just have a bottle. Please? What's happening with Jake? How is mum trying to calm him down?"

"She's locked him the cupboard under the stairs and told him he's not coming out until he stops. Don't worry about him Rach. He's got to have some discipline. He'll be right in five minutes or so. I'll go and let him out as soon as we hang up. You go and enjoy yourselves darling. We're managing here."

NO, cried Rachael, silently. YOU'RE NOT!! She said goodbye to her Dad and felt the tears sliding down her cheeks. What had she done! Poor Jake locked in the cupboard. And Ruby, without a bottle. She made her way back to their chalet and let herself in. Harry was nowhere to be seen. She lay on the bed with her face in the pillow and allowed the sobs to come freely.

Harry had made his way over to the 9 Hole Golf Course and hired some balls and some clubs and a trolley. He wasn't a bad player, and managed to play once a week at the Club near his home. Rachael wasn't happy about it though. Always moaning that it was Ok for him to have some outlet, some time alone, but all that she ever did was stay at home looking after the kids. Harry felt that he worked hard all week to earn a living for them, then he was expected to come home and help with the kids, Jake, especially. He'd then be up till all hours as Lily wouldn't go down to sleep. Oh sure, she was fine if she could fall asleep on his or Rachael's knee, but as soon as they tried to carry her up to her bed, she'd wake up crying and saying, NO, she didn't want to go to bed. Sometimes they persisted and Lily would cry herself to sleep, sometimes on her bedroom floor, sometimes on the couch. But by this time, it was usually almost midnight, and often he and Rachael just gave in and let her sleep with them. He felt he deserved a bit of time to himself. Life wasn't all about work and kids. He wished he could play golf more but he was sure Rachael wouldn't be very pleased if he suggested it. Back on the Island's Golf Course, he set up his first shot.

"Hi. You on your own?" A woman around his own age had come up beside him. She also had a set of clubs and a trolley.

Harry, surprised, had said "Yes. We've not long arrived. Thought a round would clear my head a bit. Are you on your own? You want to join me for a Round?"

"Yes, sure. I'd love to. That's one of the disadvantages of coming to a place like this on your own. Nobody to play golf with!" She had a lovely smile, thought Harry. "I'm Cassie. Pleased to meet you."

"Hi. Pleased to meet you too. I'm Harry. Let's go then." and he re-positioned his tee and took his first shot.

By the time they'd finished all 9 Holes Harry felt he knew Cassie well. Boy, could she talk, often putting him off his stroke. But he'd loved the opportunity to talk to a woman other than his wife of ten years, and their kids. Harry had told her about his three children and all the problems they had. How Rachael wouldn't stop worrying about them being with her parents, and how they were all coping. Cassie had told him that she was single having broken up with her boyfriend of three years just a few months ago, and that she lived in Byron Bay, which was about three hours from where Harry lived. She worked in a local Craft Store, selling homemade crafts and supplies, and was a bit of a hippy, she told him. Jack assured her that he'd never have guessed by the way she was dressed now; white tee shirt and navy shorts. He found her to be really good company and asked her if she'd like to play another Round tomorrow. Cassie said yes, she would love to, as long as his wife didn't mind? Jack assured her that Rachael wouldn't mind (He'd no plans to tell Rachael about Cassie) and they'd arranged to meet at 10am the next day.

After saying their farewells, Harry headed back to his chalet. Inside he found Rachael asleep on the bed. Her eyes were swollen and puffy and he knew she had been crying. He went over to the bar fridge and got out a beer. The noise woke her up.

"How did you go?" she asked, her voice groggy with sleep.

"OK. I didn't keep score, but it was good to get out there." Harry wondered whether to mention Cassie or not but decided not to. He didn't know why he didn't mention her, but something stopped him."

"You've been crying. I can tell from your eyes." Harry went and sat on the bed. "What's up?"

Rachael felt herself filling up again. "Oh Harry. It's terrible. Mum's locked Jake in the cupboard under the stairs because he had a tantrum when she wouldn't let him make a cubby out of blankets off their bed, and Ruby was crying because mum won't give her a bottle. She says she too big now for one."

Harry was furious, but with Rachael, not with her news.

"And how did you find all this out?" His voice was hard and angry.

"I went to Reception and used the landline and rang home. Dad answered and the kids were screaming in the background. Oh, Harry it was awful!"

"Why would you do that Rach? Didn't I tell you that this was our time now and to forget about the kids, just for one fucking week."

"I'm sorry Harry. I promise I really will try, starting from now. I'll try and completely forget that my disabled son has been locked in a cupboard and my fucking baby has been refused a bottle. OK?" Rachael shouted and turned away from him.

Harry stormed out onto the veranda and drank his beer. He needed to calm down as well as allowing Rachael to realise that she was jeopardising their one chance at having a relaxing week's holiday on their own. He thought of Cassie and her lovely smile, her long blonde ponytail and the way she giggled every time she went to hit the ball. No, he was glad he hadn't mentioned her to Rachael. The last thing he needed was a jealous wife.

CHAPTER 12

BIANCA

Bianca woke from a fitful night's sleep. Every noise woke her up, thinking it might be Joel returning home. But by 6am, she lay there, fully awake, the sunlight peeking through the gap in the curtains. Anger filled her. Joel hadn't come back to her on their wedding night. How dare he! How dare he treat her this way.

"I'm going to be furious with him when he finally shows his face," she thought.

Bianca decided to get up and take a walk along the beach, hoping to clear away her anger. She loved the sounds of the waves as they crashed against the shore and the salty spray from the water. She dressed in a loose-fitting shift dress and sandals and got a bottle of water from the bar fridge. As she made her way to the beach, she made sure she continually looked around her in the hope of seeing Joel, but he was nowhere to be seen. The sand beneath her feet was just starting to warm up and felt deliciously soft. She made her way down to the water's edge and paddled for a while. Then she started to walk the length of the beach. She tried to think of other things. Things other than Joel, and where he might be, but without success. He had to come back soon, surely. He'd be hungry, thirsty and hopefully realising what he'd done. Yes, he'd be back soon, she thought. After walking for the best part of an hour, Bianca rushed back to the chalet only to find that Joel still hadn't returned. Tears threatened but instead of giving in to them, Bianca decided to go back to the coffee shop and see that lovely lady again. What was she called? Tiggs, that was it. In the coffee shop, most of the tables were occupied. Bianca found a small table for two in the corner and sat down. Tiggs was at the

Expresso machine making coffees. She looked across at Bianca and smiled that lovely smile of hers.

"Be with you in a moment," she called over.

Soon she was at Bianca's table with her notepad and pen.

"Where's your other half today? Tiggs had remembered them from yesterday.

"Oh," Bianca was suddenly flustered and embarrassed. "He's playing golf, so just me this morning, I'm afraid. I didn't feel like eating breakfast so just a half strength flat white for me please Tiggs."

"Oh, so you remembered my name. I'm honoured. I'm sorry but I've forgotten yours."

"That's Ok. You must get so many people in here. Its Bianca, and my husband is Joel."

"Hello again Bianca. I'll make sure I remember if I can get my little grey cells working again!"

Both women laughed and Tiggs went away to make the coffee. Bianca sat in silence and on her own. Looking around, everybody else was in couples. There was even a group of four. Everyone was laughing, talking, and having a good time. Bianca felt the tears start again. Joel had known she'd expect something on their wedding night, surely? OK. So, he didn't like sex. But he could of least have made an effort of some kind, instead of just walking off. Quickly finishing her coffee, she walked out of the café without even saying goodbye to Tiggs. She almost ran back to the chalet but again, only to find Joel nowhere to be seen. She lay on her bed and let the tears flow. Exhausted she fell into a deep sleep, where she dreamed she was with a man, not Joel, but a very handsome man. He was making love to her. Bianca was on a bed, laying underneath him, both were totally naked and the man was pounding away inside her. She was calling out his name, asking him to go harder, faster. She could feel the tightness forming in her belly and a glorious sensation like the whole world was going to explode around her. The man planted kisses all the way down her body and his eyes were full of passion. Bianca felt her body release and she called out his name again. But it wasn't Joel's name she called. Bianca woke with a start. Oh, my God. Did I just have an orgasm in my dream, she thought? And who was the man? She couldn't remember what name she'd called out, just that it wasn't Joel's. She looked at her watch. 12.15pm. She realised she hadn't eaten so decided to go to the restaurant and get some lunch. If Joel wasn't back by five, she thought, I'll go to Reception and raise the alarm. He had to be somewhere, and he must be hungry and thirsty. Tears welled in her eyes again at the thought. She headed to the restaurant with a heavy heart.

Joel had been awake since daybreak. He'd had a good sleep and was ready to explore this part of the Island. He got up and walked to the ocean, took his shorts and tee shirt off and gone into the salty water, gingerly at first as it was still quite cold, but a little warmer once he was in. He jumped over the waves and even rode them back to shore if they were big enough. Bianca was far from his thoughts. He was just enjoying the moment and the feeling that here, he could be whoever he liked. Joel the Good, Joel the Bad or Joel the Ugly! Getting out of the water, he realised he was hungry, and there only a little water left in the bottle from yesterday. He didn't feel like going back to the main part of the Island and Bianca yet. He was enjoying this time alone. He felt that this is what he'd been needing for years. Time to think, to think about what had happened when he was a kid, about his sister, about his future. He realised it had been a big mistake marrying Bianca. She expected too much of him. She deserved better than him, he thought. Someone who could give her what she wanted, and deserved, as his wife. Sure, he loved her, but that wasn't enough, he knew that. It was every married woman's right to expect her husband to shower her with affection and to want to make love to her. He'd thought on the way to the Island that he would try harder, but when it came to it he just couldn't perform the way Bianca wanted him to. He dried himself off with his tee shirt and put his shorts and thongs back on. He wondered if he should go back and try and find the banana tree from yesterday but decided to head north and see if he could find another one. He took a small sip of what was left of his water and made his way up and over the rocks. Walking through the bush, he marvelled at the peace and serenity of it all. Birds of different kinds flew overhead and the occasional lizard scurried into the undergrowth. He liked it here. There was nobody else around. He was alone, just as he wanted it. He wondered why something in him shunned other people. He hadn't been shy at Primary School, but once the abuse had started it was like he could barely look at others. He had made a friend, David, in High School, and there had been many times when Joel was on the verge of telling him about the abuse, but something always stopped him. He didn't want to be a freak, and didn't want David to think any less of him. As much as he liked David, he couldn't be sure that he would keep the secret, and not tell anyone else. If he did, it would soon all be round the school. 'Joel The Freak'. So, he told no one. That is, not until he'd let it all out to Bianca on the night he'd asked her to marry him. Now, Joel looked skyward to see the birds that were squawking up above, but he didn't notice the thick tree branch in his path. As he fell over it, Joel felt his ankle twist and a shooting pain went up his leg. He lay on the ground, shocked for what seemed like minutes but was only seconds. He tried to get up but it was too painful. He looked down at his foot and could see that it was already starting to swell up. Fuck! What do I do now, he thought? No use shouting for help. There was nobody for miles. He tried hopping on one foot back the way he'd came but had to give up as it was too painful. He realised then that nobody knew where he was. He was sure he'd broken something and the pain was excruciating. Surely Bianca would be wondering where he was? He tried to move in what he hoped was the right direction, back to the Resort, but after hopping and crawling on his knees the pain became too much and he gave up. All he could do was to lay under a large leafy tree for shelter, and hope that help would come.

Bianca had spent the afternoon laying by the pool, trying to concentrate on her book, but couldn't stop herself worrying about Joel. Where was he? She looked at her watch. It was almost 4pm. She'd give it till 5pm then go back to the chalet, and if he wasn't there she'd go to Reception and report him as missing. Once again, everybody around her were enjoying themselves, one couple were in the water with their tongues down each other's throats, another man was laying on a beach towel with his girl's head resting on him. There was one middle-aged woman who seemed to be by herself. She was reading in a hammock. Bianca wondered what her story was and if she was here alone. Sue, in her hammock, had also noticed Bianca, and recognised her as the girl from the next chalet to hers, the one where the young man had run out of with the girl crying and running after him, just after they'd arrived. There was no sign of the man. Sue hoped they could sort out whatever their problem was. This Island was no place to be unhappy, thought Sue, and she went back to her book. At 5pm, and with her heart in her mouth, Bianca made her way back to their chalet, but there was no sign of Joel. And no signs that he'd been back either. There was nothing to it, she had to go and report him missing. He'd been gone for almost 30 hours now. Her heart was pounding as she entered the Reception building. Luckily it was empty but for a girl of about 25.

"Hi. How can I help you?" asked the girl.

"I need to report my husband as missing. He's been gone for nearly 30 hours now. We only arrived yesterday. We're on our Honeymoon, but we, well, we sort of had a row and he just took off. I haven't seen him since and I'm getting really worried about him!" Bianca blurted it all out, relieved to be talking to someone about it.

"I wouldn't worry. He's probably on the beach somewhere." The girl had a badge on that said 'Lindy'.

Bianca couldn't tell this girl all about their problems but she had to make her take Joel's disappearance more seriously.

"Look, Lindy, my husband and I have been having problems, major problems, that I thought might go away once we got here. I've walked up and down the beach and he's not there. He kind of said yesterday that he wanted to be left on his own. I'm worried he's wondered off and got lost somewhere on the Island."

"Ok. Let me call someone." Lindy picked up the phone and punched in some numbers.

Within minutes two older men were in Reception asking Bianca where and what time she had last seen Joel. Seeing her distress, the men realised this was a genuine emergency.

"Sorry, what's your name?"

Bianca told him.

"Bianca, what I'm going to do is to try and get as many of our Security Staff and any others Staff who are off duty to get together and we'll make up a search party. It would be best if you go back to your chalet and let us know if he returns. What number chalet are you?"

Bianca told them then made her way back, her heart like stone. She was really worried now. A search party? Oh God. Joel. Where the fuck are you?

CHAPTER 13

ANNA

Ken got undressed and hung his shirt and pants up. He was waiting to go into the bathroom to do his teeth but mysteriously, Anna had gone in there first, telling him she was going to change. This was something new as she always changed in their bedroom at home. After a few minutes, the bathroom door opened and Anna walked out wearing nothing more than a red and black see-through short negligee. Ken's eyes nearly fell out of his head. He could see her sagging breasts and mound of pubic hair through the thin material and the smell of perfume coming from her was overpowering. Ken was nearly sick.

"Well, darling, what do you think?" Anna asked.

She saw the look on Ken's face and misinterpreted it as lust, but to Ken it was horror. Anna did a ridicules twirl and came up to Ken's face.

"I want us to get our love back Ken. The way it used to be." And with that she put her lips to his and started to kiss him.

Repulsed, Ken pulled back.

"Erm, this is a bit sudden, isn't it? This change in you? Did you do all this for me?"

Anna, still hopeful, replied "Yes sweetheart." This is for you. I know you still love me. I've seen the way you've been looking at me lately" she smirked.

Ken didn't know what to say. Even though he didn't love his wife anymore, he couldn't be cruel to her, and he knew he had to let her down gently.

"This new you, you know. It's going to take me some time to get used to. Let's just go to bed tonight hey and try and get a good night's sleep. It's been a long day."

Anna nodded. Ok. So, he needed time. She decided to give it one more try tonight when they'd got into bed, and see how Ken felt then. Once in bed, Ken turned over, his back facing Anna. She turned and spooned him and brought her hand round to his chest. It was a funny feeling for her as they hadn't been this close for years, but she pressed on, determined to achieve her goal. She gently rubbed Ken's chest and started to nibble his ear.

"Oh fuck," thought Ken. "Here we go. I wonder what's brought this on?"

Anna's hand had made it down to Ken's groin and she put her hand inside his boxers and held on tight. Ken could stand no more and roughly pushed Anna's hand away.

"I said not tonight Anna. Let's just get some sleep."

Anna pulled away and turned over, upset. She was sure

she'd done enough to make Ken want her again. What more could she do, there was nothing else she could think of. Keep trying, her inner voice told her. Surely, he'll succumb soon. A man with his strong sex drive wouldn't be able to go with it for too much longer!

The following morning, after they'd had breakfast at the restaurant, Anna asked Ken to go to the beach with her again and together they could read and swim.

Ken had said "No, you go. I'm happy to stay in the chalet this morning and read."

No chance, he thought, after Anna had left. He was going to go in search of the girl in the red bikini, or any other vulnerable and attractive woman he could find. He'd lain in bed last night, unable to sleep. He was thinking of Ruby and had got as horny as hell. Once Anna was sound asleep, he had gone into the toilet and allowed his mind to roam freely about all the things he would do to Ruby next week and he had relieved himself, for now anyway. Today, he would find a woman who would succumb to his charms and put Ruby out of his mind, for an hour or two at least. He got dressed in board shorts and tee shirt and looked at himself in the mirror. Ken liked what he saw. Tall, strong jaw, well built, sure his hair was grey at the temples but he thought that made him look more distinguished. Yes, he'd do. Not bad for a 64-year-old. He got a bottle of water from the fridge, grabbed a beach towel, and headed out into the balmy warm morning. The cicadas were making a terrible racket and a small lizard crossed his path and ran into the shrubs. He had to admit, this was a really nice place, if only he had Ruby or a girl with whom he could indulge his passions here with him, instead of his repulsive wife. On the off chance that he'd find her there again, he headed over to the salt water pool and see if the girl in the red bikini was there, however, he was to be disappointed. She was nowhere in sight. He was just about to walk away when he noticed a woman, probably around 40, laying on her front on a beach towel in the far corner. She had her bikini top undone and a very skimpy pair of bikini bottoms. Her skin was golden brown, as though she'd been sunbathing for weeks, and her long blonde hair was tied in a loose ponytail, hanging over her shoulder. He noticed there was a cocktail glass beside her with some reddish liquid in it and one of those miniature paper umbrellas.

Ken felt a stirring in his loins. Maybe here was what he was looking for. He wandered over to her.

"Hi. Mind if I lay here?" his voice was like syrup, low and smooth.

"Sure. Help yourself," said the woman, turning onto her side so that she was facing Ken.

"Thanks." Ken spread his towel on the floor next to her and started to put sunscreen on himself.

"You want me to do your back?" the woman asked, to Ken's surprise.

"That would be lovely. Thank you. I'm Ken by the way." He handed her the tube of sunscreen lotion.

"And I'm Mandy. Mandy Milford. Pleased to meet you," she purred, her voice low and seductive.

She started to rub the sunscreen into Ken's back. Was he imagining it but were her fingers rubbing him sensually? She continued to move her hands across his shoulders and down the backs of his arms.

"I'll leave you to do your front," she laughed.

"So how long are you here for Mandy?" Ken

asked.

"Oh, I've been here for a week already and still have another week to go. I recently got divorced and this is my celebration gift to myself."

"Wow. That's wonderful. Not that you got divorced, but that you're here. Have you met anybody here yet?" Ken pried.

He needed to make sure the coast was clear for him.

"No, I haven't yet. And don't worry about my divorce darling. He was a bastard. I think he must have fucked half of the neighbourhood and we'd grown apart years ago. Still, I got a good settlement from him so I'm happy. What about you?"

"Pretty much the same as you. My wife Anna has cheated on me so many times I've lost count. We haven't been, well you know, intimate, for years now. My life is quite lonely," Ken lied. "I'm here with her now but she's gone off on her own, probably looking for some new guy to shag!" How the lies came easily to him.

Mandy looked over at Ken, feeling sorry for him. She

too was on her own mission to find someone to fuck. She had an equally high sex drive and had already had flings with 2 men in the last week. And here was another falling into her lap. He was a bit older than she usually liked but he was still quite handsome. Yes, he'd do nicely, she thought. All they had to do now was to avoid the wife.

"Why don't we go and get a drink, it's getting pretty hot out here?" she said.

Ken's eyes bore into Mandy's and said "In more ways than one, I think!" in his most sexy voice. "Here, let me tie up your bikini top" and he moved over to her and tied it. They made their way over to the Bar under the Restaurant and ordered their drinks. Theo, the Entertainments Manager, came over and asked them if they were enjoying themselves, assuming they were a couple. Ken and Mandy told Theo that they thought the Island had so much to do and was so beautiful. Theo said that he made a point every day wandering around the Resort and trying to get as many people to go and watch that night's entertainment, and he hoped he'd see them there. It was Comedy Night tonight, he said, and he was sure they'd love it. Ken looked across at Mandy and they both knew instinctively what the other was thinking. There'd be no comedy for them tonight!

"Why don't we take these to mine?" said Mandy. "We can talk better there without all this noise."

Ken knew exactly what she meant. This had been easier than he thought. An attractive, single woman was offering herself to him. How much better could it get! He was sure she would be up for it. He hoped so as they made their way back to Mandy's chalet.

Anna was jumping over the waves in the Ocean. The water was beautifully warm but salty and every now and again she got a mouthful of it, which made her choke. She was still upset that last night hadn't gone as planned. Ken obviously needed a bit more time to get used to the new her. She'd have another try tonight, although maybe something different. What though? She made her way out of the water and onto the sand to her towel and bag. She dried herself off and rubbed some more sun cream onto her face and shoulders. She was in the middle of a good book and was soon lost in it. She hadn't realised she'd fallen asleep until she awoke with a start not knowing where she was. Then she remembered. She looked at her watch and was surprised to see that it was almost 2pm. As the lunch time buffet went until 3pm, she decided to go and find Ken so that they could go and eat together, if he hadn't already eaten. She gathered up her things and made her way back to their chalet, expecting Ken to be there waiting for her, but she found it empty. Maybe Ken had got hungry and gone on ahead of her to the restaurant, she thought. She quickly got changed into one of her new sundresses and made her way to the restaurant, but there was no sign of him. Anna sat down at a small table and ordered a mineral water from the waiter. She went over to the smorgasbord and helped herself to some cold beef and salad, then went and sat to eat alone. She wondered where Ken was. He hadn't said he was going anywhere. Maybe he was still on the Golf Course, she thought, and had lost track of time. A man who she had seen around the Resort came over to her table.

"May I sit down Miss?" the man said, in a strong Italian accent.

Anna had to stop herself from giggling. It was a long

time since she'd been called Miss!

"My name is Marcello and I book the entertainments here at the Paradise Resort. What is a beautiful lady like you doing eating all alone?"

Wow, thought Anna. I could get used to this. It had been a long time since any man had spoken to her in this way. This man was very attractive, and Anna felt very drawn to him. Marcello's eyes were constantly looking around. He didn't want to bump into Sue here.

"Hi. My name's Anna. My husband seems to have gone AWOL. I thought he'd be here but he's not."

Anna felt herself blush. This man was beautiful with wonderful bone structure, thick black hair, a stubble on his face and a long Roman nose. And he was so well built. The fact that he was Italian made him even more appealing to Anna, and he'd called her beautiful and Miss! And that accent! Anna wanted to get to know him better, he was so appealing to her. This was something that had not happened to her in a very long time.

"He's probably on the Golf Course and lost

time," she said.

"But a such a beautiful lady should not dine alone. Would you like to take a walk with me after you've eaten? I know a place where no other guests ever get to see. I could take you there to show it to you."

The offer was so appealing and Marcello wore the uniform of the Resort staff, so Anna thought she would be safe enough to take a walk with this lovely Italian man.

"Come down to the Bar when you have finished your meal. I will be waiting for you there," said Marcello.

After she'd finished her meal, she made her way down to the Bar and he was waiting for her there. He took her arm, which Anna thought a little bit forward, but maybe that's how these European men do things, she thought, and they headed away from the Resort and into bushland where the path gave way to a track.

Not used to the exercise, Anna found it hard going and stopped for breath.

Marcello said "Not far now. You will find it to be worth the walk Miss Anna." Oh wow. That accent could melt butter, she thought, and yet again wondered at her attraction to him. They carried on walking and, after what seemed an eternity to her, they eventually came to a clearing. Looking down, she saw a beautiful water hole, with clear blue water. There were different types of birds in the trees trilling out their songs and the cicadas making their loud noise.

"Oh. This is beautiful," said Anna. "However did you find this?"

"I came across it one day as I was trying to escape the stress of my work," Marcello said. "You are the first person I have brought to see this beautiful place."

Anna bristled with pleasure. She was now certain that all the changes she'd made to herself had been worth it. Here was a man who obviously appreciated her.

"Tomorrow Miss Anna you and I will come here and swim, yes?"

Anna was flustered but thought that, yes, she'd love to come back here and swim with this charming man.

"Yes, I'd like that. I'd like it very much. Thank you for asking me."

"Then we will meet in front of the Reception building at 3pm. That is when my shift finishes," he said.

On the walk back Anna asked Marcello how long he had been working at the Resort. He told her he'd been there for a few years and that he was very lonely, having almost no friends on the Island. He'd only been back to see his family in Italy once in the last five years, he'd told Anna, and he missed them very much. He was a very lonely man, he told her. He asked her if she was happy in her marriage and Anna found herself telling this lovely man all about her life with Ken, his cheating, his lack of love for her, their lack of intimacy. Anna was shocked that she'd revealed so much of herself to Marcello but he was the kind of man you could talk to easily, and he was good listener. They parted at the Reception building, agreeing to meet for a swim in the secret waterhole tomorrow. Anna walked back to her chalet grinning like a Cheshire Cat, the happiest she had been for a long time. Marcello, walking back into the building, smirked to himself. Boy, had he struck lucky this week. Two women in one day. This was going to be an interesting week. He bet they were both gagging for it. Neither of them wouldn't know what had hit them once he started. He knew he was a good lover and he'd make sure that they knew it too. Which one of them would give in to him first? Neither of them were his usual type but both looked like he could seduce them. He'd been looking for an attractive younger woman for days now, without luck, so these two would have to do. The thought made him smile. His fake Italian accent had struck gold again. He loved the thrill of the chase almost as much as he loved sex itself!

CHAPTER 14

SUE

Sue woke the next morning and felt something had changed in her. Then she remembered Marcello and the secret swimming hole. He'd got too close for comfort yesterday, Sue thought, and she just wasn't used to that kind of male attention. He was lovely though, she had to admit. She wondered if she'd see him again today. In anticipation, she dressed in her swimsuit with a thin, flowery sundress over the top, and picked up her bag containing her sun cream, her book and a bottle of water, along with a towel and sunglasses, intending to head straight for the pool after eating. Once she had everything she headed out to the restaurant for breakfast. When she arrived there, the waitress asked her if she would like a table to herself or if she would like to share with another person on their own. Sue thought someone to talk to would be nice so opted for some company. She was led to a table with a man, probably in his late 60s who was already eating some fruit and drinking a glass of orange juice.

"Hello," said the waitress. "Would you mind if this lady joined you?"

"Not at all," the man stood up "Please, do join me. My name's William, but you can call me Will."

Sue sat down and the waitress made sure her napkin and cutlery were set out in front of her.

"Pleased to meet you Will. My name's Sue. How long are you here for?"

"Just till Saturday. I've been here for ten days now. I come every year since my wife died three years ago. I find it very relaxing and the surroundings are really beautiful."

"I have to agree," said Sue. "It really is beautiful. I've been divorced for two years now and thought I'd treat myself to a bit of a luxury holiday."

Sue went over to the buffet table and picked out a Danish pastry, some watermelon and a glass of apple juice. She took it back to the table and she and Will talked about other holidays they had been on. Will was well travelled and told of some fascinating adventures he'd had with his wife over the years. It was all very amicable. When it came time to go Will stood up and came over to Sue.

"Thank you for your company. It was lovely having someone to talk to. Will you be here for dinner tonight? Maybe we could share a table again?"

Sue thought for a moment and said "Yes. I'd love to share a table again tonight. Shall we say 7pm?"

"Lovely. I'll see you then." Will has very happy. Here was a lady he'd very much like to get to know!

Sue decided to take a walk along the beach. The weather was very warm this morning so once there, she took off her sundress and walked along the beach just in her swimsuit, the sand beneath her feet warm and soft. Further along, she decided to lay out her towel and have a paddle, then sunbathe and read her book. She had just dried herself off after her swim and was getting her book out of her bag when, from out of nowhere, Marcello appeared. He had on only his Speedos and carried a towel and what were obviously his tee shirt and shorts.

"Well hello Miss Sue." There was the sexy accent again. Sue felt a fluttering of butterflies in her lower regions, something she most definitely wasn't used to. "Do you mind if I join you?"

"No, not at all," said Sue. "I was just going to have a read and maybe catch some sun."

Marcello put his towel next to Sue's, a bit close she thought, and lay down on the sand beside her.

"Hey, you have not yet put the sun cream on Miss Sue. You will get burnt. Have you brought any with you?" Sue produced a tube from her bag.

"Here, allow me." was it Sue's imagination or had Marcello's voice changed slightly? He squirted a big dollop of cream on to his hand and rubbed them together. "Turn around," he ordered.

Yes, thought Sue. His voice has definitely changed but she couldn't put her finger on how. Slowly and gently, Marcello started rubbing Sue's shoulders, her neck, back and arms.

"Turn around again." There was that voice, authoritive and not as strong an Italian an accent as usual.

Sue turned, self-consciously, to face him. He put another dollop of cream onto his hands and started to rub it into Sue's neck and on the front of her shoulders. But then, to Sue's horror, his hands started to move down to the valley of her breasts. She felt like a stone stature, unable to move. Marcello then added more cream to his hands and started working on her legs, down on her feet first, but then slowly up towards her thighs. As he reached the top of her thighs, something in Sue sprang to life and she pulled away.

"Why did you pull away Sue?" Sue noticed that he'd dropped the 'Miss'.

"You have a very beautiful body, you know. Very beautiful." The Italian accent was back.

Sue, unused to been called beautiful, actually flushed and could only mumble, "Thank you."

Marcello felt that now was the time to make his move. He put his hand under Sue's chin and gently kissed her on the mouth. Shocked, Sue looked at him, his face inches away from hers. His eyes were burning dark blue and were full of desire. This is why you came here, wasn't it? Sue's subconscious told her. Looking for love. And here it was, so why refuse it? Every ounce of her being was telling her that this what not right but she made her mind up in a second. She put her mouth to his and kissed him gently. This was all Marcello needed and his kiss became more passionate and he attempted to thrust his tongue inside Sue's mouth. Sue had never had a tongue in her mouth before and found it quite distasteful. Marcello continued to explore Sue's mouth with his tongue then started to rub her neck and shoulders. His breathing got deeper and he pushed himself against Sue's hip. She felt his erection pushing into her and at first was horrified. But again, that voice inside her told her to relax. This was what she was here for. She had had very little experience of a man and his passions and this was all new to her. Her marriage to Gordon had been disastrous in the bedroom department. His experience of sex was almost nil and he wasn't a passionate man at all. He had never really shown her any affection or love, after the first flush of their meeting had worn off. And the few times they did have sex, Gordon had come so quickly that Sue wondered what all the fuss was about. Suddenly, Marcello's hand was on her breast. Sue took a deep breath and let it stay there.

"Oh, my lovely Sue. You are so beautiful. I want you so badly."

Although it barely registered with her, in the back of her mind, Sue wondered where the accent had almost disappeared to.

"Let's go to your chalet. Please sweetheart. You are the first woman to ever make me feel this way." The accent was back.

Sue was really confused. She knew the consequences of taking Marcello back to her chalet. Is that what she really wanted? But maybe to find love this is what she had to do? It took her seconds to decide. "Ok," she said in a low voice. But she was still confused by that changing accent.

Once back at Sue's chalet, Marcello wasted no time. He told Sue to lift her arms up and she did so, reluctantly. This, for Marcello, had been an easy conquest. He was as horny as hell and he knew what he wanted, and he wanted it now. Sue had butterflies in her tummy and felt sick. Was she really up for this? Part of her shouted NO but another part of her said she had to do what she had to do. Wasn't this what love was all about. This could lead to marriage and a happy life with Marcello for her. If she stopped him now, all that would be lost, probably forever. And he seemed an honest and faithful man. Sue let him take off her sundress, then slowly, take down the straps of her swimsuit. His desire was obvious as he slid the dress down over her ankles and then took off her swimsuit, until she stood before him completely naked. Sue was mortified. Only Gordon had ever seen her completely naked like this. Not knowing what else to do, Sue just stood there, unmoving. Marcello took off his board shorts and his speedos. Sue gasped at the size of his manhood, which stood proudly to attention. Marcello knew he'd got her. He saw how she looked at his erection, an erection of which he was very proud. He decided to try and stay with the fake Italian accent.

That seemed to turn the women on more, he thought. He wasn't too happy with this one though. Her boobs were saggy and she was carrying too much fat on her body. She was very plain and mousy looking but, hey, she had what he wanted and he was sure he'd be inside her very soon. Marcello chose his sex according to the responses he got from his women. Sue didn't seem particularly turned on so he decided on a 'wham bam, thank you mam' approach with her this time. He came forward and took hold of Sue's shoulders. In his best Italian accent, he said,

"My darling Sue. You are the most beautiful creature I have ever seen."

Sue could hardly move, she was so nervous. Marcello guided her by the arm to the bed and they lay together, but not for long. Within moments he was on top of her, his tongue thrusting deep inside her mouth. Sue felt paralysed with fright, so much so that when she tried to move her hips away from Marcello's huge erection, he actually though she was trying to get him inside her. Although difficult, as Sue was terrified and not in the slightest bit ready for sex, Marcello carried on. He'd never experienced a woman's reaction to him like this before so decided to try and turn her on. He grabbed her nipple between his teeth and sucked hard on it. He then bit down slightly. He knew this drove most of his women wild but Sue seemed to shy away from him.

He decided to give up trying and just get on with what it was he really wanted. He thrust himself inside her, which was no easy thing to do, given her dryness. He soon got his rhythm going and Sue felt a slight stirring in her lower regions. As Marcello pounded away, Sue though what an attractive man he was and how lucky that he'd chosen her as his lover. She decided to give him a bit of encouragement and started to meet him stroke for stroke. As he quickened, he called out her name, and with a shudder, spent himself. With younger women, he'd usually use a condom but he'd felt no need to with Sue, with her being so much older. He collapsed on her chest, panting.

He felt the need to ask, "Sue, why did you not come?"

Sue thought she had no option but to lie. She knew what 'come' meant, but she had never had an orgasm in her life.

"But I did. It was wonderful," she said.

God, he looked so handsome. And he'd chosen her. She would get used to the sex, she was sure of it. Marcello knew from experience that Sue was lying. She hadn't come at all. Abruptly, Marcello said he had to go as his shift started soon. He dressed quickly and was about to say goodbye, when Sue asked him,

"Can I see you again later tonight?"

'My darling Sue," he replied. "Unfortunately, tonight I have to work. But soon, yes?" and he walked out of the door.

Sue, left lying in the bed, felt a warm and fuzzy glow that she'd never felt before, and found that all doubts about Marcello had gone. She wondered if she'd finally found true love. She was sure Marcello liked her and had enjoyed the sex with her. Away from home, and in this Island Paradise, Sue's thoughts were different to her usual ones. She decided that she would pursue Marcello and make him actually fall in love with her. She got up, had a shower and went to the 2pm Craft Class, hoping she'd bump into Marcello somewhere around the Resort later. She found she couldn't stop smiling! Then she remembered she was meeting Will for dinner soon. She'd met two men in one day. She'd been right about coming on this holiday!

CHAPTER 15

RACHAEL

That night at dinner, there was an uneasy tension between Rachael and Harry. Both were still sulking from their earlier row over Rachael's constant worrying about the children, and her inability to actually relax and have a good time, which had been the intention of coming to the Island in the first place. Harry was thinking of Cassie and how pleasant she was to be with and talk to. Rachael tried to start the conversation between them.

"What do you fancy?" she held up her menu.

Harry turned his attention to his menu and said that he'd have the Scotch Fillet Steak with Garlic King Prawns. Rachael, who didn't have much of an appetite, decided on a small Caesar Salad. Harry made eye contact with a waiter and ordered. He also asked for a bottle of the House Wine. While they waited for their food to come, Rachael asked Harry,

"So, what have you been doing all afternoon?"

Harry thought about his answer for a minute and said "Playing golf. What about you?" He was keen to deflect the conversation away from himself.

"Oh, I had a sleep, then read a book by the pool. It was lovely. It's so warm here. I think I'm starting to get a tan."

She purposely didn't tell him she'd been crying for most of the afternoon, worrying about her poor children. She didn't want to upset Harry again. Their meal came and they ate in silence, but Rachael noticed that Harry knocked back almost the whole bottle of wine on his own. The entertainment for the night was Karaoke, something she couldn't stand, but Harry, with the wine inside him, was really up for it, and said that he'd go for an hour or so. Rachael decided to go back to Reception and ring her mum and see if things were any better. She didn't tell Harry this, just that she was going back to their chalet to read.

"Ok," Harry's speech was slightly slurred, "You go back and I'll hang around here for a bit. Might even have a bit of a sing." Rachael knew he'd drank too much wine if he was preparing to sing!

Rachael made her way over to the Reception building, took out some coins and dialled her parents' number. It took an age for her mum to answer, but when she did Rachael could hear the stress in her mum's voice and the sound of Lily crying in the background.

"Hi mum. It's me." Rachael couldn't bear to ask the question but knew she had to. "How are they?"

"Oh Rachael, these children of yours need more discipline. Jake's upstairs

with your father. They're trying to build a model plane that your dad bought for him today in the hope of distracting him. I'm not going to lie to you sweetheart, but he's been an absolute nightmare. He won't eat what I give him, then has one of his paddy's when I won't give him any chocolate or biscuits. He's ruined my good Irish linen tablecloth when he deliberately tipped his juice over it. The house is like a tip. And his language! Rachael, where did he learn such words?"

Rachael was at a loss as to how to answer her mum. She'd asked herself the same question over and over again herself. Neither she or Harry swore. Rachael could still hear her baby crying in the background.

"Mum, why is Lily crying?"

"Because I've been trying for an hour to get her to go to bed and she refuses to even go upstairs. Last night your father and I were up till almost midnight with her."

Rachael was beside herself with guilt and grief. "Mum did you give her a bottle? I told dad to get you to give her a bottle. I know you think she's too old for one, and I will try and wean her off it when we get back, but has she had one?"

"Absolutely not Rachael. She far too big for

one now. It will be easier for you when you get back. She'll be used to not having a bottle by then. I'm trying to get her to drink out of one of those baby cup things with the spout on but she refuses. The only way she'll drink is from a juice popper and a straw. We've got to keep at it darling otherwise she'll still be on the bottle when she starts school"

Rachael thought of her middle daughter. "How's Anna been?"

"Screeching at the top her voice into that damn Karaoke thingy she brought with her. Honestly Rachael, I don't know how you cope. It's only been two days and I'm a wreck already."

"Mum, do you want us to come home? It doesn't sound as though you're coping too well."

"No, darling. You stay there and enjoy yourselves. Your father and I will get through it. It's all a matter of discipline. We'll get there before the weeks' out."

Rachael had to hold back the tears. "Are you sure Mum? We can be back by tomorrow evening?"

"No, you and Harry have a good time. You've paid for it so you might as well enjoy it." Oh, I've got to go. I can hear Jake starting upstairs. Bye darling. Speak soon."

And she was gone, leaving Rachael a shaking mess, standing in the corner of Reception. She felt the tears flow down her cheeks and quickly made her way back to their chalet, where, once again, she lay on the bed and let the sobs out. Why had she thought this a good idea? They could have taken the kids on a camping trip, or down to the beach, anywhere. But to go away and leave the three of them with her parents for the first time in their lives, since Jake had been born, what was she thinking! Her Mum had said enjoy herself. How could she when all she wanted to do was go home and get her children. She stopped crying and tried to think what to do next. She didn't feel like reading but picked up her book nonetheless. She soon fell into a troubled sleep but was awakened by Harry, who had returned home and who had more than sleep on his mind. As he turned to her in the bed, he pushed his erection into her back and started to squeeze her breasts. His words were slurred and it was obvious he'd had far too much to drink, something he rarely did.

"I'm not in the mood Harry," Rachael said.

"Oh, come on baby. You know you want to really." Harry continued kneading her breasts, and tweaking her nipples. Rachael knew that it would just be best to get it over with rather than argue with Harry in this state, so she turned over and let him kiss her. His breath stunk of alcohol and as he forced his tongue into her mouth, she felt physically sick. Just get it over with, she thought. Harry made his way down to her breasts and started sucking and nipping her nipples. At home, this usually worked for her and she would be as high on lust as Harry was right now, but tonight, nothing did it for her. She helped Harry position himself on top and guided him into her. Harry immediately started pumping away and came within minutes. Rachael felt nothing. Harry kissed her and rolled over onto his side and was asleep in seconds. She lay for hours, guilt flooding every bit of her being. How could she have done this?

Harry had indeed drunk more after dinner. Much more. He had gone to the Entertainments Lounge and found the Karaoke in full swing. To his amazement, he'd looked at the stage only to see Cassie belting out 'Mamma Mia'. He waiting till she'd finished then went over to her.

"Hi again. On your own?" he asked.

"Yeah. Where's the wife?"

"She's gone back to the chalet. Karaoke's not her thing. Hey, why don't we do a number together?" Ken's enthusiasm, along with the almost full bottle of wine he'd drank at dinner made him brave enough to suggest it.

"Sure," said Cassie. "Let's go and get the book and chose a song."

Another bottle of wine later, and two songs sung together, and they both flopped down onto one of the comfy couches that were dotted around the room. At golf earlier, Cassie had told Harry that she'd felt very lonely since breaking up with her boyfriend and the Advertisement for Paradise Island, which she had seen in a magazine, had sounded like the perfect place for her to come.

Harry, quite merry at this point, had asked her "So did you come looking for love?"

"Oh, I don't think I really thought about that part of it, although it would be great if I did, but this place is so beautiful, I'm just happy to be here."

Yeah, me too, thought Harry, but with a few added extras, he smirked.

"I think we'd better call it a night hey. I'm feeling a bit tipsy and knackered after all that golf. Are we still on for another Round in the morning?"

"We sure are," said Harry. "I'm looking forward to it. Let me walk you to your chalet."

Cassie had a Rainforest chalet and the air that night was damp and sweet. They reached her door and Harry couldn't help himself and drunkenly leant in for a kiss, but Cassie was having none of it.

"Harry, you're drunk. Go home and go to bed. Sleep it off. I'll see you in the morning." And she planted a small kiss on his forehead and went inside.

Harry couldn't understand, in his drunken state, why Cassie had given him the brush off. He had been sure she was up for it tonight. Disappointed, he walked back to his chalet. He had a massive erection and had been hoping for some action with Cassie but she hadn't been game. Still, he thought, Rachael's back at ours. She'll do for tonight. He made his way back to his chalet and his wife.

CHAPTER 16

BIANCA

Bianca sat on their bed biting her fingernails, feeling sick in the pit of her stomach. The Search Party for Joel would be under way now but it was dark. She prayed that Joel would be OK. He'd never taken off before like this. She couldn't understand why he'd need to. They'd made love before. Sure, not often, but nonetheless they'd had sex, albeit of sorts. Maybe it was just that their honeymoon night had been the final straw for him and it had stressed him out. Bianca wondered if Joel thought she'd have high expectations of him for their wedding night, but she hadn't. She was fully away of Joel's capabilities in that department and was only hoping that Joel would at least try. Bianca knew that Joel never really wanted sex. She was always the instigator and it was often not very successful. Both of them knew there were problems in that department.

Outside in the Resort, ten men had gathered to try and find Joel. They split up and were each given a part of the Resort to search. There were only a few empty chalets, but these were being searched as well. Each man had a torch and they searched their own areas thoroughly, but after two hours, they assembled back in front of the Reception building. There had been no sign of Joel.

"It's pointless carrying on in the dark" said Barry, one of the security men. "Let's try further afield tomorrow when it gets light. All of you who can, meet me here at 6am and we'll keep going. Thanks everybody for tonight."

As the men dispersed, Barry went to Bianca's chalet to give her the news. She opened the door to Barry's knock.

"Have you found him? Where is he?" Bianca was full of concern.

"No, sorry, It's Bianca isn't it? No, I'm sorry darlin'. There's no sign of him on the Resort, and we've pretty much covered everywhere. We're going to meet again at first light in the morning and widen the search. If we haven't found him by noon we might have to call the SES and the Rescue Helicopter in from the mainland."

Bianca was distraught. Rescue Helicopter? Oh, my God, this is a nightmare, she thought. She had no option but to go and get into bed and wait. Joel had to be somewhere on the Island. She just hoped he wasn't hurt. She spent a sleepless night hoping and praying that Joel would come walking through the door as if nothing had happened.

The next day and word had got around, so at 6am the next morning, some 20-odd people, mostly men but a few of the female staff as well, had gathered in front of the Reception building.

"Right," said Barry. "He can't have gone too

far away. Let's break up into groups of four and search the surrounding bushland. Let's say we meet back here at 10am. Ok?"

There was a bit of a wait while people got into groups of four. Some had sticks for poking into shrubbery, everyone had a bottle of water. A few of the search party carried a First Aid Kit. They set off hopeful of finding Joel. Each group took a different path away from the Resort. They shouted "Joel" every few minutes but got no response. One group saw a blue shirt in the shrubbery ahead and picked it up excitedly. It was a men's pale blue shirt and it gave them hope to carry on.

"Hang on," said Mark, one of the men, "They said he had on a red tee shirt when he went off. This can't be his."

The small group gave a sigh of despondency.

"Let's carry on," said Mark. "He's got to be round here somewhere."

Another group, going in another direction, found a cigarette stub on the ground. One of the females picked it up excitedly.

"No, said another of the others. "He's not a smoker." They too carried on.

The sun blazed down upon them and the sky was crystal blue. All of the rescue party were feeling the effects of the heat, which increased by the hour, even so early in the morning. Keeping in touch by two-way radios, eventually, and without success, all of the groups turned around and made their way back to the Resort area.

"Right," said Barry. "We've got no option but to call for help from Mackay." He went inside and made a call on the landline to the Queensland State Emergency Services, and told them of their missing person. After explaining that they had twice sent out search parties and had no success, the SES coordinator in Mackay told Barry that they would send a larger search party and the thermal imaging rescue helicopter. Barry breathed a sigh of relief, knowing help was coming. After informing the staff members waiting outside, he decided to go and tell Bianca the news. He found her sitting on the balcony of her chalet, pale with anxiety, and the stress showing on her face, holding a coffee mug.

"Bianca Hi. Just thought I'd come and give you the news. We've had no success unfortunately so I've had to ring the SES in Mackay. We had over twenty people in the search party this morning but there's just no signs of him. He must have wandered further over to the other side of the Island. I had no option but to ring the SES."

"Yes, I know. I've just seen Lindy from Reception. She told me she'd been one of the search party this morning." Bianca's voice was barely more than a whisper. "When will they arrive?"

"I'm hoping soon," said Barry. "Look love, I'm sure they'll find him. They're even sending a helicopter. I'd suggest you stay here in the chalet just in case he returns. It'll be you he wants to see when he does get back."

As Barry made his way back to the Reception building to wait for the SES, Bianca got up and went inside. She was crawling up the walls with desperation. But there was nothing she could do. Oh Joel. Where the fuck are you? Please be OK, she said silently to herself.

Joel had lost all concept of time. He didn't have a watch on and had barely slept during the night. He didn't know when the last time he'd drunk anything and the sun was beating down on him through the gaps between the still branches of the tree he laid under. He was bathed in sweat and his heart was pounding. For what had seemed like days, he had tried to move by hopping and crawling back in what he thought was the direction of the main part of the Island. What he didn't know was that he was actually going further and deeper into the bush, further away from the Resort. With his strength gone and dehydration setting in, he could only lay under the partial shade of the palm tree and hope and wait. A huge snake slithered past him and although he was terrified of the things, he didn't have the strength to move. His mind started to wander, almost to the point of hysteria. He thought of Bianca. Maybe she'd found herself another man by now? Maybe she'd decided that getting married had been a big mistake and that she could have easily found someone else, someone who could give her the sex life and attention she needed.

After a while, Joel had convinced himself that this indeed was the case and a dark gloom came over him. He thought that maybe he would die here, and that his body would never be found. Bianca would have given up on him, of that he was now sure. A bunch of cockatoos flew over him, screeching, and a large lizard scurried past his head. He wondered why, in his lucid moments, he had gone off by himself, why he hadn't just tried to make the best of it and become more of a man with Bianca. He realised that he should have been honest with the Counsellor and continued with the sessions. He knew why he was like he was, and he knew the reason for it. He thought to himself that he really could have tried harder to face his past and the sexual assault by his father. His last thought before he passed out was that if Bianca would take him back if he was found, he would do his utmost to make things right between them.

The Queensland State Emergency Service, or SES as it is known, arrived just before noon. They had sent 10 men, all fully equipped, by boat, and told Barry that the helicopter was on its way. They all gathered together in the Craft Room, which was empty and allowed both the SES men and some Resort Staff to sit in and be briefed. The SES were insistent that all staff members should stay at the Resort but keep looking in empty chalets and on the main beaches and inland waterways close by. Barry described Joel to the SES men and what he had been wearing. He wasn't able to tell them if Joel was troubled when he had wandered off as Bianca had told nobody of their problems, only that they'd had an argument. The 10 SES men set off into the bush then split up to widen their search. They all carried a two-way Radio, plenty of water, a basic First Aid kit and some Protein Bars, as well as having sunscreen with them. They went to the sheltered coves that surrounded the Island, into the lush rainforest and poked amongst the myriad of shrubbery that was everywhere. Snakes and lizards scurried away from their path and some of the men had to brush spiders from their jackets or arms. Four hours into the search and they'd still found no signs of Joel. Over their radios, they were informed that the Rescue Helicopter had arrived and was going to go to the far end of the Island and begin its search from there. The Rescue Party all gave a sigh of relief. It had been a long, hot and hard morning.

Joel lay, half delirious from pain, dehydration and the sun, but in his haze, he thought he heard the whirring of a helicopter. He tried to stand up but couldn't, in an attempt to alert the rescuers that he was there. After circling a fair bit of the northern end of the Island with no sightings of Joel, the helicopter turned and headed back south-west. The noise for Joel became louder and as the Rescue Helicopter flew over him, an eagle-eyed crewmember spotted him lying under a lone tree in a clearing, and they hovered over him.

"REX1 to Base."

"Base receiving REX1."

"We've found him. Can't tell you much more at this stage but he doesn't look in any fit state for a ground rescue. We'll winch him up and take him to the main Resort landing pad. We'll see you when you get back. Should be with you on the ground in about 20 minutes or so. Thanks for all the efforts guys. Over and Out."

"All received. Well-done REX1. See you back there in a while. Can you give us an update about the casualty's condition once he's on board? Many thanks. Over and Out."

Jason, the Team Leader, relayed the information onto

the other SES Rescuers who didn't have a radio. Everyone was happy as they made their way back to the main Resort. The helicopter crew would send the news that Joel had been found to its Headquarters back in Mackay and they in turn would phone Paradise Island and let them know. Bianca, unable to stay in the chalet a moment longer, had made her way to the Reception building and was with the others waiting for news. Most of the other people who'd formed the original search parties were also waiting there, their faces strained. Lindy, the Receptionist, took the call from the SES in Mackay that Joel had been found and was being airlifted back to the main Resort. After the Resort's phone had rang, the smile on Lindy's face when she had answered it told them the news that they had been waiting to hear, that Joel was alive and well and was being airlifted back to the Island's helipad. Loud cheering and clapping broke out, and Bianca burst into tears and almost collapsed. Someone brought her a chair and told her that Joel would soon be at the landing pad and that they should all catch their breaths and then make their way there to greet him.

Joel couldn't believe his eyes. The massive chopper was hovering above him. He'd been found! He had been convinced that he would die in this place with nobody ever finding his body. He knew he had made a lot of distance from the main Resort since leaving, but he had no idea that he had been heading away from it all the time he had been moving. A crewmember was making his way down on a rope or wire.

He got to the ground and said "Hello there. You must be Joel? You're a hard man to track down."

All Joel could whisper was "Thank you."

The SES crewmember took stock of Joel's condition. He noticed the large swelling on Joel's ankle, his obvious state of distress and probable de-hydration and sunburn, and radioed to his colleague to drop down an ankle brace. Once he had put this on Joel's ankle, he pulled a water flask from his pocket and told Joel to drink, but to take small sips. Joel did this willingly. He didn't have the strength to take larger drinks anyway. The crewmember also took a Protein Bar out of one of his pockets.

"Here try and have a few bites of this and then we'll get you out of here."

Once the winch harness was on, the SES crewmember gave the thumbs up to his colleague, and Joel found himself flying through the air, up towards the helicopter.

Once inside, Joel, semi-conscious, realised that he'd been given a second chance. He made a vow there and then that this was the time that he would make it up to his wife.

Back at the Resort's landing pad, a group of people waited anxiously. Bianca thought she might be sick. She had no idea what condition Joel would be in. Suddenly the helicopter could be heard in the distance, and was soon in view. All eyes were firmly on it as it landed, and Bianca rushed forward but was held back by Barry.

"He's safe now, darlin'. He's here." Barry's voice was close to breaking; such had been everyone's anxiety.

The helicopter landed smoothly and Joel was stretchered out. Bianca ducked her head down to avoid the still spinning blades and ran over to him.

"Oh Joel. My God. Have you any idea what the fuck you've put me through?" But through her anger were tears of happiness. Her man was found, back safe and sound. She couldn't stop kissing him on the cheeks, the lips, his forehead. She couldn't get enough of him. The SES crew told Bianca that they were taking Joel to the Medical Room where the Island had a Nurse on call there all the time. They wheeled Joel the small distance to the medical room and once inside, the nurse introduced herself to them.

"Hi. I'm Bella. I'm the nurse here. What we'll do now is to have a look over our patient and see where we go from here. OK pet? Why don't you just take a seat over there."

The English nurse was reassuring and Bianca took the proffered chair. When Bella had removed the blanket that was covering Joel, Bianca saw the ankle brace.

"What's he done to his foot?"

"We can't tell yet pet. I'll have a good look at him then we'll decide what to do. At least he's safe now."

Bella started to check Joel over from head to toe. Finally, she turned to Bianca.

"Well pet, it looks like he might have broken his ankle, but apart from that, he's just dehydrated and possibly has sunstroke. I think he'll survive," she smiled.

Bella went outside to speak to the SES men who were just getting back.

"I think it would be a good idea to airlift him to Mackay and get his ankle looked at. I think it might be broken. Otherwise, he should be fine in a few days."

"Ok" said the pilot of REX1. I'll go and clear it with Base first, then we can get him back into the chopper."

Back inside, Joel was drinking a cup of tea and eating a sandwich which one of the men had rustled up for him. He was still slightly disorientated and in pain, and was very weak. He looked at Bianca and thought that he might have lost her. He loved her so much. He couldn't even remember why he'd gone off. Just that he shouldn't have done. Bianca reached over and kissed him. "Welcome back darling."

CHAPTER 17

ANNA

That evening, in their chalet, Anna waited for Ken to come back home and take her to dinner. When he finally came in just before 8pm, she noticed that he looked rather flushed and his hair was in disarray.

"Where've you been? I've been waiting for you for ages!" Anna had thought it best not to tell Ken about her meeting with Marcello. "Come on, get yourself smartened up so that we can go to dinner."

Ken hoped they wouldn't encounter Mandy in the

restaurant. That could get quite tricky, he thought. Anna was also thinking the same thing about Marcello. As they entered the restaurant, both of them were furtively looking round. Ken spotted Mandy at a table on her own. He thought back to this afternoon. They had taken their drinks back to Mandy's chalet and talked a bit about their respective lives back home, with Ken omitting his relationship with Ruby. Suddenly, Mandy had put down her drink.

"Sweetheart, we both know why we're here," and she moved across to Ken and started kissing him. Slowly at first, but as Ken responded, her kisses became more and more deeper. Their tongues intertwined, probing and searching, and Ken's hands started roaming around her body. He was able to knead away at her soft flesh and she was turned on in moments. He stood up and was about to tell Mandy to do the same, but she was already ahead of him and had started to take off her clothes. Ken quickly removed his own shorts and tee shirt, and together they fell onto the bed. Ken was very surprised to find that Mandy was as rough as he was and the sex was extraordinary. She met him, thrust for thrust and she was as experimental as he was. Their mouths were still locked together and Mandy bit hard on Ken's bottom lip causing him to moan louder. He soon finished, and was quickly followed by Mandy. Afterwards she lay on top of him.

"That was just what I needed," she said to him. "I like a man who knows how to make love properly. You wouldn't believe some of the sex I've had. Real drips. Some could barely get it up!"

Ken was taken aback by Mandy's frankness, although flattered that she hadn't included him in that category. But he wasn't about to reveal his own sex secrets to a woman who he hadn't long met. They lay silent for while then Ken ran his hands through Mandy's hair and down her body. Soon it was happening again, but this time better. Mandy wanted it in all conceivable positions, some that even Ken hadn't tried before, and he was proud that he was able to match her every requirement. After their epic session, Ken thought himself the luckiest man on the Island. Mandy thought herself the luckiest woman.

Now, in the restaurant with his wife, Ken tried to catch Mandy's eye, but she kept them firmly on her food. Anna had looked around but could find no sign of Marcello and breathed a sigh of relief. She would meet him for a swim in the lovely water hole tomorrow. She thought it would be so nice to spend some time with such a handsome, but lonely man. Tonight, though, it would be Ken's turn. She would try again. Only this time, she was going to try something much bolder than before. They ate their meal in silence, the noise from the chattering birds on the ledge was enough to break any awkwardness and lack of conversation between them. Afterwards, Ken, replete from his afternoon of sex, asked Anna if it she wouldn't mind going straight back to the cabin and not to the nights' entertainment. Anna mistook this for Ken wanting to be alone with her and her heart fluttered. Tonight would be the night, she thought. Once back in their chalet, Ken quickly undressed and got into bed. He rolled onto his side to go to sleep. But Anna had other ideas. She got totally naked and climbed in beside him.

"Hello darling. I've missed you," she said in what she thought was her most sexiest voice. She started to rub his back and then around to his belly. Ken was frozen with horror. He'd had enough sex for today with Mandy and the last thing he wanted was to be pawed by his wife. She continued with her stroking, knowing that surely Ken wouldn't be able to resist her for much longer. She knew it must have been days since he'd last had sex with one of his women before they'd come away, and he would surely succumb to her now. Her hand wrapped around his penis and she pushed her naked body into his back. She started slow movements, up and down, up and down, with her hand, while her other hand ran through his hair and down his back. Ken wondered what had happened to his wife, the wife who never wanted sex, and the wife who was old and dowdy, with no life in her at all. Even though he felt a stirring in his loins, he was still repulsed by Anna. What harm would it do, he thought, and turned over to her. But the sight of her greedy face and bright red lipstick, which he hadn't seen her apply, made him want to gag. He pushed her hands away from him and sat up.

"Look love, we haven't done this for ages. I need more time to get used to this new you. Can we wait a bit longer?" Ken might have been disgusted by his wife, but he couldn't find it in himself to be downright nasty.

Anna nodded her head and turned over, silently wondering to herself just what she had to do to show Ken she was a changed woman, and wanted, once again, to be the love of his life.

The next morning, after they had had breakfast, Ken told Anna that he was going to the Golf Course and would meet her back in the chalet later. Anna decided to pass the time until she met Marcello again by laying by the pool reading and swimming. Ken had no intentions of going to the Golf Course. He had arranged to go straight to Mandy's chalet. He found her there putting a skimpy bikini on.

"Hi honey. I thought we could go for a swim first. I'm all hot and sweaty. I've been out for a run on the jogging track."

Ken shook his head. "That's not a good idea. The missus said she was going to the pool and I don't want to bump into her and whichever toy boy she's managed to pick up. Why don't we get a cool shower together instead?" Ken was pleased with his idea and gave Mandy one of his special "if you know what I mean" looks.

"Sounds like a plan lover boy," Mandy was happy. She was always up for a session in the shower. Wet Sex, she called it.

They both shed their clothes in seconds and made their way into the massive double faucet shower that all the chalets had. Ken turned on the taps until the water was a slightly warm temperature and they both stepped in.

"Allow me to do the honours and wash you," said Ken. "Has to be all over though," he grinned.

He lathered up his hands with the delicious smelling floral scented liquid soap and started to wash her. He started with Mandy's back, running his soapy hands slowly down it, and around her behind in circular motions. When his hands reached between her legs, she allowed him to use circular motions and she gasped and turned around to face him.

"Do my front now," she said, her voice low and husky.

She knew Ken was powerless to resist her and he did as he was told. As his hands soaped her breasts, he pulled on her already hard nipples.

"I'm going to return the favour now," said Mandy, and she soaped up her hands and started at Ken's neck, down through his chest hair and onto his smooth belly. In an instant, she grasped him and started to massage him. Just as Ken was about to come, Mandy stopped, and turned her back to him and bent over.

"My turn now," she ordered.

Ken didn't have to be told twice and was soon inside her. Using his still soapy hands, he continued his caresses. Hearing her moans, Ken could contain himself no longer and soon allowed the precious release to overtake him. But Mandy needed more, and turned to face Ken and grabbed his hand and put it to herself. She came within seconds and they both fell into each other's arms, letting the lovely warmth of the water wash over them, cleansing them. After a while, they got out and towelled each other dry.

"We can't stay locked up in here all day," Mandy was thinking that they should make their way to the bed for another session, but Ken was, for the moment, replete, so said to her,

"Why don't we go to the Snorkelling Information Session. I think it's on at 10.30am then the actual snorkelling is later this afternoon. It would be fun to snorkel with you," he gave Mandy one of his special smiles, "And there's no chance we'll bump into my wife there. She can't stand fish or anything to do with them."

Meanwhile, Anna lay by the pool, reading. She let her mind wonder and tried to think of ways to make Ken want her again. So far, whenever she'd tried to get intimate with him, he'd outright refused her, saying that he 'needed more time'. More time for what? thought Anna. Surely by now, he should be desperate for sex. They had been away for 3 days and she knew what a high sex drive he had. It seemed that he'd rather be on the Golf Course than with her. Coming away to Paradise Island, Anna had thought that with her new look and the self-confidence it had given her, that Ken would be bound to fall in love with her again, or even just want her for the sex, which would be a start. But it didn't seem to be working. She could only keep trying, and settled her mind on new ways in which to make Ken let down his guard with her. The thought of going back to their old life didn't appeal to her at all. She thought of how she had been so lonely and unloved by Ken for many years now. What he gave her of himself was a mere pittance. She wanted more than that, though she hadn't realised it until now. She wondered what else she could do? It was obvious to her now that Ken was fobbing her off at night in bed. Maybe this was how it was always going to be.

Suddenly, frustrated, she thought "No, I'm not giving up yet. I'll try again tonight. Why should I give up now when I've come so far? Anyway, he'll soon be in need of his 'sex fix'"

She went back to reading her book, keeping her eye on her watch and remembering her 3pm meeting with Marcello.

CHAPTER 18

SUE

Sue had finished breakfast. She had stayed an hour, but hadn't seen Will there, and she could have done with some company. She made her way back to her chalet and lay on the bed, looking over the day's Itinerary of Activities on the Resort. She decided to be brave and have a go at Archery, which was on at 10am. As she walked over to the Archery Range, the birds were chirping their loud songs, and small lizards scurried about. The smell from the frangipani bushes was sweet and fragrant and Sue wondered yet again at the beauty of this place. She reached the Archery Range where there were two couples already waiting. Sue greeted them and asked if they had done any archery before. They all said no, this was their first time, so Sue relaxed a bit. Soon the Instructor came and introduced himself as Sean. He showed them how to hold their bow and how to insert the arrow. The targets seemed to be a long way away but Sean told them not to worry about that at the moment, just to get the hang of actually firing an arrow. Shy as always, Sue held back and went last. There had been much laughing from the others when their arrows had fallen two feet from their bows. When it was her turn, Sue inserted her arrow and pulled back.

"No, no, you need to pull the arrow back a lot further," said Sean.

He came across to Sue and put his arm around her shoulder and directed her arm holding the arrow to where it should be. Sue felt a delicious sensation being so close to such a good looking young man, who smelt of a mixture of shampoo and deodorant. At that moment, she really wished for a man of her own. Once Sean had let go of her, she tried to pull the arrow back.

It was really hard on her shoulder muscles, but Sue pulled as hard as she could and let the arrow go. It too fell a few feet away from her. Sean laughed and told her not to worry. She'd soon get the hang of it. An hour later and all of them had managed to hit the target. Sue, pleased with herself was sweating profusely and her shoulder was aching from the effort. The group had bonded during their session and agreed to meet again tomorrow for another try.

Sue decided she'd go for a swim and read her book, so she went back to her chalet and got changed into her swimsuit and collected the rest of the things she needed. It was while she was swimming in the pool that Will had come along, carrying his beach towel and a book. He settled himself down into one of the sun lounges, put on his glasses, and started to read. Sue got out of the water and dried herself off and wrapped her new sarong around her. She wandered over to Will.

"Hi. Nice to see you again," she said.

Will put down his book and sat up. "Hello Sue. Nice to see you too, been having a swim?"

"Yes, the water's lovely and warm. I've been

reading too, earlier."

Will pulled the sun lounge next to his closer, and asked Sue if she'd like to bring her things over and sit with him. She was happy to do so, and soon they were in deep conversation. Will told her that his wife of thirty years, Marie, had died two years ago from breast cancer. They had met at a local Club and one night he and his friend had gone over to Marie and her friend and offered to buy them a drink. Both girls had given them destroying looks and said "No thank you. We're waiting for our boyfriends."

Shrugging their shoulders, the two friends had walked away and drank on their own. The following week, the two girls were once again in the Club.

"What ya reckon," said Will's mate Ray, "Shall we give them another go?" Again, the two men went over to the girls and asked to buy them a drink. The answer was the same. "No thank you. We're waiting for our boyfriends."

This went on for some weeks and Will and Ray had decided to give up. However, one night, Will noticed one of the girls, the blonde one, looking over at him.

Ray had gone to the Gents so Will went over by himself and addressed only the blonde.

"Hi again. Sorry to bother you, but would you please allow me to buy you a drink?"

To his amazement, the blonde said yes. Her friend, sensing three was a crowd, said she had to go home and left Will and the blonde together.

"My name's Will. Pleased to meet you. What's yours?"

"I'm Marie. Pleased to meet you too, although I feel as if I know you well already after all the times you asked to buy me a drink!"

And that's how it had started. They'd gone out with each other for a year then got engaged, then married. Even though they'd tried, they never had any children but they'd enjoyed each other's company right to the end. It was a huge shock to Will when Marie had died. His level of grief was something which was unknown to him, and he struggled with it every day of his life. Now, two years later, he was still mourning her loss. Sue was distraught at hearing Will's story and felt her own story was barely worth telling. However, Will was insistent and Sue told him of meeting Gordon after so many years on her own, of her loveless marriage and of her divorce, also two years ago. She told him that she had continued teaching and was still living on her own. She was reasonably happy with her life and wasn't really sure whether or not a partner would fit in with her lifestyle, but she was here now, and if she found a new man, well, then so be it. Together they lay beside the pool in contented silence, both reading their books. After a while, Will got up and gathered up his things.

"Think I'll go and have a lie down until lunch," he said. "Maybe see you at dinner tonight?"

Sue thought for a few seconds. Although Will was a really lovely man, she really didn't fancy him at all in the way she did Marcello, and didn't really want a relationship with him. He was much older than her for a start, and she didn't find him attractive in the slightest. She quickly made up her mind. She didn't want to give him hope that a romance with her could be even remotely possible.

"I'm not sure if I'm meeting up with a girlfriend for dinner, but if not I'll see you there."

"Ok. Maybe see you tonight then," said Will as he walked off.

Sue stayed by the pool until lunchtime then went back to her chalet to change for lunch. She hoped she wouldn't bump into Will. She did, however, hope to see Marcello again. Sure enough, as she was walking to the restaurant, Marcello suddenly appeared in front of her.

"Hello the lovely Miss Sue. You are looking as beautiful as ever today." Sue blushed with the flattery. Oh, that accent melted her heart, and the butterflies flew hard in her stomach.

"What are you doing now? Are you going to have your lunch?" he said smoothly.

Sue could only stutter "Yes, I'm just on my way there now."

"What, all alone? A most beautiful woman such as you should not be on her own." Marcello moved in and put his arm around Sue's shoulders. He put his mouth to her ear and whispered, "I've got a free hour my darling Sue. Let's go back to your chalet where I can prove to you how beautiful you really are."

Sue thought about the last time she and Marcello were together the day before and felt a tingle go down her spine. Sure, she hadn't enjoyed the sex, had even been scared of it, but she loved Marcello's compliments and the fact that he had picked her out as special. She quickly decided, and said yes, and they were soon walking back to her chalet, Marcello's arm casually slung across her shoulders. Once inside, Marcello had already formulated his next plan. The last time, he hadn't turned Sue on enough to be ready for him, so this time he was going to try something different.

"My darling Sue. I am going to very slowly take off all of your clothes, then I am going to kiss you all over your beautiful body."

Sue gasped at the thought. Nobody had ever said or done that to her before. She knew that her body wasn't as good as it should be and was nervous and ashamed because of it.

Marcello, seeing Sue's face, said "Do not worry my darling Sue. You will enjoy every single kiss that Marcello gives to you. I am a great lover of beautiful women and I know how to give pleasure."

Slowly, he unzipped the back of Sue's sundress and let it fall off her shoulders and onto the floor. Sue stepped out of it, self-conscious of her big white 'granny knickers' and her plain white bra. Marcello too was disappointed, but he had only one thing on his mind and he knew that Sue could give it to him. He needed his 'daily fix', and couldn't live without it, so if it meant going with some unattractive, middle aged old woman for it, then that would have to do. He'd only found one other woman this week on the Island who had succumbed to his charms so far. He remembered that her name was Anna, and that she was old enough to be his mother! For now, though, this one would have to do. He deftly unhooked Sue's bra and her drooping breasts fell out.

"Oh Sue, your breasts, they are so beautiful. I want to suck on them like a baby!"

Sue looked down and could see nothing attractive about her breasts at all. They had long ago stopped being perky and she couldn't understand why Marcello was saying what he did. But all the same, she was flattered that he thought they were beautiful. Something told her that this man was a real charmer.

A man who had said these words to many other women? Maybe. But for now, he was saying them to her, and she was lapping it up. Marcello put his fingertips inside the elastic waist of Sue's white knickers and slowly lowered them down.

"Step out of them my darling," he ordered.

Sue did so and felt completely embarrassed and totally uncomfortable standing again before Marcello as naked as the day she was born. She realised that Marcello was also taking off his clothes, but with great speed. Soon they were both naked and Marcello took Sue in his arms and started kissing her, firstly on her cheeks then her forehead, before moving down to her neck. He'd done this so many times before that, even though he felt great distaste at Sue's unattractiveness, he continued. He liked his women to reciprocate his passion, and last night, Sue hadn't, and he'd wondered why. He hadn't come across any woman who, once turned on, hadn't appreciated his lovemaking. He continued his kisses and worked on Sue's breasts for a few moments. Sue felt nothing, but realised that if she wanted to keep Marcello happy, she had to show some response, so she decided to make a little moan.

Marcello was much encouraged by this and kept up his kissing. He led Sue to the bed and laid her down, knelt beside her and continued with his kissing. However, as his kisses got lower and lower, Sue felt panic shoot through her. Gordon had never, ever been so bold as to do anything like this during their marriage. Relax and just go with it, she thought. I really like this man. He's not going to do anything to hurt me. Sue thought she'd better say something. She didn't want to lose this beautiful man over sex.

"Oh Marcello, that feels so good," even the words sounded alien to her.

Marcello saw that as his opportunity to take it all the way and do what he knew he did best. Sue felt a tightening and some butterflies in her tummy, but was more terrified and embarrassed than anything. She decided to make a small moan again. This was enough for Marcello and he quickly mounted her. Sue gasped. She'd never experienced this level of intercourse in her life. Marcello picked up a steady rhythm, which became faster, but Sue felt nothing but fright. She wondered if she was so very different to other women. Not ever having had any close girlfriends in her life, she had never had the usual sex talks with others. This was like nothing she had ever known before, but she knew that she had to show Marcello that she was enjoying it, so she started to thrust her hips to match his and make a few moaning sounds. Marcello came within moments. Sue, who had never come in her life, didn't know what was expected of her, and said "Oh my darling, that was so good."

"But you didn't come again. Am I coming too quickly for you, my darling? Is that it?"

Marcello couldn't have cared less if Sue came or not but felt he had to ask, as it was something new for him.

"Yes, I think that's probably it darling. Never mind, as long as you enjoyed it. Maybe next time??" Sue wasn't sure if he'd want to see her again.

She wasn't so naïve to think that she was an attractive woman, but no man had ever spoken to, or touched her, like Marcello had. He must think she was special or this wouldn't be happening.

Marcello, with no other real option, said "Of course next time, my darling. I will take things slower next time and Marcello will make you come. Once you relax with me, you will come. I think that is the problem."

Oh my, thought Sue, he still wants me. His accent and his good looks alone were enough for Sue to want to see him again.

"I will come again to you tomorrow my darling. And this time it will be better for you. But now I'd better go. I have got my work to do,"

He quickly got dressed and went out without kissing her, shouting over his shoulder "Ciao baby!" Sue was left lying on the bed, happy, but wondering why such an attractive man would want her. Maybe she saw herself as unattractive because nobody had ever told her differently. Maybe Marcello saw her differently. Whatever, Sue felt like a new woman and thought she could quite easily fall in love with this man.

Marcello walked back to the Reception building and bumped into some of the other staff.

"Hi Mark," one called out to him. "What you been up to? You look flushed."

"I've been on the phone for ages trying to

organise the band for Saturday's party. I had to get some air so I've just had a bit of a walk mate," he said in a strong Australian accent. "Gotta go and get myself some lunch now. I've worked up quite an appetite with all the walking around this bloody place!" And he walked off with a smile on his face.

CHAPTER 19

RACHAEL

After their disastrous day before, Rachael woke up with a pounding headache. She got out of bed and went into the bathroom and took two Paracetamol, and drank a full glass of water. She had no idea what she should do? She couldn't even begin to relax here with the situation as it was, with her mum and the children. But she could see that Harry was getting more and more frustrated with her. She had to do something otherwise this whole holiday would have been a waste of time. She vowed there and then that she would not ring her mum again and check up on how things were. It only upset her too much. Harry stirred and opened his eyes. He didn't say his usual "Good morning," to her and Rachael felt that he was still angry from the night before. After brushing her teeth, there was a knock on the door and she went to open it.

"Hi. We haven't met yet. I'm Karen McNulty, your chalet maid for the week. You've been out every time I've been before."

Karen was dressed in the uniform of the Island staff. Her face was really pretty and her smile lit up the room. But she hesitated, detecting Rachael's mood.

"Look sweetheart if this is a bad time, I can come back later?"

Rachael looked back into the chalet, where Harry was still in bed. "Hi Karen. Yeah, sorry. It is a bit of a bad time. Can you come back later?"

"Sure thing. Sorry, it's Rachael, isn't it?" Karen said, looking at her work board. "I'll come back later on. Just leave me a note if there's anything I can get you. I'll leave you alone. Bye."

Rachael went back into the room. She looked over at Harry, who was awake and laying with his arms above his head. He looked grumpy and not in the mood for talking.

Rachael thought she'd better try. "Why don't we do the Snorkelling Class this morning and then do a snorkel later on?" she said, looking at the Island's Itinery sheet for the day.

She thought that maybe having an activity to look forward to later might improve Harry's mood. Also, it might take her mind of the kids, she thought. Panicked, Harry had to say no, he didn't want to go. He'd remembered that he'd already made arrangements with Cassie yesterday to go to the Snorkelling Session with her this morning. What had he been thinking? Of course, Rachael might have wanted to go to the Session too. He had to think quick on his feet and put his wife off.

"I've heard there's Bingo on at 10.30 this morning. Wouldn't you rather go to that instead?" Harry knew Rachael loved a game of Bingo.

"Ooh yes. That would be much better. But I

hate leaving you on your own. What will you do? Come to Bingo with me?"

Harry said no, it wasn't his thing. He might just take his book and lay by the pool for a while.

"OK," said Rachael. "We'll meet up for lunch, say around 12.30 in the restaurant. Then we can maybe try the snorkelling later on?"

OK, thought Harry. How do I get out of this one? "No, you know fish aren't my thing darling. I thought you didn't like them either?"

"Oh, I don't mind maybe looking at them Harry," Rachael said.

"You'll be more than looking at them Rach. They'll be swimming all around your legs, even touching you!"

"Oh no! I couldn't bear that. Let's not go then. I can find something else for us to do."

Harry thought quickly. "I was actually going to go and have another round of Golf, if that OK with you? I met a couple of guys there yesterday and I sort of promised them I'd see them again today."

Rachael was slightly disappointed, hoping that they could have spent all day together.

"That's OK. I'll probably go and find a nice shady spot and read my book then. What time will you be finished Golf?"

Harry wanted to spend most of the day with Cassie but knew that Rachael needed him to spend time with her too.

"How about you go to Bingo then we'll meet in the restaurant for lunch. I can then go to Golf and you can read your book by the pool and we'll meet up for dinner?" Harry hoped he wasn't pushing his luck too much.

But to his amazement, Rachael agreed. She was too worried about the children to think of much else anyway, and didn't really care what they did.

"OK then. I'll see you in the restaurant at about 12.30pm," she said.

Although she was disappointed that Harry wasn't going to spend the day with her, she didn't mind him going to Golf. She hated the game and nothing would have persuaded her to give it a try. But at least they could spend some time together today. Rachael felt the usual pangs of anxiety rise in her but quickly reminded herself of her promise not to ring her mum again this week.

Her thoughts turned back to her husband, who looked like he was about to doze off again. "Come on sleepyhead, let's go and get some breakfast!"

It was almost 10am by the time they'd finished their meal, and Harry made his way over to the beach hut where the snorkelling class was being held. Cassie was already there, along with about a dozen others. Soon, a petite young girl in staff uniform came and introduced herself as Sonia, their instructor. Sonia explained that they could only snorkel in the inlet after 2pm when it was high tide. She gave the group a general overview of the Great Barrier Reef and its Islands, some of which could be seen in the distance from Paradise Island. She explained that there were more than 1,500 species of fish living on the Reef, including clownfish, red bass, red-throat emperor, and several species of snapper and coral trout. She also told them that around 5,000 species of molluscs lived on the Reef and that the Reef was around 500,000 years old. There were many murmurs at this information, as none of them knew anything about the world-famous Reef. Sonia went on to tell them that the fish in the inlet would swim very close to them, and they should have a perfect view of many of the species that swam in the waters nearby. Finally, she said that they could hire complimentary snorkelling gear and flippers from the Reception building, and ended by wishing them all a great and wonderful experience later in the day.

"Well that was interesting. I can't wait to get out and have a go," said Harry. "Reckon you're up for it later on?" he enquired.

"Absolutely," said Cassie. "I can't wait. What have you got planned now?"

Harry, who knew Rachael would still be at Bingo, suggested they both go for a swim in the ocean. He tested the water with his foot and it was beautifully warm, with the salt coming off the spray of the waves a treat to his senses.

"Let's go back to mine first so that I can get changed, then we can go to yours so that you can change," he said.

As they made their way back to Harry's chalet, he told her that things were still not good between him and Rachael. He didn't want to go into too much detail, and just mentioned that his wife was worrying about their kids and wasn't enjoying herself. Once at his chalet, Harry changed in the bathroom, picked up a beach towel and some sun cream, then they headed over to Cassie's for her to change.

Rachael was left wondering why Harry's mood had changed. He'd been Ok earlier and she thought he'd forgiven her for their disastrous night before. She hadn't won at Bingo, which had frustrated her, as she'd got down to only wanting one number quite a few times. She looked at her watch. It was just under half an hour till she had to meet Harry in the restaurant, so she decided to take a stroll around the Resort, then make her way to the restaurant in time for lunch. She wondered how Jake was. She had decided just before they came away that they would try and find a Specialist in Sydney and take Jake to see him, to find any way, or even a different medication, to control his behaviour. She'd see a load of different area's Yellow

Pages in Reception and decided she would go there after lunch and look up a Specialist, if they had a Sydney copy. She knew they couldn't go on much longer with Jake. She was beyond exhausted with his erratic behaviour and Harry was no help, always being away from home for most of the day. Her thoughts turned to her 7-year-old daughter. Her mum had said the last time Rachael had phoned her, that Sophie driving them all mad with her Karaoke singing. Rachael knew that her singing was awful, a type of loud screeching, and the Karaoke microphone made things even worse. She also thought about her poor baby, Lily, having to do without a bottle for the first time in her life, her parents absent and staying with virtual strangers, even though they were her grandparents. Her mum had said that her and dad were up until midnight with her. At home, Rachael and Harry would try to put Lily in her own bed, but she continuously got out and came downstairs, sometimes asking for whatever a 3-year-old can think of, or another bottle, anything that would prevent her from having to stay in her own bed. Often, Rachael would lay Lily on the couch beside her and stroke her hair. Sometimes this would work, and Lily would fall asleep and could be carried back up to her own bed. But this was usually around midnight, and it mostly didn't work, so that Rachael and Harry would be forced, exhausted, to put Lily into bed with them, where she would fall soundly asleep in seconds. If Harry tried to carry her into her own bed then, she would immediately wake up and start crying again. They'd learnt that it was often easier to just keep her in with them. At least they all got some sleep.

Thinking about the children, instead of relaxing and strolling to the restaurant to meet Harry for lunch, Rachael now found herself in a heightened state of anxiety and she couldn't help herself. She quickly made her way over to the Reception building and asked if they had a Sydney Yellow Pages. Luckily, Lindy was able to find a copy, and Rachael went to the Medical Practitioners Section and looked for anybody who might specialise in children with behavioural disorders. There was one Doctor who caught her eye, and he was in Parramatta, which is a suburb of Sydney, and not that far for them to drive there to see him. Excited, she took some coins from her purse and made a call to him. His name was Dr Phillip Heachy, a Child Psychologist. After a few rings, a Receptionist answered the phone. Yes, Dr Heachy was taking on new patients, what was the problem? Rachael quickly explained Jake's background and his current level of behaviour. The Receptionist said that Dr Heachy could see Jake, but there was a three-month waiting list and the cost would be $250 for the initial consultation. Although disappointed in the waiting time, Rachael asked for an appointment, and wrote it down on a scrap of paper which was on the desk, happy that she was taking a different course of action than they'd taken before with Jake. She felt full of hope that Dr Heachy could help them. Now, still with heightened anxiety, she decided to break her promise to herself, and while she was here at the phone, she'd give her mum a quick ring. Even though it was lunchtime, the children would all be at home as it was the school holidays in New South Wales for the rest of the week. With shaking hands, she rang her mum's number, all the while telling herself to stop, and do as she'd promised herself, but something kept her going. She had to make sure everything was Ok. The phone rang and rang and eventually her dad answered. The background noise was mayhem.

"Hi dad. It's me. How are they?" Rachael was

shaking like a leaf.

"Rach, I've told you to stop worrying. We're managing," Rachael heard her mum's voice in the background shouting "No we're bloody not." It was so unlike her mum to use even the mildest swear word that Rachael panicked.

"Dad, why did mum shout that you weren't managing? Please tell me dad, what's happening? What's wrong?"

Rachael was now a mess of panic and anxiety. She heard Jake shout "Fuck off. I'm not doing it, you stupid cow."

"Dad what's happening? Why did Jake just shout that?"

"Rachael, I've told you, just go and enjoy yourself. You've only got a few more days there. We will just have to manage. They'll settle down eventually." But Rachael wasn't pacified.

"Dad, what do you mean 'they'? Are Sophie and Lily Ok?"

"Well Sophie's making a whole heap of noise

on that Karaoke thingy of hers and Lily won't stop crying for a bottle. Your mum is insistent on not giving in to her. I've told her just to bloody give her one to shut her up but you know what your mum's like. The house is like a tip and you know how she feels about the house." Rachael's dad's voice had risen and suddenly she also heard the anxiety in him.

"That's it dad. We're coming home. Today. We'll get the 4pm ferry over to Mackay and drive overnight. I can't stay here dad. It's too stressful for me. I can't stop worrying about how you and mum are coping with the three of them. I can't relax or do anything. I have to come home."

Rachael thought she heard her dad give a sigh of relief.

"No darlin' don't do that. You both stay there. We'll be Ok till Sunday."

But Rachael had made up her mind. "No dad. We're coming home today. This was the worst idea ever. I don't know why I expected you and mum to have to put up with the three of them. I'm meeting Harry for lunch soon and I'll tell him we're coming home. I'll ring you from the car tonight and we should be there sometime in the morning."

"Ok Rach." Her dad gave a sigh, probably of relief, thought Rachael. "If it would make you feel any better. I'm so sorry it hasn't worked out sweetheart. Ring me later this evening. Love you. Drive safely. Bye."

Rachael let out a huge sigh of relief. At last, they were going home to her babies. She made her way over to meet Harry at the restaurant and found him already sitting at a table, drinking a glass of wine.

"Harry, we're going home. Today. Mum and dad aren't managing the kids, so we have to go back." Rachael blurted it out as she knew Harry wouldn't be happy. Well tough! They were his kids as well.

"You've got to be joking, surely. I'm fuckin' going nowhere Rach. If you want to sod off home then you go. Christ, we can't even go away and leave the kids with your folks just for one sodden week, and you're rushing back to them. It's pathetic. Anyway, I've made plans to play golf this afternoon, so I'm going nowhere."

Rachael threw down her napkin and stood up.

"Well I'm going without you then. You stay here, you selfish bastard. If you think your stupid golf is more important than your children, then bloody well stay. They're your bloody kids as well. Why won't you come with me?"

Almost begging him, Rachael didn't realise tears were streaming down her face. She couldn't believe that Harry would let her leave on her own, making her own way back.

"I've told you, I'm going nowhere. I've earned this break and I'm going to enjoy every minute of it, so if you want to go, you bloody well go," said a furious Harry.

"Oh, don't you worry I'm going. What about the car? How will I get home?

"That's your problem," Harry hissed and stormed out of the restaurant.

In shock, Rachael walked over to the Reception building and booked herself on the afternoon ferry back to the mainland. Seeing her distress, Lindy asked if she could help. Rachael found herself confiding everything to this lovely girl. Lindy understood and told Rachael that she would be better flying home from Mackay airport. She even offered to get Rachael Qantas's number so that she could book the flight. Within ten minutes, both Rachael's ferry and flight had been booked. Lindy told her there was a taxi rank at the Landing Stage at Mackay where she could get a taxi to the airport. Rachael quickly rang her dad back and, while trying to ignore the noises in the background, told him of her plans, and what time he needed to pick her up from the airport tonight. Feeling embarrassed that Harry had chosen to stay at Paradise Island, she told her dad that she had insisted that he stay on and relax, as he worked so hard. She made her way back to the chalet with a heavy heart. Harry preferred to stay here rather than come home with her. Well, fuck him, she thought. I'm going to find a way to make him pay for this when he gets home!!

CHAPTER 20

BIANCA

The SES man told Bianca to go back to her chalet and grab an overnight bag, as Joel may have to stay at the hospital for a while. The relief was almost overwhelming her and she felt weak and tearful. She threw a few things into her beach bag, things she thought she might need, and a clean outfit for Joel, and headed back to the Island's Landing Pad. Joel had already been put back into the helicopter and Bianca was told she could sit in it with him for the journey. The flight to Mackay only took about 15 minutes as the chopper whirled through the cloudless blue sky. Apart from the noise of the rotor blades, Bianca thought it was quiet and peaceful up in the air, and she was relieved beyond measure as she was able to look across at Joel, who had his eyes closed and who had an oxygen mask on his face. Soon they had landed and Joel was being stretchered out of the chopper and into the hospital, to the Accident and Emergency Department, where the Medical Team were waiting for him. Bianca was asked to wait in the Relatives Room while the doctors gave Joel a thorough going over. She sat there motionless, thinking how lucky Joel had been, mentally punishing herself for pushing Joel too hard on their honeymoon night. Why had she thought that them being married would somehow make Joel any different? She realised that it was her own expectations that had made her push Joel too far. Her sudden guilt was overwhelming and she felt tears rolling down her cheeks. She must have sat there for half an hour when a nurse popped her head round the door and told Bianca she could go through to the cubicle in the Emergency Room where Joel was. She was told she could accompany him to X-Ray and as they walked down the short corridor she held his hand.

She felt Joel give her hand a squeeze and she once again felt so thankful that he had been found safe and well, apart from his leg, of course. She'd seen it briefly when the brace had been removed, and even she could tell that it was probably broken, it was so swollen and bruised. The X-Ray took only a matter of minutes and soon they were making their way back to the Emergency Room. A nurse bustled around Joel, giving him some more strong pain relief through his cannula and checking his blood pressure and SATS. Satisfied, she took the oxygen mask off Joel and sat the back of the bed up for him.

"What about a nice cuppa for you wee lassie?" The nurse's Scottish accent came through in a lilting tone.

"I'm sorry darlin'" she said to Joel, "but I can't give you anything until the results of your X-Ray is back, but if ya don't need surgery on that foot of yours then I'll be bringing ya a nice sandwich and a cuppa. OK?"

Bianca thanked the nurse and said, yes, a cup of tea would be lovely. Joel just nodded. He was still physically and emotionally drained from what he had just experienced. He was dehydrated and had sunstroke and the emotional roller coaster he had been on had left him beyond exhausted. The nurse bustled out through the curtains surrounding the cubicle to get Bianca's tea. The brace that the helicopter crew had fitted to Joel's ankle was back on, and as they waited for the doctor to come with the X-Ray results, Bianca pulled her chair closer to Joel. She held his hand tightly.

"Don't you ever do this to me again, do you hear?" Bianca said, with tears running down her cheeks. "Why, Joel? Why? Are you so repulsed by me that you have to run away? I've been through hell wondering what had happened to you. You could have died out there Joel! I thought you were dead my darling."

Joel's silence was deafening.

"Speak to me Joel, please!" Joel looked at Bianca. He also had tears in his eyes.

"I'm so sorry Bea. I needed time to think, to try and understand why I'm still the way I am. I realise now that I'm no good for you. I can't give you all the things a wife needs. I'll understand if you give up on me now." His voice was still weak and croaky from his ordeal.

Bianca felt her heart break. "Oh, my darling, I would never give up on you. I love you too much. We just need to find a way to work things out, so that we can both be happy."

Joel's tears were running down his cheeks now as well.

"What are we like Joel, both of us sitting her blubbering like babies." Bianca tried to lift the mood.

The lovely nurse came back in through the curtains, which surrounded the cubicle, and she pretended not to notice that both Bianca and Joel had been crying.

"Here we are, me wee darling. Get this down ya. You'll feel a lot better for it. And you, my wee man, the doctor is just at the desk now looking at your X-Rays so he won't be long." She looked over to Bianca "If there's anything you need lassie, just ask, OK?"

Bianca thanked her and sipped her tea. Naturally, as hospital tea is, it was horrible, but she felt some comfort from the heat coming from the polystyrene cup. Soon, the Doctor came back into the cubicle.

"Well, young Joel, I've had a good look at your X-Rays and you have a small fracture at the base of your tibia." He explained, "You have two main bones, which make up your leg, the tibia and the fibular. These are joined onto your foot, to put it in layman's terms. Can I just have a look at it?"

The doctor took off Joel's brace and felt around the swollen area. He was feeling if the pulse was still strong there, and asked Joel if he felt any numbness or coldness in his foot. Joel nodded and said that he felt both but only around his ankle, not on the top part of his foot.

"You're a very lucky lad you know. This could have been a lot worse. Typically, this type of small fracture will heal in 6 to 8 weeks but I'm afraid you'll have to have a cast on it for that time. We'll get that organised now and you can go home. I'll give you some strong painkillers to take with you but you can start to take Paracetamol in a day or two."

Bianca explained to the doctor that they were actually on their honeymoon at Paradise Island.

"Well, we'll give you a pair of crutches and you can go back and finish off your holiday. I've never been there myself but I've heard it's beautiful."

"It certainly is," said Bianca. "But don't you think we should just go back home?"

The doctor addressed Joel "It's up to you, but there would be no harm in going back and enjoying the rest of your holiday, even though you can't swim. I'm sure there would be things you could do there, even if you just lay by a pool and read a good book. That's what I'd do! Anyway, I'll get one of the nurses to come and put a cast on that foot and you can be on your way. All your numbers are looking much better and there's no point in keeping you in this boring place for longer than necessary," he laughed. "All the best. Drink plenty, stay out of the sun and under the shade and you'll soon feel better. Oh, and enjoy the rest of your honeymoon!" and he gave them a wink as he walked out of the cubicle.

He went out and spoke to a nurse, and soon a trolley with a bowl of water and bandages was being wheeled into the cubicle. The young nurse introduced herself.

"Hi there. I'm Kathy and I'm going to put a cast on that foot of yours. Then I'm sure it will feel a lot better."

Another nurse had come in with her, and together they set about their work. Joel grimaced at first as his foot was placed in the correct position for the cast, but soon it was all done. A porter appeared with a pair of crutches and Joel was asked to try and stand up so they could make sure they were at the right height for him. Another nurse came in and handed Bianca a small box with the words 'Endone' on the front.

"These are strong painkillers. Make sure he takes no more than 2 a day until his pain settles down, then he can just take Paracetamol when he needs to."

For some reason, the nurse addressed Bianca as though Joel was not in the room.

"He should be OK to get about using his crutches I would have thought, but if his pain gets any worse, you'll need to come back and see the Doctor again."

Bianca thanked her and gathered up her bag. Joel was a bit awkward on the crutches at first but as they made their way out of the hospital he said that he thought he was getting the hang of them. Standing outside the Hospital, Bianca asked Joel what he wanted to do.

"Let's go back to the Island Bea. We've paid for it. Like the doctor said, I can lay by the pool and read. There's a Library on the Island I think. We can eat good food, have a few drinks…"

"Whoa, oh no you can't my love. Not on those painkillers you can't anyway," Bianca teased.

"Spoilsport," said Joel just as a taxi pulled up and let out a mother and small child.

They got into the taxi and asked to be taken to the Landing Stage at the Marina. Bianca had found out that there would be a ferry leaving for Paradise Island at 6pm. She wondered as they drove through the heavy evening traffic, if anything would change now that Joel had had the chance to think about how they could change their lives and make their marriage work. A plan developed in her mind. Yes, she thought. Her plan would solve things, for now, anyway. They would just enjoy the rest of their week on the Island. There would be no talk of sex, no pressure on Joel, just be relaxed and enjoy themselves. Joel was also thinking about the rest of their time on the Island, and how he was going to overcome his fear of intimacy, but he was determined to try. Neither of them knew what the other was planning.

CHAPTER 21

ANNA

Anna opened her eyes and looked across at Ken, still sleeping. Then she remembered she was meeting Marcello at 3pm for a swim in that lovely secret waterhole. What to do till then, she wondered? Anna reached over to her bedside table and picked up the Island's list of activities for the day. Archery at 10am? No, she didn't fancy that. Wine Appreciation, Cocktail Making, Craft Class. Yes, that was what she'd like to do. She enjoyed Craft, and she would go to that. She looked over at the bedside clock. 8.15am.

Would she wake Ken to go to breakfast with her before the 10.30am Craft Class? He'd been in such a funny mood with her lately. She had been so convinced that her new look and attitude would make her appeal to him again, but it didn't seem to be working. He preferred to go off on his own all day than spend any time with her. She wondered if he'd found another woman on the Island. He wasn't a man who could go for long without sex so it was a definite possibility. If only she could follow him, the thought came to her? Yes, that's what she'd do. When he would make his excuses after dinner this evening, she would follow him. Pleased with her plan, she shook Ken awake.

"Good morning. It's breakfast time."

Ken gave a groan and opened his eyes. "What time is it?"

"It's 8.15am. I thought we could go and have breakfast then go to the beach for a while. It's such a beautiful day."

Anna had looked outside and the sky was cloudless and the bluest of blue. The palm trees rustled quietly and the sounds of the birds singing their morning songs made the Island idyllic. Across the sand, the ocean lapped gently against the breakers and Anna was yet again thankful that she had paid the extra money for a waterfront chalet. Once dressed, they both gathered up the things they would need for the morning; sun cream, books, sunglasses and towels. They both put their swimming things on under their day clothes and Anna gathered everything into her beach bag. As they left the chalet, Karen, one of the Room Attendants, stopped them and after saying good morning, asked if there was anything they needed. Ken was tempted to say "Yes, a piece of you darling!" but instead asked if they could have some more Earl Grey Teabags in their chalet. Karen said that she'd have them there by lunchtime.

As they made their way to breakfast, Anna decided to be bold and took Ken's arm. Ken was horrified. What if they bumped into Mandy? Not knowing what else to do, Ken told Anna he'd carry the beach bag and quickly removed his arm from hers.

When they arrived at the restaurant, they were shown to a table at the back along the panelled wall. Immediately, Ken was horrified to see Mandy sitting at a table further along the room. However, she was not alone. A man, probably in his 40s, was sitting with her. They were sharing from a plate of fruit salad and both had croissants on the plates in front of them. Mandy was laughing and chatting with the man, who seemed to be hanging on her every word. Ken was furious. Mandy was his, for the week anyway. He sat down opposite his hideous wife and ordered an orange juice. He had suddenly lost his appetite. They sat in silence until at last, Anna spoke.

"So, are you coming to the beach with me after this?"

She sensed that something was bothering her husband. Normally he ate like a horse at breakfast time.

Ken, downcast, replied "Yeah. Might as well. Nothing else to do."

"But Ken, there's plenty to do. Have you even looked at the Activities list in the chalet? There's all sorts of classes, Wine Appreciation, Cocktail Making, Archery, more golf perhaps?" Anna was at a loss to how to cheer her husband's mood.

"Nah. Not in the mood. I'll just have a read,"

Ken was downcast. The thought that Mandy had another man on the go made his blood boil. After they had finished breakfast he and Anna headed for the beach. He knew he wouldn't be able to read a word but put his towel down on the soft sand and took out his book.

Anna, ever the dutiful wife said "I'd better rub some sun cream onto you then."

Ken couldn't bear it. He snatched the bottle from Anna's hand and told her not to bother. He was quite capable of doing it himself. Hurt, Anna laid out her own towel and put on her glasses. She took out her book but found that she was reading the same few lines over and over again. What had gone wrong? She had convinced herself that making herself over and bringing them to this beautiful place would bring them closer together. She now realised that it hadn't worked. Anna was becoming more certain as time went on that Ken was seeing another woman. His long absences from her and his strong sex drive, along with their lack of intimacy increased her certainty. She vowed to follow through with her plan to track Ken after dinner tonight. Her mood was quickly lifted when she remembered that she was meeting Marcello at 3pm this afternoon. She couldn't wait to go back to the beautiful spot he had taken her to yesterday. And he had been so flattering to her. He genuinely seemed to like her, and that pleased Anna very much. Anna looked at her watch. 10.20am. She remembered about the craft class and decided to go to it, rather than spend the morning with her miserable husband.

Ken waited until Anna was well out of sight. He gathered his things up and made his way off the beach and back towards the restaurant, where he had last seen Mandy. When he arrived there, however, she was nowhere in sight, so he decided to go to her chalet and see if he would find her there, and more importantly, who she was with. But after knocking on Mandy's door, there was no answer. Ken walked to the saltwater pool in the hope of finding her there but had no luck. He decided he'd have a game of golf in an effort to put him in a better frame of mind. But after playing 9 Holes, Ken found his mood was still bleak. These last few days he had come to rely on Mandy for his sexual needs, plus he was getting to quite like her, and wondered if they would keep in touch when they returned home. He decided to give Mandy's chalet one last try. Walking towards it, he noticed the girl in the red bikini, as he'd come to think of her, only this time, she was walking with a man who looked in his twenties, and who was on crutches with a cast on his foot. They were walking very slowly and seemed to be chatting about something. Not in a hurry, Ken quickened his pace to catch up with them.

"Oh dear. You seem to have been in the wars. Hi, I'm Ken. Are you here till the weekend? I haven't seen you around," he lied.

"Yes, we arrived last Saturday but my husband has broken his ankle, but rather than decide to go home we've come back. It's our honeymoon you see," said Red Bikini.

"Hi. I'm Bianca and this is my husband Joel. Pleased to meet you." There was something vaguely familiar about the man, thought Bianca, but it soon went out of her head.

"I'm sorry to hear that. Look, if there's anything my wife and I can do for you just let us know. We are in chalet number 3, on the beachfront. I mean it, anything at all." Ken said this looking straight into

Bianca's eyes. This was one bikini chick he'd like to tame, he thought.

"Thank you, but I think we'll manage. We're taking it nice and easy and just enjoying the weather and the Island." Bianca didn't like the way the man's eyes looked into hers.

Then it clicked. This was the sleaze bag who had tried to chat her up by the pool on their first day. She was now keen to get away from him.

"Thank you again. Don't let us hold you up."

Ken felt the coldness in Bianca's voice but that made him all the more determined to win her round. He'd bide his time. That sickly-looking specimen of a husband of hers didn't look like he'd be up to much in the bedroom department, Ken smirked to himself. He kept walking towards Mandy's chalet but yet again she was not there. Annoyed and frustrated, Ken took himself back to his own chalet and took out one of his secret stash of Girlie Magazines that he'd brought with him. He went into the bathroom and released his frustrations there.

The hours for Anna until 3pm when she would be meeting Marcello seemed to drag by. She'd gone to the Craft Class, which had lasted till lunchtime, and then gone back to their chalet to get Ken and go to lunch. She'd found him lying on their bed, obviously sulking. No, he didn't want any lunch, thank you. He was happy just to rest here. Not caring anymore, although knowing that something was wrong with her husband, Anna had gone to lunch on her own and had then taken a good walk along the beach. When she looked at her watch, it was 2.30, time to go back to the chalet and get changed for her swim with Marcello. He was on time, and standing in front of the Reception building, waiting for her. He looked so handsome in his Island uniform, his dark hair and olive skin. Anna wondered why she hardly ever saw him in any of the public places. Even though he'd told her he booked the Entertainment on the Island, he actually only shared an office inside the Reception building, finding and booking artists for the Island's nights' entertainment. He made sure to only visit the public areas of the Resort as infrequently as possible as he didn't want to bump into the women he was seducing as the Italian 'Marcello', instead of Aussie Mark.

Unbeknownst to Anna, Marcello, as she knew him, had decided that today would be the day for him and Anna to really enjoy themselves in the water hole. After what he felt had been his success with Sue earlier, he felt cocky and invincible. He led Anna again to the waterhole, through the shrubbery and down the dirt path, and held onto her hand when she had stumbled and had somehow never let go of it. His voice, as always, was syrupy smooth, and with a strong Italian accent.

"My darling, you are yet again looking at your finest. How do you do it? How do you manage to look so, what is the word, ravishing?"

Anna blushed beetroot red and could only mutter "Oh Marcello!"

When they reached the water hole she became acutely aware that she was now going to have to take off her dress so that she could swim. She looked over at Marcello, who was already in his Speedos and had to look away quickly as his manhood was clearly on show. Without further ado, Marcello jumped into the water hole and held out his hand for Anna, who had, quite embarrassingly, taken off her dress to reveal the much hated (by Ken) swimsuit. Giggling like a schoolgirl fifty years younger, she took a deep breath, closed her eyes, and jumped in. Marcello caught her, but not before the thought had crossed his mind that he was slipping in his standards in women. Anna was much older than the women he was used to and although not ugly, like Sue she was not attractive. Marcello had searched the rest of the Island all week for other, more younger, and attractive girls to seduce, but they all seemed to be in couples this week. Anyway, he was here now, and as his only object was to give way to his lust, Anna would have to do, along with the only other woman he had managed to find, Sue. After frolicking in the lovely warm, clear water for ten minutes, Marcello decided to make his move. He grabbed Anna round the waist and pulled him to him.

"You really are very beautiful, you know," there was that accent again.

Oh, how it made Anna's butterflies flutter. She had not been flattered like this for many, many years and she was loving every minute of it. It never entered her head that she was almost old enough to be his mother, but when Marcello's lips met hers in a gentle kiss, she responded eagerly. This was what true love was all about. What she had with Ken, the life they had, that was just existing. Marcello whispered in her ear then helped her out of the water. They found a smooth area of sandy soil nearby and Marcello out his towel for them to lay on.

"You really are the most beautiful woman I have ever met," the smooth talking lothario told Anna. I can't understand why that awful husband of yours, he doesn't, how you say, appreciate your beauty. Any man would be grateful to have you as a lover, I know I certainly do."

Anna was so flattered that she immediately kissed Marcello full on his lips. He needed no further prompting. He took the straps of her swimsuit from Anna's shoulders and started to kiss her, first on her neck, her shoulders, then on her lips. Oh, how she loved it. She hadn't felt like this for years. When Marcello took off the rest of her swimsuit and started to kiss down her chest, he was slightly repulsed by her sagging breasts and wrinkled belly, but carried on nevertheless. Meanwhile, Anna was starting to experience a moment of panic. She shouldn't really be doing this. She was a married woman. But hang on, wasn't this exactly what Ken had been doing for years? She hadn't realised that sex was something she would ever have again, let alone enjoy. She let her newly found passion overtake her and returned Marcello's kisses. Within moments he was inside her. Anna climaxed almost immediately, it had been so long for her. Marcello, taking great pride in his sexual prowess, kept going for a few more moments before calling out "Sue. My dear sweet Sue," as he came. Anna was confused. Her name wasn't Sue.

CHAPTER 22

SUE

Sue had lain awake well into the night. She was sure she was in love. Sure, the sex didn't do it for her, but she was slowly falling in love with the beautiful Italian Marcello. No other man had ever meant this much too her. Gordon had been, well just Gordon. Theirs had not been a happy marriage and Gordon was not one to give out praise or flattery. And his sexual prowess was virtually non-existent. But Marcello was different. Sue knew that coming to Paradise Island this week was paying off for her. Maybe, just maybe, she thought, she'd finally found the love of her life?

She got up and headed straight for the shower. Five minutes later – she was never one to linger and waste water – she was out and drying herself. She put on extra perfume in case she bumped into Marcello this morning, and took extra care over styling her short, mousy hair. After gathering up her beach towel, sun cream, sun glasses and her book, Sue made her way to the restaurant for breakfast. As she entered, she spotted Will sitting on his own on a table in the corner, so she walked over and asked if he'd mind if she'd join him. Naturally Will was pleased to see this lovely lady, who he felt he had so much in common with, and invited her to sit down. Their conversation passed freely as Sue ate her croissant and fresh fruits and soon she and Will were down to just drinking their coffee. Will had no plans, while Sue had promised that she'd go to the Archery Range again this morning. Will said he didn't think his shoulders and arms were strong enough but would Sue mind if he came and watched her. However, always aware that she might bump into Marcello, Sue was hesitant, but had no option but to agree. Once at the Range, the people from yesterday were already there, along with a few new ones. Sue introduced Will to the small crowd, then herself, to the new people. Suddenly, and without reason, she felt slightly embarrassed, and hoped that none of them would think that she and Will were a couple. He was much older than her and not at all attractive. Sue, now used to Marcello's flattery, had begun to see herself in a different light and Will did nothing for her self-esteem, as Marcello did everything. Once again, they went through the basics with their Instructor, Sean. This time, for most of the group, hitting the target was easier. Sue was mortified that every time she hit the target, Will clapped and gave a little 'hurray'. Now she was sure that the group would think Will was her partner and she decided to dispel the image quickly.

Speaking loudly, she turned to Will and said, for all to hear, "Thank you for coming to watch Will. It was very kind of you. Stay back and watch the others if you like, but I have to get back to my chalet now as I'm meeting somebody."

Will looked crestfallen but did as he'd been told, looking over his shoulder at the departing Sue, who he really did like and had though that she'd liked him.

As it was late morning, Sue decided to go back to the chalet and get changed and go for an early lunch. There were only a few diners there, and Sue was offered a table by herself, at the edge of the restaurant, overlooking the ocean. The other diners were all in couples or groups, Sue noticed, and an uncharacteristic sense of loneliness came across her. Did she really want a man in her life, or was she so stuck in her ways that she would prefer to live on her own, as she did? The thought of Marcello made her decide that, yes, a man like him would be more than welcome in her life. He had made her feel good about herself again, like a real woman. Sue had gone through life as a nobody, someone whom people spoke to in passing, but who had paid no real attention to. Even in high school, she had been a bit of a nerd, an outcast, always with her nose in a book. Then marrying Gordon had probably been her biggest failure. Gordon had his own issues and he was shy and introverted. Sue realised that until now, until Marcello, she had never experienced passion, lust or love. The words took her by surprise. Is this what she felt for Marcello after such a short time? She was sure it was. Now all she had to do was keep him interested in her, and to persuade him that coming to live with her in Wollongong was a better proposition than his current situation. She was sure he'd find a job in one of the Clubs or Restaurants close by where she lived. After enjoying her lunch of Balmain Bugs with Thousand Island dressing and a green salad, Sue decided to have a walk around the resort in the hope of bumping into Marcello. There was a Cocktail Making class on at 2pm so she would go to that if she couldn't find him. As she was passing the Reception building, Sue noticed Marcello going inside, but he had Linda, the Receptionist with him. He must be working, she thought, so carried on walking. Looking at her watch she still had an hour and a half to go until the Cocktail Making class, so she headed to her chalet and lay on the bed reading her book.

Just before 2pm, Sue made her way over to the Entertainments area, sure she'd see Marcello there in his role as Entertainments booker, but she was disappointed. A young man, dressed in full waiter's costume was preparing bottles and glasses and little umbrellas and twiddly sticks on the long bar counter. There were only half a dozen other guests there and the young man soon started his spiel.

"Good afternoon all, I'm Jackson," he said loudly and cheerfully, as though talking to an audience of thousands. "I hope you're all looking forward to trying out some new tastes and making some gorgeous cocktails?"

One or two guests murmured an almost silent 'yes'.

"Oh, come on guys. Let's hear it, but with this time, with a bit more enthusiasm hey?"

"Yes," they all shouted back. Boy, thought Sue, where did Marcello get this guy from?

"Right folks, first of all I'm going to demonstrate how to make a Blue Lagoon. If you like to live the high life then this cocktail is for you. It is made from laraha fruit, grown on the Island of Curacao. This cocktail will transport you to the turquoise waters of a Caribbean paradise."

Picking up a cocktail glass, Jackson introduced his ingredients:

Ice cubes,

2 oz vodka

2 oz blue curacao liqueur

lemonade

a Maraschino cherry to garnish

and, of course, the little paper umbrella.

"Now how simple could this be to start us off?" boomed Jackson. "Pour your vodka and curacao over the ice cubes, top with lemonade, and finish with a flourish, your cherry and umbrella."

He invited them to take a sip each then told them they would now move onto something a bit more difficult. Sue found she was fast losing interest. She'd never been a cocktail drinker and wondered why she'd even come to this class. One of the other guests who had been standing next to her throughout Jackson's demonstration caught her eye. He was, Sue thought, in his mid 50s and beautifully dressed. He smelt of a lovely aftershave and she was instantly attracted to him. Not one to usually behave in this way, Sue put her newfound confidence down to Marcello. Suddenly, the man spoke, and Sue found it was to her he was speaking.

"I don't know about you, but I'm finding this all a bit boring. I've never been a cocktail drinker and have no idea why I thought this would be a good idea!" The man gave a small laugh.

"I was just thinking the same," said Sue. "In fact, I think I might give it a miss."

"Do you mind if I join you? Maybe we could have coffee next door?"

"That would be lovely." Sue was taken aback.

Here was another lovely man taking her out for a coffee. She wasn't used to all this male attention, or any attention, from male or female, for that matter. As they made their way to the Coffee Shop, the man introduced himself."

"I suppose I should say hi. My name's Steve. Steve Oldham."

"Hi Steve. Nice to meet you. I'm Sue. Have you been on the Island long? I haven't seen you about."

"I arrived last Sunday. I was supposed to get here on Saturday, but I was delayed with work," Steve explained. "What about you?"

"I also arrived last Saturday. I'm just here for the week though. I wish I was staying longer now. I am in love with this place!"

When they'd arrived next door, there was a buzz about the Coffee Shop as they entered. Tiggy was on her own trying to serve half a dozen people at once. She gave Sue and Steve a small wave and motioned for them to sit at a table in the corner. They picked up menus and found that they both liked the same type of coffee: Half strength skinny flat white. They laughed at the coincidence.

"Do you have a waterfront chalet or a rainforest one?" Steve asked.

"Only a rainforest one, I'm afraid. I couldn't see that paying all that extra money for a beach front one, just to hear the ocean, was worth it. What about you?"

"Same as you. And where I am is really beautiful. I can't believe how peaceful it is, even with the cacophony of noise from the birds. Anyway, I'm on a pretty tight budget at the moment. My wife left me earlier this year and is taking me to the cleaners, unfortunately." Steve's voice was quiet.

"Oh, I'm so sorry. Had you been married long?"

"22 years," said Steve. "She worked full time and gets half of everything, plus some. We've got two teenagers who are going to live with her, so I have to pay maintenance for a few years yet for them as well."

Sue, at a loss as to what to say, could only mutter "Oh dear. Where do you live?"

"I'm from Bankstown, near Sydney. I've lived there all my life."

"You're not that far from me then. Just down the Bulli Pass. I'm in Wollongong. I teach at a High School there," Sue replied.

Tiggy came to their table to take their order. "What about a nice piece of freshly baked cherry pie with your coffees," she said, after writing their order on her note pad.

"Why not. We'll share a piece hey, Sue?"

Sue agreed, and soon she and Steve were on their own again.

"So, tell me a bit about yourself," Steve seemed genuinely interested.

"Well, I got divorced from the man who was definitely not the love of my life two years ago. Seems he was more into men than he was me. I sold the house and bought an apartment overlooking Thingwall Beach. I've lived there on my own since the split. I teach History at a High School and love it as it gives me the chance to impart my knowledge onto young minds! I'll be 50 next birthday. Errm, what else can I tell you?"

"Why come to this beautiful place on your own?" Steve asked. "Are you looking for another relationship?"

Sue considered Steve's question for a moment. She wondered whether to tell him about her new-found love, Marcello, but decided to keep it to herself for now.

"Not sure. I seem to be rattling along on my own quite nicely, but I'm always wondering if there is someone out there for me. I'm getting a bit fed up of not being asked out to things just because I'm not a couple."

Tiggy had returned with their coffees and pie and set them down gently on the table.

"There you go you two. Enjoy." She bustled away to serve a newcomer into the cafe.

Keen to continue with their conversation, Steve told Sue more about himself and his life.

"I'm pretty much the same as you. I'm just starting to get used to being on my own and I don't know whether I can trust another woman again. My wife left me for a man ten years younger, you see. Makes me feel ancient. She's slowly turning the kids against me, and I'm not sure what to do next with my life, or do I just carry on as I am? I came here really just to get away from it all. Clear my head and think things through. A friend of mine came last year and told me how peaceful and relaxing it was, so I thought, why not!"

Sue nodded and made signs of sympathy. They finished their coffee and Steve said "Fancy a walk along the sand?"

Sue had hoped to bump into Marcello. When they'd last left each other, there had been no mention of when they'd meet again, and Sue was keen to arrange more time with her wonderful new man.

"Sorry Steve, but I've arranged to meet a friend. Maybe another time?"

"Sure Sue. It's been lovely talking to you. I'll look out for you again later."

What a lovely man, thought Sue, as she started her walk around the Resort in the hope of seeing Marcello. It was such a shame how his wife had treated him. But Steve was soon out of Sue's thoughts as continued her search for the new love of her life, and she revelled in the love that they both shared. Yes, coming here had been the best thing she'd ever done. Paradise Island had certainly worked its magic, she thought. She had a smile on her face like a Cheshire Cat thinking about her Italian love.

CHAPTER 23

RACHAEL

On the plane from MacKay back home, Rachael realised that there was no way of contacting Harry, other than to leave a message with Lindy in Reception for him to ring her. She hoped she wouldn't have to ring him though. God, she was so angry that he'd allowed her to go home on her own. They were his kids too. Why couldn't he understand that her parents weren't coping and they needed to cut their holiday short and go home and be with their children? Anyway, he seemed to be fine with his new golf buddies, she fumed. She wasn't going to forgive him for this for a long time. Her dad met her in the car with Jake at the airport and drove them back to his house. Jake had flung his arms around her and wouldn't let go for ages. They both sat in the back, holding hands, with Jake keeping up a constant stream of chatter, of what he'd done at school and that grandma was such a "bloody bitch" who wouldn't let him have this or do that. Rachael decided to let the swearing go for now and concentrated on just getting her children back home into their own beds. When they'd arrived at her parent's house it was past ten, but Sophie and Lily were waiting for her. After many tears and saying how much they'd missed each other, Rachael, whose Mum had already packed the children's bags ready to go, ushered them all into her dad's car, but not before seeing the terrible state her Mum's usually pristine house was in. She made a mental note to get her folks something nice as a 'thank you'. The noise from all three children on the way back home was a cacophony. The all had news to tell her, Lily particularly kept telling her that grandma wouldn't give her a bottle. Rachael told her that as soon as they got home she'd make her one. She was just so glad to be with her precious children again. All thoughts of Paradise Island were forgotten.

Back at the Resort, Harry had met up with Cassie for snorkelling. Rachael's bombshell at lunch had firstly made him angry, but then thinking about it, he thought how much of a better time he'd have without her moaning and going on about the children. He did love his children, but knew there was more to life than what he currently had. What about him, he thought? What about his quality of life? Suddenly, he realised that he wasn't really that happy. He worked hard to earn a living and was then expected to come in and deal with his not so well behaved children five days a week, then on weekends too. Sure, he realised Rachael had them for all of the rest of the time, but wasn't that they way of things? The mother looked after the kids while the man went out to work. He was 'Old School' and that's how he rationalised it to himself. Now, helping Cassie put her big black flippers on, then struggling to get his own on, made him relax. This is what a holiday should be about, he thought. And Cassie was great company. She was so easy to talk to and good on the eye as well, and he realised that he was very attracted to her. All thoughts of Rachael and the kids were forgotten and he intended to make the most of what was left of his holiday.

The ocean inlet stretched before them and he and Cassie gingerly made their way into the water. Cassie stumbled and it seemed a natural instinct for Harry to grab her hand. Somehow, he never let go of it. There was quite a large group of people already in the water, heads down looking at the fish.

When he and Cassie were about chest height, he said "OK? How about we put our heads in and see the fish?"

Still holding onto her hand, they both put their heads in the water, their snorkels sticking up above. There were thousands of fish, mostly tiny grey ones but every now and again, a bigger, more colourful one came into view. Harry came up for air and Cassie followed.

"Great hey? Did you see that orange and blue one with the big fin?" Harry still had hold of Cassie's hand.

"I know. It was amazing. Thank you so much for suggesting this. I don't know that I would have been game to do it on my own," Cassie replied.

They spent the next hour in the water, enjoying trying to spot the different species of fish. When they'd had enough they got out and found their towels, which they'd left on the bank, and dried themselves off.

"I've got some news Cass. Rachael's gone home this afternoon. She told me at lunchtime that we had to go back home as her folks weren't dealing with the kids with the same kid gloves that she treats them with, and they weren't coping. I hope you don't think I'm selfish and horrible, but I told her I deserved a break, and didn't see why I should go home just because she was so determined to. So here I am, on my own." Cassie was silent. "You think I'm really awful don't you?" Harry took Cassie's silence as disapproval.

"No, not really. Were her parents really not coping or was it just Rachael worrying?" Cassie asked.

"Rachael said they weren't, but they've had three kids of their own so they should know how to deal with them. I know Jake can be a handful, and Lily's not the easiest of kids, especially at night, but it was only ever for a week. I don't think it was too much to ask that we have a little time to ourselves. Anyway, she's chosen them over me, so she can go and get stuffed." Harry was back to being angry again.

After they had handed their snorkelling equipment back in, they stood looking out to the ocean.

"It's really beautiful here, isn't it?" Cassie was lost in the moment.

Harry was also starting to relax. "Let's take a walk along the beach, then maybe you'd care to join me for dinner?"

"That would be lovely." Cassie really liked this man, although with his baggage, it would be hard to allow things to progress, she thought. Still she'd live for the moment, the way she always did.

Rachael had made Lily a bottle and put her to bed. Amazingly, she had stayed there and fallen straight to sleep within minutes, something she'd never done all her life since being a small baby. Sophie was in bed reading a book and Jake was in the bath. Rachael wondered what Harry was doing now. Probably feeling guilty, she hoped. She didn't regret her decision to come home early from Paradise Island. It was good to be back with her kids in her own house.

She poured herself a glass of wine and put the TV on. It felt good to be back to normality. That's all she had wanted, she thought. Going away had been a bad idea. She should have known there was nobody she could leave her children with and expect them to look after them with their behaviours. But she'd sure as heck give Harry a hard time when he arrived home on Sunday! How dare he not support her, especially where their children were concerned. She hoped he was as miserable on his own, as she now hoped he'd be. She'd make him wish he'd agreed to come home with her when he got back. All kinds of revenge plans took up her thoughts that night as she lay in bed trying to get off to sleep.

CHAPTER 24

BIANCA

After arriving back on the Island, Bianca and Joel had made their way, slowly with Joel on his new crutches, back to their chalet. Joel was exhausted, and after settling him into bed, Bianca had rung Reception and arranged for dinner to be delivered to them in their chalet. Lindy said she'd be more than happy to do so, under the circumstances, and Bianca had put their Order in. Half an hour later there was a knock on the door, and one of the Island's staff had a trolley with plates of food and cutlery. Joel sat himself up in the bed.

"There was no need for this Bea. I could have made it down to the restaurant."

"No way matey. Not tonight. Maybe tomorrow. I just want you to rest for now and get your strength back. Look at you. You're exhausted."

They ate their meal in silence then Bianca put the empty plates outside the chalet to be collected.

"How about a movie?" Bianca asked. "There's quite a good selection here." She walked over to the TV stand and started to look through the dozen or so movies that were in every chalet. She read them all out to Joel and he decided on one. Bianca turned the TV on and inserted the disc into the player. Lying beside Joel, holding onto his hand and watching the movie felt good. She had done a lot of thinking while he was missing and decided to change how she approached the intimate side of their marriage. From now on, she was not even going to mention sex or intimacy to him. She would try and talk him into going to speak to a counsellor and maybe their GP when they got home, but she wasn't going to rush him. He had to be the one to decide when and how to do things, otherwise it would never work. When the movie finished, Bianca decided she and Joel would talk about her new plan, to take the pressure off him, but when she looked over at him, he was fast asleep. The talk would have to wait until tomorrow.

While he'd been missing, Joel had also been thinking about his relationship with Bianca. If she took him back, that's if he was found alive, he was going to do everything he could to make himself into the perfect husband. He would go to counselling, maybe his doctor could recommend some medication, he was willing to give anything a try. He realised that he loved Bianca very much, and it was not fair on her that he wasn't what a husband should be to his wife. He'd forced himself to remember the abuse he'd received from his father, for the abuse his sister had had to endure. This was the first time he'd been able to think about it since it had ended. He visualised, with some pain, his father's lecherous face, his foul breath, especially when he'd been drinking, the lewd acts themselves, and the guilt and pain that he had carried with him all these years. He knew, without a doubt, that this was what was stopping him having a proper intimate relationship with Bianca. If he was found alive, he intended to do something about it and face his demons head on! The thought gave him comfort.

The next morning, Joel was feeling much better. He had a shower, although with a plastic bag over his leg, and got dressed in shorts and tee shirt. He told Bianca that he wanted to try and walk, with his crutches, to the restaurant for breakfast. They made slow progress and along the way they'd bumped into the sleazy old man who had tried to make a move on Bianca on their first day. The way he had looked into her eyes as he spoke had sent a shiver down Bianca's spine. She had sent him on his way with some cold words, and a look that said "Leave us alone. We don't want your help!" Arriving at the restaurant, they faced the problem of getting Joel up the stairs but, although slow, he managed to make it all the way up. The effort made him exhausted and Bianca realised they'd have to think of another way to eat. Once Joel had recovered his breath, they chose a table overlooking the ocean, even though Bianca didn't much like the close proximity of the many colourful parrots sitting on the ledge waiting to pounce on the leftovers. She ordered Eggs Benedict with smoked salmon and Joel had an avocado omelette. They ate in silence then ordered coffee. Bianca decided that now was the time to tell Joel of her plan.

"Darling, I've done a lot of thinking over the last few days. I thought I'd lost you forever and it was more than I could bare."

Joel, interrupted her, "Bea I'm safe now ..."

"No Joel, let me say what I have to say. I need to. I've done a lot of thinking and we've never really had a proper talk about our problems. You clam up every time I try and bring it up, so from now on, we won't mention it at all. I'm happy just to be with you. Let's forget about the sex. We need never mention it again until you're ready, if ever. I'm just so glad you're alive and not seriously injured."

Joel looked into his wife's eyes and saw the love there.

"Bea, now it's my turn to say something. While I was away, for want of a better word, I had the chance to do a lot of thinking myself. I actually thought about what happened to Jacqui and I, in detail, for the first time since we ran away all those years ago. I saw my father's face, smelt his breath, felt his abuse and the pain. I realise now that I can't go on living my life carrying something like that around with me, especially now that I've got you. As soon as we get back home I'm going to see a counsellor again and this time I'm going to tell her the truth!"

Bianca didn't understand. "What, you didn't tell the truth last time you saw Wendy?"

"No, Bea. I told her a load of bullshit and she gave me some breathing exercises to do. I just wasn't in the right headspace to tell the truth, but I think I am now."

'Sweetheart, that's wonderful that you've realised that. I hope you can go through with it, not for my sake but for yours. For now, though, I say we just enjoy what time we've got left here. Let's just do what you can. Read, relax by the pool, look out over the ocean, eat and drink, well orange juice for you for now, and we don't even think about anything else. Deal?"

"Deal," said Joel, "but I promise I'm going to get help and change just as soon as I can. I love you so much you deserve so much better than me Bea."

"OK. That's enough of feeling sorry for

yourself mister. Let's make our way downstairs and get you into a comfy chair and see what today's entertainment is. I think swimming's out for you my darling!"

They spent the rest of the day at the Entertainment Centre under the restaurant. Firstly, there was the Cocktail Making and Tasting, then Bingo, where Joel managed to win a hundred dollars, making him grin from ear to ear. He'd never played Bingo before and had found it hard at first but caught on fast. After lunch, there was a band on, and even though it was not their kind of music, they sat together happily holding onto each other's hands. A small group of people had set up tables in a corner and happily played card games for a few hours. Then Bianca had gone upstairs to the restaurant and brought them down plates of ham, cheese and salads, so that Joel wouldn't have to struggle upstairs again.

Finally, Joel had said "Bea I have to get out of here for a while. I'm getting Cabin Fever."

Bea suddenly thought of something. "Hang on for five minutes Joel. I'll be right back."

She quickly made her way over to Reception and asked Lindy if the Island had a wheelchair. Yes, they did and yes, Bianca could borrow it until they went home on Saturday. Joel's face was a picture when Bianca walked back into the room with a wheelchair in tow.

"Right Sir. In you get. Let's make life a little easier for you and go and explore a bit and get you some fresh air!"

Later that night, in bed, Joel gently kissed Bianca's lips.

"I love you so much, you know Bea. We are going to work this out. I'm just so determined to. When I was away, I realised a lot, and I'm determined that this time, I'm going to get my problems sorted out."

Normally, Bianca would have tried to initiate sex from Joel's kiss but now, she just kissed him back, rubbed his chest and said "And I love you too my darling. Night night. Sleep tight."

"Don't let the bed bugs bite," laughed Joel.

CHAPTER 25

ANNA

Sitting at breakfast the next morning, Anna and Ken ate in silence. Ken was still smarting that Mandy had another man. He hadn't managed to track her down yet to find out who the man was, but he was going to make sure he did today, even if it took him all day to do so. He felt his anger grow. Mandy was his. He had planned to creep out last night when Anna was asleep and go to Mandy's chalet, but he'd fallen asleep before he could do so. He felt a sudden determination that he would find her today and, if necessary, use his charms on her for what he needed. Anna had also planned to sneak out last night, but her plan was to follow Ken. However, as the night wore on he showed no signs of going anywhere and she soon realised that he was asleep. She decided to continue with her mission today, so sure was she that he was seeing somebody.

"I'm going to spend the day by the pool with my book," Anna lied. "Want to join me?" She knew full well that Ken would say no, which he did.

"No, I've arranged to play golf again with some of the others today. I think we're going snorkelling this afternoon. But we can meet up for lunch if you like?"

Ken knew there was no way Anna would go snorkelling but felt he had to justify their long separation that day by having lunch with her. Anna agreed and said she'd meet Ken in the Restaurant about 12.30pm. Together they went back to the chalet to get what they needed; beach towel, sun cream, sunglasses and a book for Anna, and glasses, hat and sun cream for Ken. They both went their separate ways out of the chalet, but not far down the pathway, Anna turned, and picked up Ken's trail. Instead of walking towards the Golf Course, Ken was actually walking further into the rainforest. Keeping her distance, Anna watched him. Ken stopped at a chalet and tapped on the door. A woman, probably in her 40s, from what Anna could see, opened it. She had shoulder length copper hair and a figure to die for. She was in just a tee shirt and her long legs and arms were tanned, as though she spent a lot of time in the sun. Anna moved a bit closer so that she could hear what Ken and the woman were saying.

"I've been looking for you all yesterday. Where were you? I saw you in the Restaurant with another man." Ken's words came out in a rush, so afraid all of a sudden that he might have lost Mandy.

"Ken, you may think so, but I'm not exclusively yours, you know. So what if I fancied seeing someone else? We'll both be going home in a few days, probably never to see each other again."

Ken was mortified by this, but with the knowledge that Mandy's sex drive was as high as his own, he put on his sexiest voice and said "Can I come in Sweetheart?"

"Of course you can. Actually, I've been waiting for you!"

Ken went in and the chalet door shut. Anna stood rooted to the spot. So, she'd been right all along. She knew it! But for some reason, she wasn't angry this time. What she had done with Marcello yesterday at the waterhole had been just as bad. She was glad now that she'd met Marcello. He was giving her a purpose in life and some much-needed self-confidence back.

As she walked over to the Pool, she realised that she and Ken were probably finished. Their marriage was well and truly over. She'd done everything she could to make herself more attractive to him but it hadn't worked. And she would never be able to compete with the likes of the woman she'd just seen open the door to her husband. Ken had been doing his own thing for far too long and Anna wondered why she had ever thought she could win him back in the last few weeks. Meeting, and making love with Marcello had taught her that she could love and be loved again. She wondered if there was any way they would be able to keep in touch? She could hardly ask him to give up his job on the Island and come and live with her. Or could she? The thought gained momentum in her mind. Soon endless possibilities seemed possible for her and Marcello. She had three more days on the Island to persuade him to make a new life with her. She decided to go and seek him out instead of going to the pool, the happiest she had been in a long, long time. For the first time, Anna realised that she now knew her marriage to Ken was over. It had taken this holiday to show her that. She'd have to make time to talk to him next time they were on their own, she thought. She would tell him that she thought it was time they both moved on. She realised, too, that she was falling in love with her gorgeous Marcello, and she wanted to try and make him realise that a life with her back home in Sydney could be wonderful for them both. It would be a great opportunity for him. He could leave his job here on the Island and get one close to her place, well, the place she would buy once Ken's and her house had been sold She'd broach the subject with him next time she saw him and see how he felt. She knew he really liked her. He may even be falling in love with her, she thought. She smiled at that. A new beginning. That's what she was going to have.

Ken and Mandy were in the shower together. They had already made love once, and were about to do it again. However, Mandy suddenly decided she'd had enough for now. She'd already had rough and vigorous sex early this morning with Tony, another sex crazy man she'd met yesterday, who was much younger and more attractive to her than Ken.

"No more for now Ken," she said as she stood under the powerful stream of water from her showerhead and let the soap wash off her. She got out of the shower leaving Ken wondering what was wrong. Mandy was always up for more than one session. The other man he'd seen her with suddenly came to his mind. He got out of the shower and they both towel dried themselves off.

"Is it that guy I saw you with yesterday? Are you having it off with him as well?" Ken was getting angry. He didn't like sharing his women.

"Look, darling, as I said before, I am not your property. We're only here for a week. If I want to have sex with somebody else, I will. I'm a free agent Ken. You can't dictate to me who I can and can't sleep with! What makes you think you're so special anyway that

I'd only want you?"

This hurt Ken to the core. He'd never had a woman say anything like this to him before.

"I thought what we had was good. I thought maybe we could continue meeting up once we're back home? You don't live that far away."

Mandy was nonplussed. "Ken, I'm not here looking for a relationship. I've got enough guys at home to keep me satisfied. I don't want another man in my everyday life. I'm happy as I am with my cat for company at home. You and your wife should give it another try. Have you talked to her about things?"

Ken was horrified. He hated, no, despised, Anna, especially with her new look and the way she was now trying to seduce him after years of being more like a housekeeper to him than a wife. The old Anna had been his staple back home, the one who allowed him to do anything he wanted without question, always having his meals ready, his clothes washed and ironed, the house clean and tidy. But this new version of her, well, to put it mildly, he really didn't like her at all. He realised at that moment that what he and Anna had had years ago could never be got back. He thought of Ruby back in Sydney. Yes, he could see a future with her, but not with his wife.

"No, I can't talk to my wife. I'm positive its over between us, has been for years. I think I probably need to move on. I thought I'd found that someone special with you Mandy. Are you sure we can't at least keep in touch after we leave here?"

Mandy took hold of Ken's face in her hands. "Look baby, we've got three more days here. Let's not talk about the future, but just live in the now." Feeling guilty, she said "Come on let's go to bed and I'll give you the best sex you've ever had!"

Ken dutifully followed her into the bedroom. He had a lot to think about, he realised. But not now, as he grabbed Mandy around the waist and threw her on the bed!

CHAPTER 26

SUE

After her coffee with Steve, Sue had walked around the Resort looking for Marcello. She hadn't found him, but had bumped into Will near the pool. He had his swimming things with him and asked Sue to join him. Still hoping to meet Marcello, Sue had told Will that there was something she needed to do and maybe she'd join him later. Heading back to her chalet, Sue thought she saw Marcello in the distance, but he was with a small group of people walking towards the Reception building. Once back in her chalet, she realised that she now had two choices. Stay in the chalet and read her book, or go and join Will at the pool. It was a beautiful warm day and the sun was shining, with a cloudless blue sky above. She decided to join Will at the pool. He was quite good company and Sue felt in need of someone to talk to. She quickly changed and gathered up what she'd need and started to make her way out of the chalet. As she was leaving, she noticed a slip of paper near the door, which she hadn't noticed when she'd, came in. She picked it up and read it. *'8pm tonight. Be ready for me. M.'*

Sue felt the butterflies in her tummy going crazy. She was seeing Marcello, tonight. She decided she was going to pull out all the stops with him now. She'd play the part of the perfect lover if it killed her.

Marcello, or Mark, as he really was, had just finished work for the day. One of the other workers had asked him what plans he had for the rest of his day.

"Just gonna have a swim then go and watch some tele," he said in his strong Aussie accent.

"You're a boring old git," said Pete, one of his colleagues. "You hardly ever come out with us. A few pints would do you good."

Marcello laughed and said "I told you mate, I'm on the wagon. I'm trying to get fit. No alcohol for me from now on. Home, a microwave meal and some tele. That'll do me!"

He didn't mention that his plans were somewhat different. He'd told none of his workmates about his secret life. Once outside, he had immediately bumped into Anna, who was on her way back to her chalet after being at the pool. Not knowing if her husband was back at their chalet, Marcello had suggested to her that they take a walk down the path away from the Resort. Once out of sight, Marcello held onto Anna's hand. Soon they came to a clearing in the bushes and Marcello invited her to lay down with him there. Anna didn't need no persuading. She'd realised now that Marcello was the love of her life. Good, thought Marcello. I've got Anna now and Sue tonight. In two more days, a new crop of visitors would be arriving onto Paradise Island. Marcello hoped he would be able to find a younger, more attractive woman he could seduce with his 'Italian Charm' to meet his needs. His lust grew at the thought. He smirked. Happy days indeed!

Sue spent a pleasant couple of hours at the pool chatting with Will. She didn't know what had made her do it, but she told Will that she thought she'd found the love of her life on the Island. Of how that love had hit her so strong and so quickly, and how she planned to take things further with him once she got home. She never mentioned any names and Will immediately thought Sue was talking about him. He was flushed with pleasure at the thought of this lovely woman and how they could become a couple. He guessed Sue didn't want to come right out and ask him, so went along with her, waiting for the right moment to tell her that, yes, he felt the same way.

Realising that she'd had enough of talking to Will, Sue decided to go back to her chalet and have a glass of wine on the verandah to contemplate her future. Saying goodbye to Will, she left him contemplating his future with her. He too had not necessarily come here looking for love, but it seemed he had finally found it. Back at her chalet, Sue got a miniature bottle of wine out of the bar fridge and poured it into a crystal glass. She looked at Marcello's note again and felt the love they had for each other surge through her. Out on the verandah, sipping her wine, she looked at the Entertainment list for the day and saw that Bingo was on in the Entertainments Lounge shortly. Sue didn't mind the odd game of Bingo so decided to go to pass the time until this evening. When she arrived there, she sat at a table with a lovely young couple. The man had broken his ankle and had a cast on his leg. They were on their honeymoon, they told Sue and said that the man, whose name was Joel, had fallen whilst walking in the bush, and that he'd been rescued by a helicopter. While Sue found it fascinating, she wasn't always listening properly to what the couple were saying, as her mind was full of Marcello. When Bingo started, she found it hard to concentrate on the numbers, so full was her mind of the new love of her life.

Tonight, she was going to make certain that Marcello had found the love of his life as well. Marking off the numbers, suddenly Sue realised she only wanted one number, 50. This was her age next birthday and Sue thought it was a sign that everything was finally falling into place for her. When the caller said "Fifty, 5 – 0" Sue shouted "BINGO". She'd won $150 and the thrill it gave her, along with her finding her new love, made her feel the happiest she had ever been.

After Bingo had finished, Sue said farewell to Joel and his wife, Bianca. She looked at her watch and saw that it was time for an early dinner, before she had to go back for her night of love with Marcello at 8pm. She had an easy meal of Steak and Chips, a dessert of sticky toffee pudding, then made her way back to her chalet. It was 7pm and she had an hour to prepare herself for Marcello. She took a longer than usual shower, making sure that her whole body smelt of the delicious body wash that was provided in every chalet, she shampooed her hair twice, as her mother had taught her to do if you wanted really soft hair, then she towel-dried herself and used the electric blow drier on her hair. She plumped up the pillows on the bed and smoothed down the cover. Looking around her, Sue decided that everything was perfect. Now all she had to do was wait for his knock on the door.

Sue knew that she hadn't been the perfect lover to Marcello and didn't want to lose him because of it. She had planned in her mind to make tonight the night that Marcello would really understand just how much she loved him, and how she wanted to please him. She had decided to use her, not so knowledgeable, powers of seduction on him, in the hope of showing him that she was, indeed, the woman for him. At precisely 8pm there was a short tap on her door. Sue took a deep breath, took one last look in the mirror, and opened the door. Marcello stood there in all his glory. He had a perfectly ironed crisp white shirt on and tight, dark blue jeans. His mass of dark black hair was immaculately combed back and Sue thought he couldn't look more handsome if he tried.

"Hello again, my darling Sue," he said in his best Italian accent. "I have been waiting for this time to come all day. I have not been able to concentrate on my work for thinking of you." Marcello, who was well practiced at his chat up lines, once again wondered how he got away with it time and time again.

Sue was stood in front of him like a love-sick teenager.

"Hello my handsome man. I too have been thinking about you all day. I'm so glad you're here. Let me get you a drink from the fridge."

Sue pulled out a bottle of lager and a miniature gin and a bottle of tonic and got two glasses.

"Lager OK or would you prefer a G & T?"

"Lager please, my darling Sue. No glass though. I'll have it straight from the bottle." His lie about being on the wagon to his friends made him give a quiet chuckle to himself.

Sue was beginning to feel a lust, something she never had done before, and was keen to get to know Marcello into her arms. However, feeling that she shouldn't be too pushy, she suggested they take their drinks onto the verandah. This was the last thing Marcello wanted to do. Any one of the other staff members, or even Anna, might see him if he sat out there with her. No, he had to think quickly.

He took her drink from her and placed both his bottle and Sue's drink on the table. "Plenty of time to drink later my darling. I can't wait any longer to hold you in my arms," and he grabbed Sue around the waist and pulled her close to him.

Marcello had only one thing on his mind. The last thing he wanted to do anyway was to talk to Sue. He was sure she would have to be one of the most boring women he had ever fucked, and there had been many.

Sue could feel Marcello's erection pushing against her hip. She decided that now was the time for her to act, to use her previously unused powers of seduction that she thought would work.

"Darling, let me take off your clothes, really slowly," she said.

Marcello almost gagged at the new 'seductive' voice that Sue had just put on. A change had certainly come over her. Oh well, he thought, let's just go with it, as long as the end result is the same! Sue slowly removed Marcello's shirt, then his pants, his loafers, and, finally, with some difficulty and much embarrassment on her part, his underpants, which, she noticed, were Calvin Klein's. Marcello was proud of his body and not in the least embarrassed. His erection stood tall, his abs taunt. What wasn't there to admire, he thought? Sue started to rub her hands over Marcello's chest, though avoiding any contact with his erection. At the moment, that was a step too far for her, although she knew she had to overcome it, and soon.

After a while, Marcello said "Now it's my turn my darling. Only this time I am so, how you say, horny, that I am going to rip your clothes off you so I can once again gaze at your splendid body!"

Oh my God, thought Marcello. How can I say this shit with a straight face? And they fall for my stupid fake accent every time! True to his word, Sue's summer dress and bra and knickers (there was no way Marcello could call them panties. Sue's were like the ones his Nona used to wear when he was a boy!) were roughly taken off in record time and they were soon laying side by side, naked, on the bed. Sue decided to quickly take the initiative and started to kiss Marcello, first on his face, then neck and down onto his chest.

"Ok," thought Marcello. "Maybe this is how Sue gets turned on and she's just been too embarrassed before. I'll let her do her thing for now."

Thinking that Sue wasn't going to stop at his erection, he grabbed the back of her head and pulled it down onto to him. Sue was mortified. No, she couldn't do it. Definitely not. But before she knew it, she had done it, and it was the worst experience of her life. Vile. How was she ever to overcome something like this? How could people actually enjoy doing this? Was this something that all most men expected a woman to do? Marcello then mounted her. It was his turn now to dictate the sex, which, after all, was what he was here for, not foreplay with some unattractive, saggy, middle-aged woman who, if there had been anything better on offer in this weeks' crowd, he wouldn't have touched with a barge pole.

Sue, still shocked from before, didn't even think to let out a fake moan. Marcello just pounded away at her and then came within minutes. Marcello knew that there were only 2 more days to go until the next group of guests arrived at the Resort, so decided that pleasantries to Sue were now not worth the bother. He'd got what he wanted from her all week. No need to try to get his way now.

Sue had now regained her composure, and said "Darling, once again, you are so virile. You made me feel so good." She looked at him with adoring eyes, something which made Marcello panic.

This wasn't what he had wanted. He just wanted a week of casual sex until it was time for her to go home.

Sue plucked up the courage to say "Darling, there is something I'd like to talk to you about, but not now. Can you meet me in the restaurant for lunch tomorrow so that we can talk?"

Sue had decided to ask Marcello to come and live with her, to share his life with her. She was sure now of their love for each other. Marcello freaked out. No way could he be seen in the restaurant with Sue. That would give the game away. All of the staff there knew him as Mark, an Aussie bloke. No, Marcello had to make his excuse and think of one quickly.

"I'm so sorry my darling but tomorrow I have to work until late. We have a special Tribute Night coming up soon as I still have to complete the arrangements for the Band. But after work, yes, I will come to you here and we can talk then, yes?"

Disappointed that she wouldn't see him all day tomorrow until late, Sue could only agree. It was Ok. She'd ask him then. Marcello quickly got dressed and without looking back said "Ciao baby. See you tomorrow." And he was gone. Sue wondered why Marcello never wanted to talk to her, or spend any time during the day with her. He obviously loved her as much as she loved him. It would never have even crossed her mind that he was just using her and that soon she would be last weeks' news. A suspicion that he was a 'wham bam, thank you man' type of man thought was quickly pushed to the back of her mind. He loved her and she loved him. She was sure they could make a go of it away from Paradise Island. Once again, she felt happy and smiled as she made her way to the shower, waiting for tomorrow when she'd be with him again, and tell him of her plans.

CHAPTER 27

RACHAEL

The day after getting back home, Rachael had decided to give the two eldest children the day off school. They had lain in bed until just after 8am and were soon making their usual noise. Jake wanted chocolate biscuits for breakfast and rather than get into a fight with him so soon, Rachael had given in and let him have two. She'd made Lily a bottle, telling herself that she would keep doing so until next week, then start to wean her baby off it. Sophie had come down wearing a pink tutu and her sparkly orange top.

Rachael had to laugh. Her older daughter certainly needed to learn some dress sense.

"Mum, can we paint my nails? Grandma wouldn't let me."

"Sure sweetheart. Just let's have some breakfast first."

As they were talking, the phone rang. Rachael jumped at the sudden sound but it was only her mum.

"How are you Rach? Have they settled down yet? They were a nightmare for us here!"

"Yes, Mum," Rachael, replied, guilt coursing through her. "They're all just having their breakfast. We had a lay in. I'm keeping Jake and Sophie off school today to get them back into their normal house routine. It's just so good to be back home. Thank you and dad so much for having them though."

"That's Ok sweetheart. I'm sorry you felt it necessary to come home early. We could have managed for the extra few days, you know. Well I hope you haven't given in and given Lily a bottle. I think I've managed to wean her off it. She's far too big for one anyway. I keep telling your father, our Rachael has to stop treating her like a baby. She'll be going to Nursery soon, and she won't be able to have a bottle there."

"No Mum," Rachael lied. "I haven't given her one." Anything to get rid of her mother, she thought.

"Ok. Well you take it easy, and if you speak to Harry, send him our love. Bye for now darling. I have to go and tackle this pigsty of a house. Bye."

Phew, thought Rachael. Give Harry our love? Oh yes, sure she would, the bastard. She'd find a way to make him pay for staying behind, she was sure of it. Rachael realised and for her and the kids, life had returned to normal, for now, at least.

Back on Paradise Island, Jack and Cassie had walked along the beach for an hour before going back to their respective chalets to change for dinner. They met back up again outside Harry's chalet and made their way to the Restaurant. Over dinner, they chatted about the lives and their jobs, their younger days and where they had gone to school. Before they knew it, they had drunk a full bottle of red, and Harry motioned to the waiter to bring them another bottle. They sat chatting well into the evening, eating dessert, and then having their coffee.

"How about we go downstairs and see what entertainment they've got on tonight?" Harry suggested.

Cassie readily agreed and they made their way downstairs to the Lounge Bar. Both were quite tipsy after the wine they'd drank with dinner, but that didn't stop Harry from ordering himself a whisky and soda and a Toblerone Cocktail for Cassie. Cassie had only ever had one of these cocktails once before. They were made out of Tia Maria, Kalua, chocolate sauce, honey, milk and cream. She thought they were delicious and offered Harry a taste. He pulled a face after taking a sip and said that it was far too sweet for him and he'd stick with his whisky and soda. They found themselves a comfy two-seater lounge at the right of the stage and sat down happily with their drinks. The band had already started up, but were really loud. Harry shouted across to Cassie that they were quite good, but had to shout it three times before she could hear him. There was already half a dozen or so couples up dancing, and

Harry, who usually despised dancing, now with the wine and whisky inside him, grabbed Cassie's hand and pulled her onto the dance floor. Neither of them were good dancers but they didn't care. They were bordering on being fully drunk and thought they looked great. When the band started up with a slow number, it was a natural progression for Harry to take hold of Cassie around the waist, pull her body close in to his, and muzzle into her neck. As they swayed to the music, their bodies got closer and closer together. Although he had no control over it, Harry felt his erection growing. Cassie also felt it pushing into her. Soon his muzzling became small kisses on her neck, then her cheeks and finally on her mouth. Both felt the passion, or was it lust, rising in them?

Harry whispered in Cassie's ear "Let's go back to my place. We can raid the mini bar."

Cassie, realised she was now very drunk, and thought she should be sensible, but could only say "Ok. Let's go."

Back in Harry's chalet, he took a bottle of lager and a miniature bottle of whisky and some lemonade. He poured the whisky with a good measure of lemonade into a glass and handed it to Cassie.

"Let's go and sit outside on the verandah. It's such a lovely evening," Cassie suggested.

Harry, who had never, in ten years of married life, cheated on his wife, had other things on his mind, but agreed to take their drinks outside. Although now quite late, there was still a lot of noise from the rainforest's inhabitants. The cicada's songs, the frogs croaking and the late-night birds' cries made for a cacophony of sound. The air was warm and balmy and smelt delicious of frangipani and lilies and other flowering bushes outside his chalet. Harry and Cassie sat with their drinks and continued to find out more about each other's lives back home. Harry told her of his children and the difficulties they had, especially with Jake, and also with Lily not going to bed properly every night. Their middle child, Sophie, was the only one who didn't really give them problems, he told Cassie. In his drunken state, Harry was feeling morose and said that he was sick and tired of his whole life being about Rachael and the kids. He wanted more but couldn't see a way of changing things. Cassie told him that her life was much less complicated. She worked as a Secretary to a Director of a large Insurance Company, owned her own apartment, had a cat called, originally, Kitty, and had a group of friends who she could rely on and go out with whenever she felt like it. She liked her life and didn't want to change it. Soon, the presence of the mozzies became a nuisance and Harry suggested they go back inside.

"You want another drink?" asked Cassie heading to the bar fridge.

"No, it's you I want." Harry knew he was very drunk but at the moment he didn't even give Rachael a thought.

He made his way over to Cassie and took her in his arms. She was equally as drunk and she returned Harry's kisses, feeling as passionate as he was. They fell onto the bed and Harry started to take off Cassie's jeans and tee shirt, just as she tried to take off Harry's. They both started laughing as they twisted and turned, getting each other's clothes off, and soon they were both naked. Harry hadn't seen another woman naked in ten years and the sight of Cassie's naked body and pert breasts (Rachael's were saggy from having the children) made him hornier than ever. For a brief moment, Harry had doubts about the size of his penis, as most men do in these circumstances, and hoped Cassie wouldn't be disappointed in him. He didn't know if he was a good lover or not. Rachael certainly never told him he was. They just 'did it' once or twice a week and it was usually over within five minutes. Now, here with Cassie, Harry realised he was about to do the wrong thing by cheating on Rachael, but she had been the one who had buggered off home, leaving him here on his own. Why not have a bit of fun, he thought to himself, as he started kissing Cassie's neck and throat. His hand found her breasts and he marvelled at the softness of them. Her nipples were hard and when he squeezed them, she let out a little moan. Harry couldn't wait any longer and helped Cassie straddle him. Once inside her, and still fondling her breasts, Harry grabbed Cassie's hips and they got into a rhythm. Cassie came first with a loud moan, her whole-body shuddering, and was soon followed by Harry, who called out her name as he came. They lay on top of each other panting.

Afterwards, when it was over, they lay side by side, Cassie's head laying across Harry's arm. In his drunken, hazy state, he said,

"I think I've fallen in love with you Cassie."

"What are you going to do about it? You're a married man with kids," an equally drunken Cassie said.

"I don't know. That's the problem." Minutes later, they were both asleep, drunk, but sated and happy.

The following morning, they woke to bright sunshine streaming in through the gap in the blinds. Both had terrible hangovers and they were aghast at what they had done the night before. Cassie had made it a point never, ever, to sleep with a married man. It was against her principals, and Harry had never once cheated on Rachael in their ten years of marriage. In the past, it had also been against his principals.

"Good morning beautiful girl," Harry looked into Cassie's eyes.

Although still full of sleep, he was sure he saw the same love in them that he was starting to feel for her.

"Fancy some breakfast? But I'll get us some Panadol first to deal with my headache, and I'm assuming you've got one too?"

"Ouch. I sure have," Cassie put her hand on her forehead.

Harry went into his shower bag and took out two Panadol each and got a glass of water. They lay in silence, allowing the medicine to do its work. After twenty minutes, Cassie was ready to get up.

"I'm going to jump in the shower, if that's ok?" she said.

"Mind if I join you?" Harry didn't know what made him say it but both he and Cassie knew the meaning behind his words.

A nod of her head, and soon they were both in the chalet's double shower, each standing under a stream of hot water to try and get their hung-over bodies working again. After a few minutes, Harry once again wrapped his arms around Cassie, more than ready for more lovemaking.

"Just feel I've got to tell you," said Cassie "I think I love you too!"

Back home, Rachael had had a happy day back

with her kids. Now, with the older two in bed, and Lily almost asleep lying beside her on the lounge, she started to feel sorry for Harry, left alone. She felt bad for leaving him behind on the Island, where he was probably missing her terribly. He would lonely and bored, stuck in his chalet, not wanting to lose face by giving in and coming home early. Suddenly missing him, she decided to contact Reception on the Island in the morning, and leave a message for him to give her a ring. Even though she was still mad with him, she wanted to tell him she was sorry she'd left him there alone, and that she loved him. Yes, she decided, she'd do that in the morning after breakfast. He would be home in three more days anyway, and her vow to make him pay for not coming home with her was evaporating with every passing hour. She knew how much he would have missed her! They had never been apart in ten years of marriage. She also knew he wouldn't be able to enjoy himself on his own. Suddenly sleepy, she carried Lily up to their bed and laid her down gently on Harry's side, got undressed and got in beside her baby. This was what she had come home for. How could she have even thought about leaving the kids in the first place? And why hadn't Harry supported her in coming home early with her? With her mind going around in circles, she fell in to a deeply troubled sleep.

CHAPTER 28

BIANCA

Bianca and Joel were again at Bingo. Yesterday, they had sat with a lovely lady called Sue. She hadn't talked much and Bianca had thought that she had something on her mind. Sue had mentioned something about finding the love of her life on the Island but that was all. Today though, they didn't win anything, and Joel had said he'd found it "mind numbingly boring" and didn't want to come again, his happiness at yesterday's win forgotten. The night before, they had lain in bed talking for a while, but both Bianca and Joel had made sure they hadn't discussed the subject of their sex life together. For Joel, Bianca's promise that she wouldn't mention the problem again had been a real relief. He was determined to get some help when they got back home, and become a proper husband to his new wife. When he had kissed her goodnight, he had allowed his lips to linger for a few extra seconds on hers, and this gave Bianca great hope, but she kept to her promise and didn't try to take things further with him. Now, Bingo had finished and Bianca again went upstairs to the Restaurant to bring them both down some lunch. It saved Joel having to use all his energy getting up and down stairs, and she'd cleared it with the staff manager earlier. Eating their lunch, Bianca had pulled out the list of the Island's activities for the rest of the day, but there was so much they couldn't do because of Joel's injury.

"Do you know what, darling? How about we take a book and lay by the pool. Just relax and take in this lovely weather?"

"That would be wonderful. I'm not really up to much else. I've been a huge disappointment to you haven't I Bea? There is so much you could be doing but you're stuck with me like this!" Joel felt guilty that his wife was having to forego the Island's activities.

"No sweetheart. I'm only happy that you are safe and well. Anyway, lazing by the pool with a book sounds absolutely perfect to me. Come on let's go and find the Library and chose you a book. I've already got one."

The wheelchair again came in handy, as Bianca was able to push Joel in it to the Library. Once there, they spent a pleasant twenty minutes choosing him a book he fancied. They then went back to their chalet for Bianca to change into her swimmers and a sarong, and for Joel to put on his sleeveless tank top. They gathered the rest of the things they needed and headed to the pool. Luckily, there were two sunbeds free side by side and they were soon laying on them.

Bianca, eager for a swim on such a warm day, said to Joel "Do you mind if I have a swim? I don't want you to be upset at missing out!"

"Sure. Of course I don't mind. You go and cool off. I'm fine." Joel secretly wished he could also have a swim, but was resigned to his situation.

While he watched his wife, diving under the water and swimming the length of the pool, he thought what a lucky man he was. What other new wife would put up with a piss weak man who didn't want sex? He was almost in tears with frustration with himself. Why hadn't he fixed his problems months, or even years, ago? Bianca deserved better than him. He was such a failure, a pathetic specimen of a man.

By the time Bianca had got out of the pool and was drying herself off next to him, Joel was in the pits of depression. As far as he could see there was no easy way out of his predicament. Sure, he would go to counselling when they got home but could he be fixed, so ingrained was his childhood abuse within him? He'd tried to make an effort in bed many times since he'd been with Bianca but something always stopped him being able to enjoy, or even do the sex act itself.

"Come on man. Pull yourself out of this mood," he told himself. "At least keep trying. Don't just give up."

Bianca gave him a peck on the lips and said "I love

you, you know that, don't you?" She then lay on her sun lounge beside him and picked up her book. Joel made a promise to himself that tonight he was going to try his very best to make love to his wife. Even if it wasn't mad passionate love, he'd try to make what love he could.

They spent the rest of the day reading by the pool. Bianca went into the water once more to cool off, but Joel stayed reading on his sun lounge. They had both brought a bottle of water with them from the chalet's bar fridge but that had ran out and Bianca had gone to the Island's shop to buy them bottles of diet Coke. The girl serving her recognised Bianca as being one of the honeymooners she had given out badges to on their first day on the Island.

"Hello. Remember me? I'm Elise. I was in Reception when you first arrived. I gave you and your husband Honeymooners badges. How are you enjoying yourselves?" But then Elise remembered that it was this poor girl's new husband that had gone missing and had to be rescued by the helicopter. "Oh dear. I'm so sorry. I only just remembered about your husband having to be rescued. How is he?"

Bianca suddenly found herself embarrassed for both herself and Joel, but then realised that this girl would know nothing of their personal problems, so said,

"He's doing fine thanks Elise. Can't do much but we decided to come back and not go home as we'd paid for this honeymoon so we might as well come back and enjoy what we could. We've been by the pool reading all afternoon. It's been lovely. I just feel so sorry for Joel not being able to have a swim, with his leg in the cast, but we're still enjoying ourselves."

Bianca made her way back to Joel and the pool with their drinks and once again marvelled at the beauty of Paradise Island and all it had to offer, even if they did have to just lay by the pool.

That night, after dinner, they stayed downstairs in the Entertainments Lounge and listened to the band for a while. Then a comedian came on. He was very good and soon both Bianca and Joel had tears of laughter running down their cheeks. Bianca thought she had never seen Joel laugh like this before, or look so happy. Her plan of not pushing, or even mentioning, sex was paying off. Joel had promised her he would get proper counselling and go and talk to his Doctor when they got home, so she was full of hope for the future. She'd put her own needs to the side until Joel was more able to get better, she thought. Back at their chalet Joel suggested they sit on the verandah for a while with a glass of wine. As they sipped the cool liquid, Joel opened up, really opened up, to Bianca about his feelings for her and how inadequate he felt. He promised he would get some proper counselling as soon as they got back. Bianca reminded him of a clinic she had researched months ago which helped adults and children who had experienced abuse, to which Joel had dismissed out of hand at the time. In fact, he'd stopped Bianca from talking about it, saying he wasn't interested. However, he was now keen to go and get some help.

"Bea, I want to make our marriage work more than anything. You know how much I love you. I just can't believe I haven't done something about it sooner."

"Joel, it doesn't matter. Really it doesn't. Let's just take it easy for now until you can get better. I'm fine. I've realised this past few days that it's not all about sex. I love you for who you are, a kind, caring and considerate man. I'll be with you all the way sweetheart. I love you too!" They went indoors and got ready for bed. It was a beautifully barmy night and they were both sticky with sweat.

"Let's put a plastic bag over your leg and get into our lovely double shower together. I'm all sweaty," Bianca was already stripping off.

Joel stood for a second and admired his wife's beautiful body. Again, he wondered why someone so beautiful as her would want a useless piece of shit like him. Pull yourself together, he told himself. You're going to get help when you get home if it's the last thing you do. He quickly got undressed, wrapped the plastic bag onto his leg and followed Bianca into the huge shower with its two faucets. Each standing under one, Joel picked up the top of the range quality body wash that came with the chalet and squirted some onto his hands.

"Here, Bea. Let me wash you. I'd like to."

This was something that had never happened before and Bianca was shocked, but as Joel's hands soaped her body, she relaxed and started to enjoy the experience. Joel found it not as bad as he'd thought and actually enjoyed the feeling of his wife's soapy soft body. Without meaning to, Joel found his hands between Bianca's legs. Instinct told him what he had to do and soon Bianca was gently moaning.

"Joel, you don't have to do this you know," she said breathlessly.

"I want to Bea. I want to show you that one day I am going to be a real husband to you. Just close your eyes baby and enjoy it." Bianca didn't need telling twice, so she did.

CHAPTER 29

ANNA

Anna had spent a few hours with a woman, Julie, that she'd met in the coffee shop earlier in the week, at the Pool. They'd arranged to meet today, and had found two sun lounges free. They talked of how beautiful the Island was and of their lives back home. After a while, and she didn't know why, but in a moment of weakness, Anna had told Julie that her husband had been cheating on her with another woman on the Island, and that she had seen the two of them together this morning. She told Julie that she was now certain their marriage was over, that they didn't love each other anymore, and that they had just been existing together for years. She also told her about all the affairs that she suspected Ken of having, and the lies he'd told her over the years. Anna confessed that for a long time she felt as though she had just been Ken's housekeeper. She was going to have to sort something out when they got home, as she couldn't go on any longer as she had been. Anna also told her new friend that she thought that she herself had found the love of her life here on the Island, but had given little else away. Julie told Anna that her partner, Stella, (yes, she laughed, I'm Gay!) had found another girl on the Island whom she was spending a lot of time with. Julie was afraid she was losing her lover of five years and told Anna that they were more or less in the same boat. Feeling that she had made a new friend who she could keep in touch with once she got home, the two women exchanged phone numbers and vowed to ring each other regularly. Anna told Julie that she had to get back as she was meeting another friend for coffee.

"Maybe I'll see you tonight at Dinner? If not, want to meet for coffee tomorrow, say around 10am?" Julie asked.

"Sure. I'd love to." Anna was keen to get away now and said her goodbyes. In fact, she was hoping to go in search of Marcello, and headed down towards the Reception building.

Unbelievably for Anna, just as she reached the pathway to Reception, Marcello was walking out, towards her.

"Hello my darling Anna. I was hoping to see you." Marcello had his Italian smooth voice on, and his dark brown eyes bore right through her. She felt the now familiar butterflies in her tummy. Without another word, Marcello took hold of Anna's hand and they started to walk down a path, through the rainforest and past all the chalets there. They were soon on a dirt path with only bush on either side. Eventually, they came to a clearing. Anna guessed why Marcello had brought her down here but was powerless to do anything else other than go along with him. He was, after all, she realised, the man she was starting to love. She knew that she loved him more than she ever had Ken and felt that he was starting to love her back. She had two days left on Paradise Island in which to pluck up the courage to ask Marcello to come and live with her, and start a new life. She felt as though he would say yes, he would love to, as Anna didn't feel that he found his job here on the Island very fulfilling. When they arrived at a secluded spot, they sat down in a clearing, Marcello laying out his jacket for Anna on the ground.

"Anna, my darling, I can't believe I have found you. You are the most beautiful woman I have ever known." Oh, how easy this was, thought Marcello.

These women were like putty in his hands. All that he had to remember was to keep the fake Italian accent up and to keep flattering them. He'd been doing it for so long now, it was almost second nature. What did surprise him was that he never got found out. All his work colleagues knew him as Aussie Mark, one of the blokes, but as Marcello he was careful in what he did. And working away from the main Resort in an office at the back of the Reception building made his life a lot easier. This time though, he was keen to get on with it. He didn't have much time, and he certainly didn't fancy Anna one little bit, but he only wanted one thing and was eager to get started. Anna who liked to take things more slowly, with some foreplay, got no choice in the matter this time. Mark quickly unzipped his jeans and took down Anna's new lacy knickers (bought specially to try and win Ken back so long ago now, it seemed,) and pushed himself inside her. It was over in moments and Anna had barely started.

"Keep going darling," she asked. "I want you so badly." But Marcello had had enough and quickly withdrew and zipped up his jeans.

"I can't stay longer my darling Anna. I have to get back to work. They think I am getting things ready for tonight's entertainment in the Lounge."

Anna was bitterly disappointed and pulled her lacy knickers back up. She felt that it was now or never, and said "Marcello, darling, I only have two days left here. There is something I want to ask you…"

Marcello cut her off, and said her would meet her tomorrow at this same place.

"But what about tonight? Can't we get together after Dinner? I know my husband will not want to hang round with me when he would rather be with his latest woman. We could even go to my chalet. I'm sure he won't be there."

Horrified at the thought of being seen with Anna in the main Resort, Marcello had to try and think up some excuse. Anyway, he was seeing Sue tonight. He had to think quickly.

"I'm sorry my darling, but I have arranged with some of the other guys to have a card night tonight. I can't let them down. Meet me outside Reception tomorrow at 3pm. Then we can talk. Ok?"

Anna had no option but to agree. She was running out of time to ask him to start a new life with her. She was sure he would say yes. The life she could offer him would be far better than the life he had now, surely. She vowed to look after him. Really look after him. Wait on him hand and foot and become the lover she always dreamed of. Ok, so it would have to wait until tomorrow before she would tell him her plans, but so sure of success was she, that another day wouldn't matter.

Ken and Mandy had spent the afternoon walking along the Beach, holding hands and talking about their lives. Ken omitted the part about the many affairs he'd had, instead blaming his wife for doing so, and for paying him no attention at all. Mandy felt so sorry for him. She herself had had quite a lot of lovers over the years, but there was something about Ken that she was getting to like. Plus, he was a damn good lover, she thought.

"Sweetie, I know that my marriage to Anna is over but I don't know how to get out of it. We still have a mortgage together and all the furniture and things. I can't just walk out on all that!"

"Why not? Ken, you are your own person. If you aren't happy with Anna, why not do something about it? Move out, put the house on the market, divide the proceeds, decide who gets which bits of furniture, or let her have the bloody lot and buy some more. It's that easy if you really want to do it."

"Yeah, I know," said Ken, "But I've been with her for so long and there is so much stuff in the house, I don't know if I have the guts to actually do it."

"Of course you have. You are a strong man. Who cares about possessions anyway? Your happiness is what matters most. Find yourself your perfect woman, one who you really love, and build yourself a new life with her."

"Mandy, I think I have found that girl. One that I can truly love. Can't you guess who that is? It's you. You're the one. I think I've fallen in love with you."

"Ken, you know I don't want to settle down. I'm happy with my life the way it is. Sure, we could meet up now and again, but live together? No, sorry. It's not what I want at this time in my life."

Although bitterly disappointed, Ken thought of Ruby, back in Sydney. He thought of the wonderful times he'd had with her and if Mandy didn't want him, he was sure Ruby would. He decided to tell Mandy about her.

'Well, there is a girl back home. Her name's Ruby. I've been getting on really well with her. I suppose I could see how things go when we get back home and then see if she'll have me. Yeah. I am strong. I could move out of the house. Sell it, then buy something smaller. I think coming here, to Paradise Island, was probably one of the best things I've ever done. Its put everything into perspective for me. Our marriage has been over for a long time. Even here, Anna and I have hardly spent more than a few hours together. She's probably been off shagging anything with a dick, that's the way she is." Ken wondered why he felt he had to lie about Anna now. He knew she wasn't like that.

She would have been terribly lonely on her own this week, probably sad that he hadn't spent much time with her. He wondered how she'd cope if he left her. He knew she'd never get another man, that's for sure. Who'd have her?

Ken and Mandy made their way along from the Beach and back to Mandy's chalet. Only two more days left and they might never see each other again, who knew? Once back at her chalet, Mandy pulled Ken into a tight embrace.

"Whatever you decide to do sweetheart, you'll survive. I know you will. Just do what's right for you. You've had to put up with a cheating wife for so many years. Go to Ruby if that's what you want. You deserve a bit of happiness."

Ken felt guilty all of a sudden for lying about Anna. She hadn't been a bad wife to him, just a boring one. Ken needed the constant reassurance that only a good sexual partner could give him. That's why he'd had so many affairs over the years, he thought. Anna deserved a life too, he suddenly realised. It was then that he decided he would leave her as soon as they got home. Make a clean break and start again. Anna could then re-build a new life for herself. He pulled Mandy into him tighter, feeling his erection grow. Soon they were on the bed doing what they both did best.

CHAPTER 30

SUE

Sue and Will were having lunch together. Will, sure that it was him that Sue had talked about falling in love with, was waiting for the perfect opportunity to make his move. They chatted about this and that, avoiding the subject of romance, and drank their coffee. Will suggested they go to the pool again, as the day had turned quite hot. They made their way back to their respective chalets and got changed and gathered together all the things they'd need. They met back at the pool but there weren't two sun lounges free, so they lay their towels down on the grassy bank at the side of the pool. Will decided to make his move.

"Here Sue, let me put some sun cream on your shoulders." Will was not game to suggest putting cream on any other part of Sue. He was 'Old School' and didn't believe in being too forward.

Sue, although feeling uncomfortable, agreed, and Will took great pleasure in rubbing the cream into her shoulders. He expected Sue to return the favour but she couldn't think of anything worse. To her Will was old, much too old, and she found nothing physically attractive about him at all. Her deep love for Marcello was all she needed. She just knew he would agree to make a new life with her in Wollongong. She had so much to offer him and he was so obviously in love with her. She had only today and tomorrow left to build up the courage to ask him, although she was sure he'd say yes. She was seeing him again tonight. She would ask him then.

Will, feeling he was on a roll, said to Sue "You know, I never thought I'd ever find another woman to love after my wife died. Meeting you, Sue, has been the best thing that's happened to me in a long time.

And to know you feel the same, well it's just wonderful!" There, he'd said it.

Sue was horrified. How could she let Will know that he was not the man she'd fallen in love with? How and when had she given him that impression? Sure, she'd found him easy to talk to and spend some time with, but she had never intended, or even wanted him to think that she felt anything else for him. She had no choice. She couldn't allow Will to think he was the one.

"Will, I think you may have got the wrong end of the stick. I'm so sorry, but it's not you I have fallen in love with. His name is Marcello and he works here on the Island. I've never before met a man who makes me feel so alive and loved. In fact, I plan on asking him to come and live with me, to give up his job here, and move to Wollongong with me." Sue blurted it all out, both embarrassed and feeling pity for Will.

"Look, I think I'd better go. I'm so sorry Will. I never realised you thought there was anything between us. I'm so sorry." Sue quickly picked up her things and almost ran from the pool.

Sue was feeling so embarrassed that Will had thought she had fallen for him. With her head down, making her way along the path back to her chalet, she never saw the man coming the opposite way to her and they bumped into each other.

"Hello again." It was Steve who she'd had coffee with yesterday after the boring Cocktail Making class. "Who are you running away from?" he asked kindly.

Sue blurted out the whole sorry mess with Will. Steve took her arm and told her he was taking her for a coffee. They turned around and made their way to the Coffee Shop where Tiggy was serving. This time, they were able to give their identical orders to her.

"I've still got some of that cherry tart left from yesterday. Want a piece of that too?" Tiggy smiled.

Over their pie and coffee, Sue told Steve the whole story again of Will. She also told him about Marcello.

"I'd be careful of these so called Italian Lotharios in places like this," Steve warned Sue. "They often have a silver tongue just to get what they want out of a woman, but that's it. They really feel nothing for you at all. Sorry to burst your bubble Sue, but you have to give this some serious thought."

"Oh no," said Sue." Marcello is the real thing. He and I are in love and I'm hoping to ask him to come and live with me, give up his job here and get one in Wollongong."

Steve was very sceptical but said nothing. Sue would have to learn the hard way, if that's indeed what this Marcello was. Their talk went onto other things. The music and books they liked, the places they had visited. It was amazing that they had so much in common. And he was so easy to talk to and so good looking as well. If I hadn't met Marcello, thought Sue, I'd find this man really attractive. They finished their coffee and pie then said their goodbyes. Sue made her way back to her chalet to have a read and a rest before dinner. Then at 8pm her lover would arrive. She couldn't wait.

Mark, or Marcello, had almost had enough of Anna and Sue. He was now waiting for Saturday, for the new influx of Visitors to arrive. He liked his women to be at least marginally attractive and Anna and Sue certainly hadn't fitted the bill this week. As a sex addict, Mark's sexual appetite was huge. He was now sitting in his staff apartment at the back of the Resort with a Girlie Magazine. When he had landed the job on Paradise Island he had immediately seen it as his opportunity to get as much sex as he'd wanted. Surely there would be plenty of lonely women coming on holiday alone. However, this was not always the case and most were loved-up couples, or, like Sue and Anna, lonely older women who he didn't fancy one bit, but who always gave him the one thing he needed, especially after he had changed into the wonderful, smooth Italian accented 'Marcello' and used his flattery on them. The women, whatever their ages, always seemed to fall for it, and Mark was never without at least two women each week. He'd got to like some of them, but at the end of the day, he couldn't allow himself to feel anything for them. They had to go home at the end of each week and there was no way he was going to leave his well-paid, cushy job here with all the benefits it had to offer him. He looked at his watch. Almost 8pm. Only twice more with Sue and then she'd be gone. At 8pm sharp, he knocked on Sue's door. Naturally, she was waiting for him. The look of love in her eyes almost made him feel sick. But he'd had this look before, many times and could handle it.

"Hello my darling. How are you tonight? Have you had a good day?"

Sue immediately put her arms around him. "It's been Ok but I would have rather have spent it with you. Don't you ever get a day off?"

"Not very often my darling Sue. They give me time off during the day but usually all's I want to do is sleep or go for a swim in my private waterhole." Marcello was the master at getting out of tight questions.

Feeling that the time was not yet right, Sue put off asking Marcello the question she wanted to ask him, instead she kissed him, deeply this time, on the lips, and told him how much she'd missed him. Marcello just wanted to get this over with and quickly took off Sue's sundress and knickers. Soon they were on the bed, Marcello suckling on Sue's saggy breasts. He had no wanting to try anything different with her now, and there was no need to shower her with compliments.

He'd had the only thing that he had wanted from her all week. Without any foreplay, he thrust himself into her, taking her breath away. Sue, for the first time in her life, felt stirrings deep in her loins. The faster Marcello went, the stronger her feelings were becoming. Sue wondered if this meant she was going to finally have an orgasm. She'd had no previous experience with these feelings before and now knew that it must mean that what she felt for Marcello was real. He was moaning and saying her name. Telling her that he loved her as he himself came inside her. Him suddenly stopping and pulling out of her made Sue feel as though she hadn't quite been satisfied. All this was new to her, she thought. They'd soon find a happy medium though when they were together back home and Marcello would teach her more about sex. Sue wanted to talk to him now about their future, but to her surprise, he quickly pulled on his jeans and said,

"I have to go my darling. I have some work I need to finish off tonight. How about I meet you tomorrow outside the Reception building and we'll go to the waterhole? About 3pm yes?"

Sue agreed, vowing that, as tomorrow was her last full

day on the Island, she had to talk to him then.

After he had gone, Sue got into the shower and experimented with her soapy hands on her body. She was trying to get back the same feeling she'd just had with Marcello inside her. But try as she might, nothing happened. It didn't matter where she touched or what she did. She felt nothing. Tomorrow, my darling, she thought. Tomorrow and I will offer you a whole new life. The two of us, together at last. Now she knew for sure that coming to Paradise Island had been meant to be. She'd found true love at last, of that she had no doubt. She and Marcello would soon be together, for always.

CHAPTER 31

RACHAEL

Rachael arose early the next morning. She realised she would have to wait until Paradise Island's Reception office opened at 9am before she could phone them and leave a message for Harry to ring her. She wanted to tell him she was sorry she had left him to come home early, to try and explain to him why she'd done so, and how much she had been worried and missing the children. She wanted to tell him to drive home safely and that she had a surprise for him when he got back. She went into the kitchen and did last night's supper dishes and got the children up for school. She didn't want them staying off for another day. At 8.30am the two eldest were picked up by the other 'School Run' mum and at 9am she rang the Island and left her message with Lindy on Reception, asking her to get Harry to phone her at home. Lindy said she'd get a note taken to Harry's chalet straight away. She put on the TV and settled down, waiting for his call. Lily was playing with some blocks in the corner, sucking away on her bottle of milk and was quite happy to be back at home again with her mummy and not that nasty granny.

Harry and Cassie were in the shower together and didn't hear the knock on the chalet door and the delivery of Harry's note to ring his wife. Now that they were no longer embarrassed, and felt comfortable in front of each other, they found that sex for them was like nothing they'd had before. Both were dreading tomorrow when they'd have to go their separate ways and leave the Island.

"Cass, you know I don't want to leave you, don't you?" Harry whispered in her ear as he kissed her.

"Me neither my darling. But we don't have much choice. I can't come between a man and wife. It's just something I can't do. I'm sure we'll soon forget each other once we're back to our normal lives."

"I'll never forget you Cass. I thought I loved my life back home with Rachael and the kids, but I realise with you I feel free and happy, like I used to before I was married. I want that feeling back again Cass. I'm prepared to give up everything for you. Please just think about it hey. For me?"

"Look Harry, I think we've had what is called a holiday romance. I tell you what, go home tomorrow. I'll give you my mobile number and ring me in four weeks' time and tell me you still want to give up everything. I bet you won't."

Harry, upset and aware that he only had today left with Cassie, made love to her again, gently and sweetly. If this was to be one of the last times he'd be with her, he wanted to make it as memorable as possible. After they got out of the shower, dried off and got dressed, Cassie suggested they go to breakfast and then spend their final day at the beach. Harry gathered up all the things he would need and as they were walking out of his chalet, he noticed a folded note. Picking it up and reading it, the only words on it were 'Ring Home'. Harry panicked, thinking something was wrong and told Cassie to go on ahead and get her thing. He would meet her at the Restaurant after he'd phoned home. He wondered what the hell the problem was. He and Rachael had parted on a bad note and there had to be something wrong for her to leave him a message to ring her. He made his way quickly over to the Reception building and changed a ten dollar note into coins for the phone. He dialled his home number and Rachael answered on the second ring. With his heart pounding in his chest, and fearing the worst, Harry said "Rachael. It's me. What's happened?"

"Nothing's happened darling. I just wanted to say sorry for leaving you on your own. Have you been really miserable?"

Harry was furious. "Rachael, I thought something was wrong. I'm shaking like a fucking leaf here!"

"But why, Harry? I only asked them to get you to give me a ring."

"Well the bloody note just said 'Ring Home'. Naturally I thought something was wrong. And no, I fucking haven't been really miserable if you really want to know. I've been having a ball. Just remember, it was you who left me to it here on my own." Harry was still angry.

Hearing Rachael's voice made him even more sure that he didn't want to go back home to the daily grind which was his life. He wanted Cassie but knew there was no way he could have her, not yet anyway.

"I'm getting the 3pm ferry back to Mackay tomorrow and I'll drive straight through. I'll phone you when I'm an hour away. Don't wait up for me." And he hung up.

Fuck her, he thought. She thinks more of the kids than she does of me. Now that he'd found real happiness, he was angry that it couldn't be his, not until he'd given his life with Rachael and the kids another go anyway. Cassie had made him promise that.

Harry made his way over to the Restaurant and Cassie was waiting for him there on a table for two next to the open balcony, looking out onto the Ocean.

"Hey. Everything Ok?" she asked him.

"Yeah. She just wanted to see what time I'm getting back tomorrow." Harry looked around him. The palm trees, the birds, the soft, white sand and the clear blue Ocean. He didn't want to leave all this tomorrow, but especially he didn't want to leave Cassie. After they'd had breakfast of croissants and fresh fruit salad, they walked along the beach holding hands, the soft sand beneath their feet.

"Cass, I don't want to go back. I don't want to go back to Rachael and the kids. Please tell me we can be together. I love you and I know you love me. It's that simple. We can be together."

Cassie let out a sigh. "Harry, I think I love you too. But I barely know the real you, and you don't really know the real me. We've been together for a week. You and Rachael have ten years under your belt, and three kids together. All this, this Island Resort life, it's not real. We're not real. You have to go home. Get back to normal. I'm going back to work on Monday. I have to get back to my normal life. Harry, as much as I might be in love, or in lust with you, you aren't part of my normal life. Why don't we just see what happens. Let's go home, get back to normal, and then see how we feel. We can keep in touch whatever happens anyway." Cassie was adamant.

Harry, realising she was right, felt a deep depression come over him. They'd reached the end of the beach and turned to walk back. But somehow, he felt he had to have one last try.

"Cassie, if life doesn't get any better for both of us once we get back home, promise me you'll consider a future with me?"

"Harry, I promise. But for now, let's just see what happens hey! Let's go back to my chalet and make the most of our last day together, even better let's go on the Sunset Champagne Cruise. I think it leaves at 6pm."

Harry put his arm across Cassie's shoulders and pulled her to him.

"Just don't forget. I do love you, you know. I think the Cruise sounds like a perfect ending to our time here."

At 6pm they boarded the boat that would take

them on the Cruise. A staff member in Island uniform explained that, to make the most of the Sunset, the boat would circle the Island before dropping anchor just as the sun began to set. There would then be champagne and cheese and biscuits for them to enjoy before returning back to the jetty. The ocean was beautifully calm and the smell of the salty sea invigorating. Harry kept his arm around Cassie, still sad that tomorrow they had to leave each other. But soon the beauty of the Island's perimeter and the spray from the sea lifted Harry's mood. Once the boat had anchored, the sky had already turned multiple shades or reds, yellows and orange, all swirling together. The sun looked massive and was hidden halfway behind the skyline. It was a beautiful sight and Harry and Cassie toasted each other with champagne.

"I will get you eventually, you know Cassie."

"We'll see," was all she could reply.

Later, back at Cassie's chalet, they made soft, gentle love well into the night, making sure every moment counted. How can life ever be the same, thought Harry? What am I going to do, thought Cassie?

CHAPTER 32

BIANCA

Joel woke up on their last full day on the Island and immediately knew something was wrong. He had pins and needles in his foot, and all of his leg was numb. He shook Bianca awake and told her.

"Can you feel this, Joel?" she said, running her nail down his thigh.

'No, not really. I can feel that something is touching me but it's a very weak sensation." Joel was panicking now.

Bianca felt she had to stay calm for Joel's sake. "Ok. I'm sure it's nothing, but let's get you dressed and I'll ring Reception.

As soon as Joel was dressed, Bianca picked up the phone by the bed and rang Lindy.

"Hi Lindy. Sorry to bother you but I need some advice. Do you have the Nurse's number?" Lindy gave Bianca the number and she called it."

"Hi, sorry to bother you but I need advice. It's Bianca. You remember me? My husband had to be airlifted off the Island at the beginning of the week. He'd broken his ankle."

"Yes sweetheart. I remember you. I was the one who checked your husband over when he had his accident. What's happened?

"It's Joel. He's got pins and needles in his foot and his leg is numb, right up to his thigh. I'm really worried about him. What should we do?"

The nurse immediately thought of nerve damage. "I think the best thing to do pet is to bring him here to the clinic. We've got a wheelchair in

Reception. I'll have it brought to your chalet."

"No, I've already got it," replied Bianca. "I'll bring him down straight away."

Ok pet," said the lovely English nurse. "I'll be waiting for you."

Bianca hung up the phone and told Joel what was happening.

"Oh no. This is all I need Bea. The day before we go home as well."

He sat in the wheelchair and Bianca pushed him over to the Nurse's clinic. Once there, Joel's blood pressure was taken (what does that have to do with his leg, thought Bianca,) and his temperature as part of the initial routine assessment. The nurse then prodded Joel's leg on his thigh, the leg which had the cast on it, with a small sharp instrument.

"Can you feel that, pet?" she asked Joel.

"I can feel something but it's a very dull type of feeling. It feels numb."

"And what about the pins and needles? Can

you point out to me where about they are?"

Joel pointed to his toes and foot and around his fractured ankle.

"Darlin' I'm not sure but it looks like you might have some nerve damage there. I think the best thing to do is to take you back to the mainland hospital and get them to have a proper look at you. Our own helicopter can take you if you like, although it will cost you. But it will save you all that time on a bumpy boat. Have you got travel insurance?"

"No," said Bianca," but don't worry about the cost. The most important thing is to get Joel to the hospital as soon as possible. Can you arrange for the helicopter please?" Bianca was now worried sick but tried to keep her voice calm.

"Are you going home tomorrow pet?" the nurse asked.

"Yes. We're supposed to be anyway."

"Well what I suggest you do while I'm arranging the helicopter is to leave this lovely young husband of yours here with me and go back to your chalet and pack all your things up, just in case you don't come back tonight. Bring them back here and everything should be arranged by then."

No wonder this lovely lady was a nurse, thought Bianca. She was such a kind and caring person. The Island was lucky to have her. Bianca went back to the chalet and stuffed all of their possessions into the two large sports bags they'd brought with them. She remembered their toothbrushes and hairbrushes in the bathroom and got those as well. Joel's box of painkillers were still on the bedside table, and Bianca put those in the bag. With a final look round, she said "Bye bye lovely chalet. Hope to see you again one day!" She then made her way back to the Island's clinic and Joel.

All of the arrangements had been made and soon Joel was being helped into the helicopter. Bianca followed and took the seat next to him. Before they knew it, they were hovering over the Island. Its beauty took Bianca's breath away. She vowed to come back one day. One day when all of their problems were sorted out. Paradise Island was a magical place. It had just been such a shame the way things had turned out for them. Next time, she thought, we'll really be able to enjoy all you have to offer. With that they flew higher and were soon over the ocean. Not long afterwards, they were landing on the Helipad Landing Pad at the Mackay Hospital. A nurse with a wheelchair was waiting for them and Joel was taken straight into the Accident and Emergency Department. One of the nurses who had been there when Joel had first injured his ankle earlier in the week remembered him.

"What have you been doing to yourself?" she asked

"I don't know," replied Joel. "I woke up this morning with pins and needles in my foot, and my leg seems to be numb."

"Ok honey. The doctor won't be long. Get yourself up on this bed. Do you want a blanket?" Joel said yes, he'd love one and the nurse went away to get it.

Bianca took Joel's hand in hers. "Don't worry sweetheart. I'm sure it's nothing," she said.

But Joel was starting to panic. "What if I lose my leg Bea? What would I do then?"

"You won't lose your leg Joel. Let's wait and see what the doctor says. The nurse on the Island seemed to think you might have some nerve damage. I'm sure they can fix that these days." After waiting half an hour, a doctor came into the cubicle and got some background information on what had originally happened and what had changed since. When Joel had explained, the doctor said that they would do another X-Ray then possibly an ultra sound. They could do the X-Ray with Joel's cast on but if he needed an ultra sound they'd have to take the cast off for that. A porter was called and another wheelchair appeared. Joel and Bianca made their way to the X-Ray department down the corridor, whey had to wait for a while to get the X-Ray done, as there were people there before them. It was soon Joel's turn and Bianca was asked to wait outside. Five minutes later Joel re-appeared.

"Let's get you back to your bed mate," said the friendly Porter who was pushing Joel's wheelchair.

"I'm a Porter too, you know," said Joel to the man. "I work at The Princess Mary Hospital in Brisbane. I've been there since I was 17."

"It's not a bad job, hey mate," the Porter said. "You meet some nice folk and it's not too difficult to push someone round all day," he laughed.

They had arrived back at Joel's cubicle and the nurse said that Joel's X-Ray results wouldn't take long and the doctor would be back in soon.

While they waited, Bianca once again took Joel's hand.

"What if I lose my leg Bea?" Joel was still worried.

"Sweetheart. Let's not talk about something, which is not going to happen. Let's talk about going back to Paradise Island again next year when everything is better. You can go to counselling, maybe see the GP, there might be something he can give you to relax, and not worry so much. I can even come to the counselling sessions with you if you like, or you can go on your own, it doesn't matter. But once you're all sorted, and your leg is better, let's book another week, or even two weeks, back to Paradise Island and really enjoy ourselves next time!

"What, you mean Sun, Sea and Sex?" laughed

Joel.

It was good to hear him make light of such a huge problem in his life and Bianca felt they were making some progress.

The doctor came back into the cubicle about half an hour later and said that, unfortunately, nothing new was showing up on the X-Ray so the next step was to remove Joel's cast and do an Ultra Sound. First though, the doctor wanted to have a look at Joel's foot and leg. He went and arranged for a nurse to come in and take off Joel's cast then, using a similar sharp object as to the one Bella had used back on the Island, he poked Joel's leg and foot, asking him to describe the sensations he was feeling. It appeared that it was the whole right side of Joel's leg that was affected with the numbness, while the pins and needles were in his whole foot.

"I think we will get that Ultra Sound done now young man," the doctor said. "I'm suspecting you've got a bit of nerve damage there as well as the fracture. I'll go and arrange it. You might have a bit of a wait but just rest and keep that leg raised."

After the doctor had left, the nurse explained to them that nerve damage can sometimes take a few days to appear after a fracture. There was nothing to worry about. In the majority of cases, she said, rest and elevation of the leg, along with painkillers, usually worked within 6 weeks of the injury. Relieved, Joel thanked her and smiled for the first time that day.

Later, his Ultra Sound showed that there was indeed some nerve damage and a new cast was put back on.

"When are you due to go back home?" the doctor asked.

"Our flight is tomorrow, at 6pm," Bianca told him.

"I'd like to keep you in overnight, just to keep an eye on you, and it will save you having to do the journey all the way back to Paradise Island. Let's say we can discharge you around 3pm tomorrow afternoon. That will give you chance to get to the airport. Ask the cabin crew on the aircraft if there is a spare seat and if so, try and keep your leg elevated. I'm sure they could give you a cushion to put under your leg. The day after you get home, I want you to go to your local hospital and present to Emergency. I will arrange for you to have a letter to give them and they can check to make sure nothing has changed. Just remember, rest and elevate the leg as often as you can, Ok?" It was obvious the doctor had finished.

"Thank you doctor. I will do," said a relieved Joel.

"I'll get one of the nurses to arrange a bed for you for tonight. Your wife can stay with you. Then you can go home tomorrow. All the best to both of you." And he was gone.

Soon, a porter once again pushed Joel up to Men's Surgical Ward, where he was put in a single room with a smaller camp-type bed beside the hospital bed for Bianca. There was a TV on a ceiling mount above the bed. Joel's leg was throbbing and Bianca went and found a nurse who would give him painkillers. They spent a pleasant night in the cosy room watching TV from their respective beds, relieved that Joel's leg would be OK in a month or so. At just after 3pm the next day, Joel was discharged with his crutches, and he and Bianca took a taxi to the airport. They were happy to be on their way home. Their honeymoon, disastrous as it had been, had been an eye opener for both of them. Now the hard work must begin, for both Joel's leg and his intimacy problems. As their plane took off, Bianca thought, next time when we come to visit you, Paradise Island, everything will be perfect!

CHAPTER 33

ANNA

Last day today, thought Anna, as she was getting dressed. She had slept in and it was almost ten. She looked over at Ken, still asleep in bed. He hadn't come home until almost 1am. Anna knew where he'd been. There had been no need to ask him. She roused him now and asked if he wanted to go to breakfast but, still sleepy, he'd said, no, he'd get something later and just wanted to go back to sleep. Anna didn't feel like breakfast either but thought she'd make her way to the coffee shop and get some coffee and maybe a muffin.

Walking along the path towards the main building, Anna bumped into a woman she had seen around the Island a lot this week, but had never spoken to. The woman was a bit younger than herself, but had always been on her own whenever Anna had seen her. She decided to say hello.

"Hi. I've seen you around but we've never spoken. Do you go home tomorrow?" Anna asked.

"Yes," said the woman. "I've had a great time. What a lovely magical place this is. I'm Sue. Nice to meet you, even if I do have to go home tomorrow," she laughed.

"Yeah, me too. I'm Anna by the way. Are you here on your own? I've never seen you with anybody."

"Yes, I came on my own. Had a bad divorce a while ago and needed to kick start my life again. I'm just on my way to the coffee shop. Fancy joining me?"

"I'd love to. Thanks," said Anna.

Tiggy was once again rushing round, taking orders and making coffees and serving cake, pies and suchlike.

"Hi ladies. Take a seat. I'll be with you in a

tick," she said.

Sue and Anna sat down and soon Tiggy was there to take their orders. Once they'd both asked for a coffee, Anna told Sue a bit about herself and her marriage to Ken.

"Coming here has really opened my eyes you know," she said. "I've realised that Ken has treated me really badly over the years and I've only ever been his housekeeper for far too long. I've now realised that I must leave him, start afresh, and now think about my own happiness for a change."

"You poor thing," said Sue. "After my divorce, I vowed never to trust another man again. I realise now that I never really loved him anyway. He was never even a real man."

Anna couldn't wait to tell Sue her good news. "Well, I've been really lucky coming here. I've found a man who I can really love and who loves me back. He makes me feel like a woman again, attractive, self-confident and loved. In fact, I'm going to ask him today if he'll leave all this behind and come and start a new life with me. I know I've only known him for a week but we are besotted with each other. I can't think about anything else but him."

Sue was astounded. Here was another woman in the same boat as her.

"I can't believe it Anna. I've also found a man who loves me for who I am, here on the Island. He makes me feel, well, same as you really, like a real woman, and he is madly in love with me and I with him. It looks like we've both struck it lucky this week. I'm also going to ask him later today if he'll come and live with me. I've got my own apartment in Wollongong and I'm sure Marcello will be able to find a job somewhere close by..."

Sue looked at Anna's face. She had gone ashen.

"Did you just say Marcello?" Anna felt her stomach fall.

"Yes. I've really fallen for him. I think he's the love of my life. Why, do you know him? He's the Entertainment Booker here on the Island."

Anna could barely get the words out. "Oh yes. I know him alright. He has to be the same Marcello that I have fallen in love with too. There can't be two men here with that name. Speaks with an Italian accent?"

Anna was hoping Sue would say no, but, yes, he did, said Sue.

"I don't suppose he's taken you to his 'Secret Waterhole' has he?"

Sue was feeling sick. "Yes," she whispered.

"I think we've both been played Sue."

"I met another man, Steve, who warned me that Marcello could be a lothario, someone who preys on women," Sue said. "Oh, my God. I won't believe it. I'm sure he loves me Anna, I think he's just been stringing you along. He told me over and over again that he loves me."

"He's told me the same thing Sue. I'm so sorry."

Sue started to cry. Silent tears were running down her cheeks. "I won't believe it until I hear it from his own mouth."

Anna was shell-shocked. "Ok. There's only one thing we can do Sue. We have to go and find him and have it out with him."

"Oh God. I don't think I could bear it if he told me he didn't really love me. I'm sure he'll have a good explanation for all this. Ok. Let's go and find him."

The pair of them made their way to the Reception building. As usual, Lindy was behind the desk, on the phone. While they waited for her to finish her call, Anna got hold of Sue's hand. Although both had just as much at stake as the other, Anna felt that Sue would fall to pieces if indeed Marcello had been playing them both along. Lindy hung up the phone.

It was Anna who spoke. "We'd like to speak to Marcello please, your Entertainment Booker"

Lindy smiled at her. "There's nobody of that name works here love. Our Entertainments Manager is called Theo but we've got a Mark who books our Acts."

"No, he said his name was Marcello. Speaks with an Italian accent."

Both Anna and Sue now felt sick.

Lindy was perplexed. "No, sorry. Our booker is Mark, but he's an Aussie, although I do think his parents may be Italian. Do you want me to get him?"

"Yes please," said Anna.

Lindy picked up the phone and punched in a number.

"Hi Mark. Can you come out to Reception for a minute? Ok. Bye"

"He's on his way out ladies. Is there a problem? I don't understand."

"Neither do we," said Anna. The internal office door opened and Marcello, or Mark, walked through.

Hi Lindy. What's up?" he said in a broad Aussie accent. Then he saw Sue and Anna.

"Oh." Suddenly he was lost for words.

Sue stepped forward, towards the desk. "Tell me this is all a dream. Tell me you are Marcello, the same Marcello who told me he loved me more than any other woman he'd ever met? You can't, can you, MARK?"

Now it was Anna's turn. "Yes MARK. Tell me you never used your smooth Italian accent to tell me I was the most beautiful woman you'd ever seen? Tell me you didn't call out Sue's name when you were fucking me?" Anna was now furious.

Mark said to Lindy "Can you give us five minutes?" Lindy, amazed at what was going on really wanted to stay but agreed to give them some privacy.

"Look, both of you," Mark started. "It was never meant to be serious, with either of you. It was just a bit of fun..."

"Fun? Fun? You sick, evil, bastard. It was never FUN," Sue was sobbing now. "I thought you loved me. I certainly loved you. Do you know what, I was planning to ask you today to give up your job here and come and start a new life with me."

"So was I," said Anna, quietly. "You've certainly played us both haven't you, you creep. Is that how you get your kicks? Making love to venerable woman, having them believe you are in love with them, then watching them leave the Island, ready for you to prey on your next victim?" Anna was now beyond angry, she was humiliated and felt used and dirty.

Sue was taking it much worse. She felt she had to give it one last try.

"Marcello, I mean Mark, did you ever love me, really love me?"

Mark's bravado was letting him down. "Come on girls. It was all in a bit of fun. Yes, I do like women, but old, unattractive ones like you two? You've got to be joking. I only chose you two because there was nothing more attractive in this week. I'm sorry if I've upset you girls but hey, it was all a bit of fun. Surely you can see that. You couldn't possibly think I had any real feelings for either of you, could you?"

Sue screamed out "You bastard. You filthy rotten bastard. I've never hated anyone more than I hate you now!" Sue walked up to him and slapped him, hard, across the face. Mark reeled back.

Anna had heard enough. She took hold of Sue's hand. "Come on Sue, let's get out of here." She started to walk out but turned back and looked Mark in the eyes.

"Oh and by the way, yes, we will be making an official complaint to the Management."

Back at her chalet, Anna was laying on the bed sobbing. Although she was still in shock, she felt almost bereaved. She'd planned a whole new life with Marcello at the centre of it, and now it was all in ruins. As Ken came back in, he heard Anna's sobs. He had never heard her cry like this, ever. He went over and sat on the bed beside her.

"What on earth has happened? What's wrong?" He stopped short of actually touching her, but his tone was full of concern.

Through her sobs, Anna told him "Its nothing. I'm fine."

"No, it's not fine. Look at the state of you. Tell me what's happened."

Suddenly Anna was full of fury.

"Ok. I'll tell you what's happened. Like you, I have also been having an affair here this week. His name is Marcello, although today, I've just found out that it's actually Mark. He told me he loved me and I loved him. Yes, we did have sex and I was planning to leave you and start a new life with him. But it seems he was just playing both me and another woman along. He actually choses a different woman, or women, each week when new arrivals come, and uses a smooth, fake Italian accent to woo them for sex.. So, no new life for me, Ken. But one thing I've realised this week is that you and I are finished. I'm sick of your lies and your cheating. I've put up with it for years, but no more. I've always known, you know. All about the women and the lies. I've put up with washing your dirty clothes, making your meals, cleaning the house, everything except being loved by you. I want you out of the house as soon as we get home. I'm sure you've got someone lined up already that will take you in."

Anna was breathless from her confession. She expected Ken to put up some sort of fight, but he just stood up and sighed.

"Anna, this week has also made me realise that you deserve someone better than me. What we had, well, it's long gone. I know you think that too. Yes, I've lied and had affairs. I admit it. I'm thankful for what you've done for me all these years, looking after me and never confronting me. I think you're right. We need to split up and start again. Don't worry, I'll move out as soon as we get back. We can put the house on the market and each buy something smaller. I know you've tried, these last few weeks, to make yourself smarter, but if you did that for me sweetheart, then it didn't work unfortunately. I'm so sorry that it didn't. I've long acknowledged that my sexual needs, and my emotional needs as well, haven't been the same as yours, that's why I've had affairs and lied to you. I realise now that I should have been open and honest with you years ago, and allowed both of us to start over again. I'm sorry. I don't know what else to say." Ken, too, was almost in tears.

"Well that's that then, I suppose," said Anna. "At least we now both know where we stand. This week, Marcello has made me feel more loved and more like a real woman than you ever have Ken. The fact that it was all a load of bullshit hurts me more than you will ever know. I'll never, ever, trust another man again. I'll be happy on my own. I'm not going to wish you happiness Ken, in fact I wish you only misery, the same as you've made my life all these years."

Ken didn't know what to say. He was hoping to keep this split as amicable as possible, even for their daughter's sake, but it looked like Anna didn't feel the same way. Ken was starting to feel slightly sick. Anna didn't want him and Mandy didn't want him. He thought of Ruby, back in Sydney, and hoped that she would be waiting for him. He realised that there wasn't a doubt in his mind that she wouldn't be.

"Look, Anna, we go home tomorrow. What are we going to do until then?"

Anna was still mad. "Why don't you go to your whore and spend your last night with her?"

"Ok," Ken said. "If that's what you want." He walked out of their chalet, his head on his chest, reeling from the news that Anna had been with another man this week, and realising that his marriage was finally over. His last night on the Island would be spent with Mandy, if she'd have him. He made his way to her chalet, more upset than he'd been in his life.

CHAPTER 34

SUE

After saying goodbye to Anna after their confrontation with Marcello, or Mark as she'd now have to think of him, Sue, blinded by tears and not knowing what to do next, bumped into Steve again.

"Hey, what's wrong? What's happened Sue?"

But Sue was too upset to talk. Her whole future had just been destroyed by an evil, conniving bastard. It was too much for her to take in. Sensing her deep distress, Steve took her arm and led her to the coffee shop. He ordered them both a large coffee and waited until Sue had calmed down enough to talk to him.

Eventually she said, "You were right about Marcello, although that isn't his real name. It's Mark and he isn't Italian. He's also not an Entertainments Manager, but just the one who books the Acts. He's as Aussie as you and I. I've just met another woman, Anna, and it appears that we have both been played like a fiddle by this creep. He told her the same things that he told me, took her swimming to a supposedly secret waterhole, as he did me, told her he loved her, that she was beautiful, just like he told me, and had sex with her, just as he did with me. I can't believe that we've both been taken in by this monster!"

Sue then told Steve about their encounter in Reception with Mark and how stupid and foolish she now felt. Her whole future was ruined, all the plans she'd secretly made for her and Marcello had gone.

"I hate to say "I told you so" but I've seen his type before. Preying on vulnerable women. I knew he sounded too good to be true. Look, put all of this into perspective," Steve placed his hand over Sue's. "At least you know now why he did what he did. It was all for his own sexual gratification, nothing more. That's no reflection on you Sue. You're a lovely woman. Any man would be lucky to have you. You're kind, considerate and a really lovely woman. There are better men than this Marcello, or should I say, Mark, in the world. You've just got to find him!"

"Oh Steve, I don't think I could ever trust another man again. Not after this. He built up my confidence and my self-esteem to a level which nobody else ever has done in my whole life. And he's destroyed it again in minutes."

They sat drinking their coffees in silence for a while.

"Look, I hope you don't think this presumptuous of me, but as it's our last night here, can I take you for dinner? So that you're not on your own like this? Plus, it's the Finale Night Fancy Dress Show tonight. There's a load of dress ups for hire. We could come as two Greeks dressed in togas!" Steve was concerned for Sue and tried to lift her mood.

"I don't really feel like eating or doing anything right now Steve, but yes, as it's my last night here it would be silly to lay on my bed crying all night.

I'd like the company. Let's go and hire the togas."

"Ok," said Steve. "We'll go and see what they've still got left at the costume hire. See if they really do have togas," he laughed.

Amazingly, the hire shop did have two togas, with silver belts and matching headdresses. Sue and Steve hired one each.

"Surely we don't go to dinner dressed in these?" Sue asked Steve.

The woman behind the counter overheard. "Yes, you can. Most of the others are going to. It should be fun."

"Ok. Dinner in togas it is." Steve took the bag and he and Sue left the shop.

"Right, you go back and have a shower and get changed and I'll meet you back in the restaurant. Say 6pm?"

"Ok," said Sue, "and by the way, thanks for being there for me, Steve. I don't know what I'd have done without you."

"Anytime Sue. I want you to promise me we'll keep in touch when we get home. You're a very special lady and I'm lucky to have met you."

Sue went back to her chalet and stripped off. She felt dirty and helpless. She got into the shower and allowed the tears to come again. They soon turned into sobs and she broke all her own rules about having short showers, until finally, she'd shed all the tears she could. Now she was angry and started to plan revenge on Marcello. She wanted to hurt him and humiliate him as he had done to her. But as she got dressed, she realised that not only was that not possible, as she was leaving tomorrow, but it would achieve nothing and make her no better than him. Somehow, making her way to the restaurant to meet Steve, Sue became philosophical. She hadn't been the only one Marcello had hurt. There was that other poor woman, Anna as well, plus who knew how many others over the years. She hoped she would see Anna again before they left tomorrow. She got dressed into her Toga and met up with Steve at the Restaurant. Once there, they both laughed at each other dressed up in their togas. All around them were other guests dressed up, one as a pumpkin, and another as a Smurf. There were quite a few Hawaiian Hula Girls and their men with just the colourful leis around their necks. Steve was the perfect gentleman. He pulled the chair out for Sue to sit down, placed the pure white linen napkin across he knees and ordered a bottle of wine. Sue wasn't usually a drinker, but tonight she felt she deserved to have a glass. Steve had been right. There was a fun atmosphere in the restaurant, and Theo was mingling amongst the tables, telling everyone how great they looked. Everything was really colourful and it lifted Sue's spirits. Rather than be upset, she was now angry. Angry that she had so easily been taken in by that awful man's charms and his fake accent. She thought back to all the things he'd said to her, about her being the most beautiful woman he'd ever seen, how much he's loved her. Oh God. What a fool she'd been. She'd believed every word he'd said to her and it had all been fake. The worst thing was that he'd admitted to doing this all the time, picking out women every week just to fulfil his own sexual needs.

"Hey. Wakey wakey. You're daydreaming," said Steve. Sue had been almost in a trance thinking of how she had been treated. "You know you can't spend the next few months, years, I don't know, thinking about what might have been. The man is a creep, a predator. I think before you leave tomorrow, you need to find this other woman. What did you say her name was, Anna? and go and report him to the Resort Manager. He needs to lose his job over this."

This seemed like the perfect revenge for Sue and agreed with Steve that that's what she'd do. Before she left, she would find Anna and together they'd make sure that sleaze bag bastard Marcello, or Mark, would pay for what he'd done to them.

Sue and Steve spent the rest of the night, after dinner, singing and dancing at the Fancy Dress Party. Sue had drunk two glasses of wine and was feeling very merry. Amazingly, she could now look back on Marcello without getting upset. Steve made sure that he was always by her side. Always ready to take her mind off things and make her laugh. After a while, Sue, exhausted from dancing, suggested they go into the cocktail bar and sit down for a while so that she could get her breath back.

"Why not try a cocktail? Have you ever had one?" Steve asked.

"No, never. But go on, I'll give one a try. You chose one for me. Surprise me." Sue was so happy she'd met this lovely man. He seemed so caring and had certainly looked after her today.

Steve came back carrying a bottle of lager and a cocktail glass.

"Here we go. I thought I'd start you off with a classic Martini. I think it's Gin and Vermouth, not sure, but I hope you like it. Squeeze the lime wedge into it if you like."

They took their drinks and sat on one of the room's comfy lounges. Steve told her about his childhood. His father had left his mother when he was only five and he'd never seen him again. He could just barely picture his father's face but had no real memories of him.

"That is so sad," said Sue, "How did your mother cope? Do you have brothers and sisters?"

"Just one sister, Jane. She's two years older than me. Mum did pretty well. She worked two jobs most times just to send Jane and I to a good school. When I graduated, I went to Sydney Uni and got my degree in English. Now I teach the bloody thing to migrants. I'm getting a bit bored with it all, if I'm honest, and sick of the Sydney scene. I have been contemplating moving up North, up here somewhere in Queensland, and starting again. We'll see."

"As you know," said Sue, "I teach History. But I love it. I'd give anything to go back a hundred years, even further, just to see what it was like."

"Yeah, I wouldn't mind doing that as well. I bet we wouldn't believe how different everything was back then. No electricity, no TV, no phones, iPads, or video games. I wonder what those people back then would think of us now?"

Sue laughed. "We'll never know Steve. You said you lived on your own now. Your wife has left you?" Sue saw the look on Steve's face. "Oh, sorry. I don't mean to pry."

"It's fine Sue. Everything was great for the first few years. We got married very young. I was only 22 and she was 20. Our marriage lasted for 20 years, then she decided she wanted to go and live on her own with the two girls. She never really gave me a plausible explanation, just that she just didn't love me anymore.

She said she needed to 'grow and find herself', whatever that means. It's taken me a few months to get over it but I'm surviving. I've had a couple of girlfriends since, well, one night stands really, but nobody who has stayed around long enough. I've kind of resigned myself to being a bachelor all my life now."

Sue told Steve about her childhood, of which she only had good memories, and of going to Wollongong Uni to get her Teaching Degree, specialising in History. She told him about being on her own for so long and not being able to make friends easily, then about meeting and marrying Gordon, another teacher at her school, and about their non-existent love life, their lack of anything that they had in common. Finally, and embarrassed, she told him of finding Gordon in bed with another man. She said that their divorce had been quick and easy and she'd been glad really that he was out of her life. She told him of her lovely apartment overlooking the beach in Wollongong, and even though she got lonely at times, her life was pretty much settled. Sue looked at this lovely man. In her slightly drunken haze, she had forgotten all about Marcello. She liked the look of Steve, his strong jaw, his lovely blue eyes.

"Steve, I hope you don't think I'm being to forward, but could we keep in touch? After we get home?"

"There's nothing I'd like better Sue. It's been lovely meeting you. And I'm just so sorry that your experience here this week has been ruined."

"No, Steve. It hasn't been ruined. I've learnt that I am capable of love and that I've got get some sort of self-confidence back. Oh, and I've met you. So, it hasn't been all bad," she once again thought how attractive he was.

They smiled at each other and Steve put his hand over Sue's and gave it a squeeze.

"You will be Ok you know."

"So will you," said Sue as she sipped her drink.

CHAPTER 35

RACHAEL

The kids were driving her mad and all thoughts of having been to Paradise Island were forgotten. Last night, alone in bed, Rachael had wished she had stayed there with Harry. What he'd said about her mum and dad coping would have been true. She'd needed the break and she'd thrown it all away. Now it was back to drudge Ville. Jake was refusing to get dressed for school. He wanted to go in his pyjamas, he'd said. But one thing that had happened while she was away was that Rachael had realised she was too easy on her children. Her mum had been right, and she had stuck her ground, grabbed Jake by the arm and almost pushed him into his bedroom.

"If you don't get dressed into your uniform right now, you get no chocolate biscuits when you get home this afternoon. Get dressed. Now!" She shouted the last words so loud she was sure the neighbours could have heard her.

Jake looked shocked at his usually placid mum, but shouted after her "Ok you stupid witch. But I want two biscuits when I get home. OK?"

Again, not up to a fight with her son so soon after getting back home, Rachael had just taken Jake by the arm and gave him a slight push into his room. Sophie had got dressed nicely, as she usually did and was brushing her hair, singing away to herself.

She's a mini me, thought Rachael.

"Come on sweetheart. Almost time for Lucy's mum to get here."

It was Rachael's turn off from driving them to school this week. Lily was still asleep and Rachael looked down on her baby, empty bottle laying at the side of the cot. She really needs to start going into a proper bed, thought Rachael, and I have to start weaning her off that bottle. I'll get Harry to go and buy a bed for her when he gets home, and I'll start weaning her off the bottle on Monday.

The horn of a car beeped outside and soon Jake and Sophie were in the car, Jake in his uniform, and on their way to school at last. Sarah, from next door, was coming over for a coffee for the first time since Rachael had got back from Paradise Island. As usual, she arrived on the dot of ten, Rachael having feverishly tidied the house before her arrival. Sarah was horrified to hear that Rachael had spent the whole first three days of her holiday worrying about the kids and had actually left Harry there on his own.

"Rachael, what were you thinking? This was the trip you had to have, the one where you'd get your mojo back for the next ten years' worth of dealing with Jake. Your parents could have coped. You should have let them cope. When is Harry back?"

"On Sunday. He leaves the Island tomorrow afternoon, then he will drive through the night I think.

I'm not really sure. When I phoned him on Thursday he as good as told me to, well you know, f... off."

"I'm not surprised Rachael. If I had walked out on my husband when we were supposed to be having a relaxing luxurious holiday on a beautiful Island Resort, he'd be pretty pissed off as well. What was he supposed to do all by himself?"

"I don't know why I felt I had to come home Sairs. I just did. I couldn't relax for worrying. Now I feel so bad that poor Harry has been lonely and stuck in the chalet all day not wanting to do anything by himself. Almost everyone else there were in couples, you see."

"Oh well," said Sarah. "You're going to have to find a way to make it up to him when he gets home!"

"Oh, I'm going to. I just feel so bad leaving him there on his own. I'm going to show him that he is married to the perfect woman, you'll see!"

It was the morning of their final day on Paradise Island and Harry and Cassie had already made love twice since waking up together. The first time had been fast and passionate, the second time, slow and gentle. Again, Harry had professed his love to Cassie and she to him, but she was determined that they both go back to their own lives, and then see how they felt at some point in the future. After showering together before going to breakfast, Harry had an idea.

"Hey Cass, as this is our last day here, why don't we hire a couple of jet skis and go out on the ocean?"

"Yeah, I'd be up for that, although I've never been on a jet ski before in my life. I'll warn you now, I'll probably fall off a dozen times though," she laughed.

After their last breakfast on the Island, Harry and Cassie did most of their packing, then gathered up what they would need and went down to the beach, where the jet skis were moored. The Instructor in charge, Ian, asked them if they were a honeymoon couple and Cassie flushed bright red. Harry had told him, no, they were there together on holiday. Cassie took off her sarong, leaving herself just in her swimmers. Harry was in tee shirt and board shorts, and he gave Cassie an admiring glance. Boy, he thought, she looks so good in that swimsuit. He felt his erection growing, but soon Ian was giving them a few basic lessons and rules, telling them how far they could go out, and how to use the controls. He then helped them push the jet skis out onto the water. Harry climbed aboard easily, however, Cassie had to be helped on, while laughing, until tears were running down her cheeks. Once on, they started the jet skis up. Harry, who had never been on one in his life, seemed to take to it like a duck to water, but Cassie went so slowly she was almost at a standstill. Then she kept stalling it and Harry looked back at her, laughing. Soon though, she had got the hang of it and they spent a pleasant hour riding around part of the Island's perimeter.

Harry looked at his watch as their hour was up and they made their way back to the mooring. Harry jumped off his jet ski as though he'd been doing it all his life, but Cassie did a very un-ladylike slide off hers. Both agreed that the experience had been exhilarating and Cassie vowed that they would do it again one day. Harry took her in his arms, both of them standing in the warm, soft sand.

"Do you really mean that Cass? Will we come back together one day, together, as a couple?"

"Hey come on, I thought we'd sorted all that out. Let's go and get a coffee then maybe, just maybe, I might let us be a couple for one last time before we have to go home this afternoon."

After lunch, they both went back to their respective chalets and finished off their packing. When he'd finished, Harry made his way over to Cassie's chalet and found that she too had just finished. He took her in his arms and looked deep onto her eyes.

"I'm going to miss you some much, you know that Cass, don't you?"

"Yes, my darling, and I'm going to miss you too. I'm just about to start crying Harry. You'd better do something to make me stop."

Harry took her hand and together they lay side by side on her bed. Harry had meant their last lovemaking to be slow and full of love but, without knowing why, it became fast and furious. He couldn't kiss Cassie's body enough, and felt he had to get as much of her as possible, something that would stay in his memory and would keep him going until he saw her again, because he was determined that he would see her again. Cassie was what he wanted, he knew that. All he had to do when he got home was to make her realise that as well. As he thrust himself deep inside her, he could see that she was starting to silently cry. He came quickly but realised that Cassie hadn't. He asked her if she wanted him to carry on, but she just shook her head and burst into tears.

By 2.45pm, they were standing on the jetty waiting for the ferry to take them back to the mainland, and home. Harry felt like he'd been hit in the stomach. He thought of Rachael and the kids waiting for him back home, about his job, and the relentlessness of his daily grind. He realised the lack of passion and freedom he had with Rachael and the love, and lust, he felt for Cassie. He moved closer to her and took her hand. Cassie was also thinking about her life. Maybe she took it for granted that all was well in her world. Sure, she didn't want to come between a man and his wife, and especially as they had children, but she also loved Harry and wondered what the future would bring. Soon the ferry had pulled up alongside and they boarded, still holding hands. Once everyone was on board, the propellers started up and soon they were on their way. As they went further out into the ocean, they looked back at the piece of paradise they had just been on for the past week. Soon a new group of people would be taking their place on the Island.

Cassie, with tears in her eyes, said a silent "Goodbye Paradise Island. I hope I come back." She looked at Harry and knew that he was thinking the same.

CHAPTER 36

ANNA

Anna's first thought upon waking was that today, she was going home. Going back to her old life, no longer living amongst the beauty of the Island, but to life in the suburbs, a three bedroom, single story brick house with barely a tree in sight. Then it hit her. She and Ken were going to split up. They would put the house on the market for sale and split the proceeds. She'd only be able to afford to buy a small apartment, as prices in Sydney had rocketed in recent years. She wondered what Ken would do. She knew he had been seeing someone back home and wondered if he'd move in with her. He'd promised to move out as soon as they got back home and part of her was sad for all the wasted years, and the love they'd shared when they'd first got together. But then she thought of all Ken's lies and cheating and her determination to be rid of him returned. Even though she'd been played like a fool by Marcello (she would never think of him as Mark), he had taught her that she could be a woman that somebody could love, as well as learning to love herself again, and believe in her own abilities to be able to be on her own if she had to be. Ken had probably spent the night at his lover's chalet. She wondered what her name was, something exotic probably. Anna got up and showered, then packed everything except what she would need for her last few hours on the Island. She decided to go to breakfast, then have a walk along the beach, maybe a swim in the ocean. She looked at the List of the last day's activities. There was a Beauty Seminar and Demonstration on in the Spa Salon at 11am. It sounded just what she needed and she decided to go to that after her swim, and before lunch. She hoped that she wouldn't bump into Ken and his lover before they had to leave today, as there was nothing more to say to each other. She just wanted to get home as quickly as possible without argument now. Anna quickly packed all of her own things, apart from what she needed today. Ken could do his own, she thought.

Breakfast was croissants and fresh fruit and a pot of coffee. Anna looked around the restaurant at all the happy couples, chatting away with each other. They all looked tanned and happy. Today, there would be a new influx of guests to Paradise Island and Anna was suddenly sorry to be going home. Maybe one day, she thought, I can come back with someone I actually love and who genuinely loves me back.

She dabbed at her mouth with the linen napkin and gathered up her beach bag and made her way over to the beach. Slipping out of her beach shoes, the sand soft and warm under her feet, even at this early hour, Anna walked the length of the beach to the first rock cove, then turned around and walked halfway back. She passed couples, hand in hand, and the odd single person out for a morning jog, then set down her towel, took off her sundress and rubbed some sun cream into her shoulders and face.

At this time of day there was little chance of getting burnt, but she did it just to be sure. The water was slightly colder than usual but she managed to brave it until she was chest high. Not having to worry about how her hair looked anymore, she plunged herself under the water. In some ways, it was like a baptism. She felt free and alive again. And, although she despised him with all her heart, she had to thank Marcello for making her feel like this. After fifteen minutes, she'd had enough and got out and dried herself off with her towel and lay on it to dry herself off properly under the morning sun. When she next looked at her watch, it was almost 11am, so she put her sundress back on and made her way over to the Spa Salon.

There was a dozen or so women already at the Salon, but the demonstration hadn't yet started. Across the room, Anna spotted a familiar face, Sue. She went over to her and took her hand.

"Hi Sue. How you holding up?"

Sue's eyes were puffy, which told Anna that she had done a lot of crying over that love rat!

"Hello Anna. Yeah, I'm ok. Still getting over the shock and the disappointment, but I'll be alright. I have to be, don't I? I've got no other choice but to just get on with things. I go back to work on Monday. Get my boring life back on track. What about you?"

"I'm ok. Ken and I talked last night and we're definitely going to split up. He's moving out as soon as we get back home. Probably got it all sorted already, if I know him."

They were interrupted by a tall, slim blonde woman, about thirty, dressed in the white dress of a beautician. Her hair, skin and nails were, as was to be expected, immaculate. She introduced herself as Natasha and ran through what they could expect from the class and the demonstration. The course lasted for an hour an Anna and Sue came out with a few hundred dollars' worth of face creams each.

"I reckon it's not a Class at all," said Anna. "They just do it to sell you the beauty products and silly old us fell for it!"

Sue laughed and agreed. "Hey, it's lunch time. Fancy coming to lunch with me? This will be our last meal here, and I'd love some company."

"Sure. Why not. I'd love to. Maybe we could compare notes on Marcello's prowess?" Anna had said it jokingly but a dark shadow crossed Sue's face.

"I'd rather not, if that's ok with you. I'm still pretty cut up about it all."

Sue hadn't told Anna about lying awake for most of last night, crying, first with sadness and disappointment, then with anger and frustration, at Marcello.

"Sure Sue. We don't have to even mention his name. Let's just go and enjoy our final meal here."

They made their way to the restaurant and got their food, then some freshly brewed coffee. They talked about each other's lives and what they wanted from the future. Anna wanted to see more of her daughter and grandson, while Sue just hoped to get over Marcello. She was heartbroken, she confided to Anna, and didn't think she'd ever get over the disappointment and the humiliation.

"You will Sue. Just give it time. Remember,

there's someone out there for all of us if we look hard enough." She scribbled her mobile phone number on a piece of paper from her bag. "Here, take this. Let's keep in touch. Sydney's not far from me and we can meet up whenever you like. You can come to me, or I can come to Sydney. I love it there anyway and don't get there as much as I'd like to."

"I'd love that," said Sue, sipping the last of her coffee. "We could take it in turns to visit each other. And I've got a spare bed so you can stay over if you want to."

Anna agreed that she'd love to stay. "I don't know what's going to happen when our house sells but I'll certainly be buying a two-bedroom place so that the family can come and stay over, so you can stay over at mine as well." Anna got hold of Sue's hand. "Here's to the start of a good friendship hey."

"Yeah," said Sue, "To us!" and they chinked their coffee cups together, and both said a silent goodbye to Paradise Island.

Ken and Mandy walked into the restaurant together. This was to be their last meal on the Island as well. After a morning of rather robust sex, they were both famished. As they were being shown to their table, Ken spotted Anna, sitting with a dowdy, middle-aged woman he had seen about the Island a few times. He wondered what they were talking about, but more importantly, he didn't want Anna to see him and Mandy and come over and start talking.

"The wife's over there," he said to Mandy, pointing to Anna and Sue. "I'm surprised she's not having lunch with the toy boy she's been having it off with for the last few days," he lied. "Let's sit in the corner over there. I don't want her to see us."

Ken steered Mandy to a quiet table. After they'd got their food and ordered a last bottle of wine, Mandy got hold of one of Ken's hands.

"Ken, I just want to say it's been a great week and I've really enjoyed myself. I know you and your wife are going to split up and I hope you find whatever it is you're looking for in life. You're a great guy and any woman would be lucky to have you."

Ken, still upset that Mandy didn't want him in her life said "Sweetheart, can't I persuade you to at least give us a chance. We make a great team together, and, well, I think I've fallen in love with you."

"No, Ken. Stop right there. I've always been honest with you, haven't I? I don't want a permanent relationship. I'm happy with my life as it is. It's been fun while it lasted but, hey, we go home in a few hours. You will have forgotten all about me by this time next week anyway," she joked.

Ken was crestfallen. He'd never been so rejected before in his life. He always got the woman, always. They finished their meal in silence, then Mandy said "Look, we've got just over two hours until the ferry takes us back to Mackay. Why don't we just go and sit on the beach and be thankful for what we've both had this week with each other. Maybe you could think about what's going to happen when you get back home tonight."

So that's what they did. They found a lovely secluded spot halfway down the main beach and sat looking out over the ocean. The palm trees swayed in the soft breeze and the salty smell of the sea seemed to be the perfect ending to a remarkable week.

Ken and Anna had both realised that their marriage was over, indeed it had been over for some time now. He hoped the split would be amicable as Anna had been a lot happier here than she was at home. He wondered how he should leave their house, once he was back home. He'd spend the night in the spare room then pack all of his things up the following morning. Then he would phone Ruby as soon as he could, and arrange to go around and see her. He thought about how pleased she would be to see him, and went over in his head what he would say to her, how to ask her if he could move in with her while he sold his house, then they could choose another apartment together. Maybe Ruby would want a baby. She wasn't exactly over the hill yet, and there was still plenty of gunpowder in his gun, even at his age. Mandy broke into his thoughts.

"I hope it works out for you Ken. I really do. I've had a wonderful time this week. Maybe if you're ever in need of a chat you could give me a call sometime?"

Ken said, yes, he would, but he knew deep down that he never would. Mandy had made her position very clear that there was no room in her life for him.

He looked at his watch. "We'd better get going. I've got some last things to pack. I suppose this is it then."

Mandy took his face in her hands and kissed him long and hard on the lips.

"Ok, let's go. I'll see you at the jetty soon. They walked hand in hand and parted when they reached Ken's chalet. Mandy let go of his hand and walked away without looking back.

CHAPTER 37

TIME TO GO HOME

It was 2.45pm and there were a number of people waiting on the jetty for the ferry to take them back to the mainland, and home. Sue and Anna were standing together, however Ken was standing alone, away from Anna. Harry and Cassie were standing together, but saying nothing. They both knew where they stood and there was nothing more that Harry could say to Cassie that would change her mind. She'd made it perfectly clear that she wanted him to try again with his family, try and make things work. Then, in a few months' time, if things hadn't changed, maybe they could talk. Mandy hadn't yet appeared, and Ken kept looking over at the path in the hope of seeing her. Just before 3pm, she turned up, but to Ken's horror, she ignored him completely and started talking to another man who was also standing waiting on the jetty. Ken was furious. He looked over at Anna who was with the woman he had seen her with that morning. He was having no second thoughts about their breaking up. He knew Ruby would be waiting for him back in Sydney and he hoped she'd welcome him back with open arms. He was glad he and Anna had come to Paradise Island. It had clarified a lot of things for both of them. What they had together was long gone and he realised, for the first time, that Anna deserved better than him and what he could offer her. He tried to catch Mandy's eye but she was in full conversation with the younger man on the other side of the jetty. Ken suddenly felt old. He'd never been rejected before and this thing with Mandy had really taken its toll on him. He started to think about Ruby and what he'd do to her tomorrow and his confidence came flooding back. He couldn't wait. He knew Ruby would be as pleased to see him as he was to see her.

Anna and Sue, while waiting for the ferry, had been comparing notes on Marcello. Sue was now much more angry than devastated. She and Anna had been played by a two-timing bastard and she hated him for it. The fact that he had different women on the Island every week made matters even worse for her. She felt used and stupid and ridicules, all the things she supposed the others who'd found out about Marcello felt when they realised that they'd been played. One good thing had come out of the week though. She had met a lovely man, Steve, who had not only given her comfort when she'd found out about Marcello, but with whom had so much in common, that she felt they would remain firm friends. Steve had given Sue his number and she'd promised to call him soon. The other man she'd met, Will, had soon taken the hint that Sue felt nothing for him. They had had lunch together a few days ago and Sue had laid her cards on the table, telling Will that she wasn't looking for a relationship. She wanted to let him down gently as she guessed he had become besotted with her. Will had felt badly let down, having thought he was in with a chance but once Sue had told him about Marcello, he had actually been sympathetic towards her. They parted friends and promised to keep in touch, although Sue didn't think she would.

Now on the jetty with Anna, Sue looked up and saw Steve coming down the path. She asked Anna if she'd mind excusing her for a minute and went over to meet him.

"Hi Steve. I'm glad I've seen you before we go. I just wanted to say thank you for all you did for me and to say goodbye. I really hope we can keep in touch?

Steve was all tanned and smiles. "Hello Sue. I was hoping to see you. I'd love to keep in touch. What that yellow-bellied snake did to you and your friend was disgraceful. I hope you've put in a complaint!"

"Yes, we did it this morning. Apparently, we are not the first women to complain about him. There have been many others. The Manager intimated that he could lose his job now. I really hope he does. I could never forgive him for what he did. I thought I'd finally found someone who could love me as I am, and I know I'm no oil painting!"

Steve jumped in, "Hey, less of that. You're lovely, and witty and intelligent. Any man would be lucky to have you. Oh look, here comes the ferry. I'll let you get back to your friend. Keep in touch hey?"

To her surprise, Steve leant over and gave Sue a peck on the cheek.

"I'd like that very much," said Sue, and she made her way back to Anna.

Once everyone was loaded onto the ferry, the engines roared into life and soon the boat was heading away from the jetty. Everyone on board had their own personal memories of being on Paradise Island but for some, it meant change. Change in their lives, change about how they felt about each other and themselves.

Bianca and Joel had already gone home to try and sort out their problems. Both had seen each other with new eyes and were determined to make life easier and understand each other better. Joel had a broken ankle to deal with but in the long run, they both felt that everything would be alright.

Ken and Anna had realised that their marriage was over and had been for a long time. Ken was hoping for a happy reunion with Ruby back in Sydney and Anna was going to take it one step at a time, maybe find a part time job, sell the house and get herself a small apartment. Maybe she'd even get herself the dog she'd been promising herself for years but could never get, as Ken hated them.

Rachael, at home with the three children, had forgiven Harry for not going home with her and couldn't wait for his return. But Harry had realised that there was more to his life than work, Rachael and the kids. He was in love with Cassie and, although he'd promised her he'd give it another go with Rachael, he knew deep down, that Cassie and he would get together soon.

And finally, Sue. She hadn't really gone to Paradise Island looking for love, although she would have welcomed it, but what Marcello had done for her, as much as she now hated him, was to give her some confidence that she could find love at some point in her life. She had also made a wonderful friend in Steve, and she hoped that she would keep in touch with him and maybe see where it went from there.

As the ferry drew further and further away, they all looked back at Paradise Island, receding into the background, and they were all in wonder at how beautiful a place it was and how, for some, it had worked its magic. For others, it had changed their lives forever.

EPILOGUE

12 MONTHS LATER

BIANCA

Bianca was folding her clothes ready for packing in the suitcase. Joel hadn't even started.

"Joel. Come on. Get packing or we're going to be late," she called out.

"Ok. I'm coming, I'm coming." Joel rushed into their bedroom and got his suitcase down from the top of the wardrobe. He threw it onto the bed next to Bianca's then wrapped his arms around her.

"Can't we just go as nudists? Take no clothes with us at all?"

Bianca laughed. "You wish!"

The sound of a baby's cry interrupted them.

"Ok Kye darling. Mummy's coming."

She quickly went into the baby's nursery. Bianca still wasn't used to having another little person in the house. Kye was only two months old and demanded a lot of attention. She picked him up out of his crib and sat rocking with him in the chair near the window. Who would have thought that she, Bianca, would have a tiny baby to look after, one who was her whole world? Well along with Joel, of course. It was exactly twelve months since they'd gone to Paradise Island, torn apart by Joel's inability and disgust at any sort of intimacy or lovemaking. Today, her and Joel were going back to Paradise Island, only this time it really would be Sun, Sand and Sex, she thought. There would be no problems with Joel's performing this time. They were leaving Kye with Bianca's best friend, Jen, for the week, and let the Island work its magic once more.

After they had returned home a year ago, Joel with his foot in a cast and a break in his ankle, they had both visited their local doctor, and for the first time in his life, Joel had spoken openly and honestly about his childhood abuse, to anyone other than his wife. Bianca was shocked by the full story and realised that Joel had kept parts of the abuse from her. Anger at Joel's father didn't begin to cover how she felt.

Their doctor was kind and sympathetic and had given them a referral to a local therapist. This therapist didn't come cheap, the doctor warned them, but Bianca and Joel were happy to spend the money, if it even had a small chance of working. A week later, they were both sitting in the therapist's room. Her name was Wendy Thompson, she told them, and she had almost twenty years dealing with people with sexual and abuse problems. She started off by getting a picture of Joel and Bianca's daily lives as they were now, and how Joel's problems were currently affecting them. Joel had said that he didn't feel like the husband Bianca deserved, that he didn't feel like a real man. That he just wanted to make his wife happy, and maybe one day have a family with her. Bianca said that, although initially, she couldn't understand why Joel didn't want her, or seem to even find her sexually attractive, she had soon become angry and frustrated at his behaviour. However, in an attempt to help him relax and give him a change of scenery, maybe even time to think things through, they had recently gone on holiday to a lovely, relaxing Island in Queensland. Bianca told Wendy that Joel, obviously full of frustration and resentment at her, had wandered off and had become lost a long way from the Island's main Resort.

During this time, Bianca said she had done a lot of thinking, and had taken stock of hers and Joel's situation. She realised then that she loved him too much just to abandon him. She had decided that if he was found safely, that she would put the intimate side of their marriage on hold, and hope that there was something she could do to help Joel through what must be a very difficult time in his life. Wendy kept nodding her head as both Joel and Bianca spoke.

"So, what is it Joel that you'd like to get out of our sessions?"

Joel thought for a minute, then said "I'd like to be like any other man. I've got a beautiful wife, and I'd like nothing more than to be able to make love to her. To feel passion, something I've heard about but never felt. I'd like to make Bianca the centre of my universe."

"Good," said Wendy. "And what about you,

Bianca? What do you expect to happen, coming to these sessions?"

"It's just like Joel said, really. I want us to be a proper couple. To experience lovemaking together, happily and as often as we both want to. I don't want to be the one who always has to make the first move, and then be disappointed again when I feel Joel doesn't want me, or find me attractive. That's it really. If this counselling works, then wonderful. If it doesn't, then we will just have to search for something else that will."

Wendy was again nodding her head. "Joel, tell me, when Bianca approaches you to have sex, what do you feel? Both in your body and in your head?"

"I can't describe it really, as I've had no real experience in making love and having sex." He turned to Bianca. "Sorry Bea. That came out all wrong. What I was trying to say was that the sex we have had together, well, I've nothing to compare it to. I feel nothing, nothing at all. I've read all about lust and passion, but I don't know what they are meant to feel like. When I touch you, it's like, I don't know, it's as if something tightens round my whole body, and it makes me scared beyond belief. I…" Joel stopped mid-sentence.

Wendy patted him on the knee. "It's Ok Joel. We can stop now if you want."

Joel shook his head. "No, Wendy. If I don't get it out now, nothing's ever going to change. Whenever Bianca wants sex, I can feel my father's face pushing into mine. I can smell his breath, stinking of booze and his body of sweat. I can see my sister Jacqui laying on her bed crying that she's hurting. Wow!" Joel's eyes filled with tears and he seemed to be staring into a place far away. "Sorry," he said moments later. "I can never forget those feelings I've carried around with me all these years. One thing's for sure though Bea, is that I know how much I love you, even if I don't show it."

Bianca's eyes filled with tears. "It's Ok darling. We don't have to carry on with this."

"Yes Bea, we do. We need to get me sorted out

Wendy agreed with Joel and told the two young people that they had come a long way today.

"You two seem made for each other. I'm sure

between us, we can make things a lot better for you. Now I'm going to give you some homework to do and I want both of you to tell me how you felt about it when you come next week. I want you to do absolutely nothing else in bed but stroke each other's faces. Do it for as long as you want, but make sure you feel every part of the face. Run your fingers over each other's lips. I want you to both look into each other's eyes as you're doing it. We'll call this 'Stage 1'. Ok? I'll look forward to hearing how you both found it next week."

That night, Bianca and Joel, feeling slightly silly, had done just as they'd been instructed. Joel elected to go first and Bianca ran her fingers, softly over his face, touching his eyes, his cheeks, his ears and his lips. Bianca found this to be very erotic. It had been so long since she'd had sex and she felt the need in her growing. But she had to stick to Wendy's homework otherwise this wasn't going to work.

"How does that feel? Ok?"

Joel had his eyes closed. "It feels lovely. It's making me very relaxed. Keep going." Bianca had kept on stroking Joel's face then turned on her back and said "Ok, my go now."

Joel had touched Bianca's face properly, and for the first time, gently running his fingers over her face and neck. He felt relaxed and enjoyed the soft, smooth feel of her skin but felt no stirring down below.

"This is not working Bee. I'm feeling nothing down there."

"Sweetheart, the whole idea of this is so that eventually, you will feel aroused. Give it time. This is only the first night. Come on, keep going for a bit longer. Do I feel good to you?"

"You know you do Bee. Your skin is so smooth. I love you."

The following week, during their session with Wendy, Joel told her of his frustration at not feeling aroused. Wendy explained that it was going to take time and practice. Joel had denied himself the pleasure of arousal for so long that it was now second nature to him, and he had to un-learn his behaviour.

"Your homework for next week is going to intensify your relationship and hopefully be a bit more fulfilling for you both," Wendy told them. "Now I want you to keep touching each other, but this time, I want you both to touch the other wherever you feel comfortable doing so. If the other one says stop, then you must stop immediately. Under no circumstances are you to actually take it further and have sex, however much you may want to. Understand?"

Joel looked at Wendy in disbelief. He was nowhere near that stage yet. Wendy, saw Joel's face.

"Sorry Joel. I never meant that you may have sex, but I had to mention it just in case. It's important at this stage that when the time comes, you really, really want Bianca, and feel an almighty passion inside you that you've never had before. OK?"

That night, for some reason, was uncomfortable for both Bianca and Joel. After a shower, they both got into bed with their pyjamas on and lay on their backs for a while. Joel broke the silence.

"Ok. Shall we give it a go Bea?"

"I will if you will," Bianca quipped back.

"I suppose it would be a good idea if we got out of our PJ's?"

Still feeling slightly apprehensive, Bianca agreed and they both got naked.

"I went first last time, so it's your turn now," said Joel, building up his courage for what he was about to do.

Bianca started by again stroking Joel's face, then his neck. He had always pulled away from her touch in the past and she was afraid he would do so again. But as she moved her hand further down his chest, she was surprised that he didn't.

"How're you going?" she asked him.

"Keep going. It feels good. I can't believe this is what I've been missing all these years!"

Bianca had reached Joel's pubic area and she ran her hand through the wiry hair there. Tentatively, she stroked his penis, which she was surprised to discover, was semi erect. She remembered Wendy's words about no sex and stopped.

"Ok. That's enough for you for now. Your go now," and she lay on her back waiting for Joel to start his homework. He also started stroking his wife's face and neck, then her shoulders. His fingers were doing small swirling motions which was driving Bianca wild, although she had to keep it hidden. When his hand reached her breasts, he wavered for a moment. In his mind, this was a really crucial time for him. He had to overcome his fear of intimacy. It was now or never. He gently held onto one of Bianca's small breasts and found the nipple. He twisted it between his finger and thumb and Bianca let out a small moan. Remembering Wendy's words, he suddenly stopped.

"Well done, darling. You did really well. I know how hard that must have been for you."

"I actually started to feel something Bea. Something deep down in my belly. I think this is going to work."

"We'll keep going darling until it does. Don't worry, we'll soon be at it like rabbits."

Six weeks into their sessions with Wendy, and Joel and Bianca continued to make progress, with Joel constantly wanting to open up about his past abuse, which Wendy said was a huge step forward for him. This week, Wendy told them that she felt they were actually ready to try and make love and told them to go back over all of their homework and see how they felt. She advised them to do whatever they were both comfortable with. But if Joel said 'Stop', then they must stop.

That night, it had seemed so natural to them and Joel was able to have sex with his wife because he wanted to not because he had to. He quickly got an erection when Bianca stroked his body and, even though he came too quickly during sex, they waited ten minutes then did it again, this time more slowly so that Bianca could be satisfied too. Not long afterwards, they were making love almost every night. Their homework had paid off and Joel was like a new man. He couldn't get enough of Bianca. But then, after a while, Bianca realised she had missed a period. Because of their past history, she never thought she would ever become pregnant. Could she be? There was only one way to find out. When she saw the lines appear on the tester, she burst into tears. She and Joel were going to have their miracle baby. She couldn't believe it. When she'd told Joel, they had sat crying together, and had sat well up into the night discussing parenting, schools, baby foods and names.

The pregnancy went like a dream. Bianca had barely any morning sickness, no high blood pressure, the only problem was that Bianca was feeling like a beached whale, towards the end. They still had regular sex, but it was not as regular or as manic as before. It was now soft and gentle, slow and full of love. Joel's problems had been long forgotten and their whole focus now was on their baby. They'd found out it was to be a little boy, and had decided to name him Kye. His birth was a long drawn out affair. Bianca hadn't known pain like it existed, but once her baby boy was put in her arms, with Joel beside her, tears streaming down his face, Bianca felt a happiness and fulfilment she never knew was possible. Now they were going back to Paradise Island again to make up for their disastrous time there last year. And this time, it really was going to be Sun, Sand and Sex! Love had really blossomed. They were a family at last and Joel was the husband he had always wanted to be to his wife! The Island had once again worked its magic!!

ANNA

Anna woke up and stretched her arms above her head, rubbed her eyes and turned on her side. She stroked the shoulder of her man, Rob, and he woke up and kissed her. The both loved Sundays when they didn't have to get up for work and could have breakfast in bed together and read the papers. Rob went downstairs and brought back a mug of steaming coffee for her, then went out to get the Sunday papers. While she was sipping her coffee, Anna gloried in her new life. She was the happiest she'd been in a long time. When she and Ken had returned from Paradise Island a year ago (where had the time gone!), Ken had been as good as his word and had packed most of his things up and driven off in his car, leaving Anna to contemplate an empty house and life on her own. She had been slightly apprehensive as she hadn't lived on her own since she and Ken had been married, although with Ken away so much with his latest fling, she thought, she should be used to being on her own. She spent the following few weeks pottering around the house, reading magazines and tending to their small garden. Ken had arranged for an Estate Agent to value the house and there was soon a 'For Sale' sign outside. The first week the house had been open for inspection, there had been quite a lot of prospective buyers come through but no offers.

One day, Anna was reading the local paper when an Ad caught her eye. The local Library was asking for volunteers to read stories to the children twice a week. Anna, by now bored, had thought what a wonderful opportunity it would be to get out of the house. And she'd always liked small children. She rang the number given immediately, and was asked to go and see a lady called Pat the following day. Anna and Pat had hit it off immediately and before she knew it, Anna was arriving at the Library the following week, having obtained her 'Working with Children"

Licence, to start her first session. Anna was a hit, and the children loved her. Soon, Pat was asking Anna to come in and help out in other areas. One was sorting books to take in the Mobile Library to the local Aged Care Home. Anna loved it. It gave her a purpose in life. She never got to see much of her own daughter and grandchild, and this was the perfect solution to her loneliness. After the second viewing of their house, an offer had been made. She and Ken had accepted it, which was more than they had expected. Four weeks later, Anna had packed up, with the help of her daughter and son-in-law, and, to some extent, Ken, and had rented a small, furnished apartment in the eastern suburb, having divided the proceeds from the sale with her husband. They had sold all of their furniture, as it was big and clumsy, and had divided the rest of their material possessions amazingly amicably. She had only taken a six-month lease on the apartment, which she thought would give her plenty of time to have a look round and find her perfect forever home.

Ken was sitting smoking on the small balcony table, which overlooked the park. He had a bottle of beer and a packet of smoky bacon chips and his mood was glum. After he and Anna had arrived home from

Paradise Island, he had, true to his word, packed up most of his clothes and belongings, put them all into the back of his car and picked up his phone to ring Ruby. But then he decided, no, he wouldn't ring her. He'd surprise her and just turn up. Naturally, she'd be overjoyed to see him and there was no doubt in his mind that she'd let him stay with her. Then maybe they could get a new, bigger place of their own. He had driven to Ruby's and parked his car in the only available space, further up the street. He walked back and knocked on her door, then he'd knocked again when she hadn't answered. Eventually Ruby opened the door. She was wearing the silk dressing gown that he'd bought her just before he went away.

"Ken! What are you doing here?" Ruby was obviously surprised to see him.

"God, have I missed you sweetheart," and he started to move past her into the house.

Behind her, a man, probably in his mid to late thirties, appeared, wrapped only with a towel around his waist. It was obvious to Ken what had been going on. The man said

"Oh Hi. You must be Ruby's dad?"

"No, I'm not Ruby's bloody dad." He looked at Ruby. "I think you've got some explaining to do. Who the hell is he?"

Ruby turned to the younger man and told him to go back inside then partially closed the front door and came out to Ken.

"Look Ken, I'm sorry. Chris and I met last week, just after you'd left. He's been here ever since. We've got a real connection. I really like him and we think we have a future together. I'm so sorry but what we had is over. I'd better get back in. Good luck Ken. I mean that. We had some great times hey." And she was gone.

Ken stood shell shocked on the front. First Mandy, on the Island, and now Ruby. He had never experienced such rejection before. Now there was the small matter of where he'd go. He certainly wasn't going back to his own house. As he walked back to his car, Ken felt the lowest he had ever felt in his life. He thought Ruby had loved him and would wait until he got back for him. He thought he'd loved Mandy, but she too had rejected him, calling him 'a holiday fling'. He got into his car and thought about where he could go. There were some Serviced Apartments in Bromley High Street so he made his way there. Although extortionately expensive, he'd booked himself in for a few days. It would give him a chance to see where he went from here. He was due back at work on Monday. All the Real Estate Agents would be closed tomorrow, it being a Sunday, so he'd have to wait to find an apartment to rent.

Back at work and during his lunch break on Monday, he had gone into the Estate Agents across the road from his office and asked the pretty Receptionist what they had to rent. Unable to break the habits of a lifetime, he found himself flirting with her, but the girl just gave him a look that said 'what are you? Some kind of weirdo or something?' Ken immediately felt flat again. How could he be losing his touch after only a week? Luckily, they did have a first-floor apartment in Manly to rent, and Ken arranged with one of the Agents to go and view it after work. When he'd seen it, Ken realised it wasn't the luxurious bachelor pad he'd hoped it would be, but it was decent enough and had a nice little balcony with a good view over the park. He told the Agent he'd take it straight away, and they had gone back to the Agent's Office where Ken had signed a 6 months Lease, and paid over the required Bond and Rent. As it was fully furnished he moved in the next day after work. He decided to celebrate, and go out to a local bar and get hammered, pick up a girl and spend the night screwing her, in order to get his confidence back. After three whiskies and two pints, he had approached a woman, obviously on her own, who looked in her late thirties or early forties.

"Hello darlin'" he slurred. "Fancy another?"

"No thanks grandad," said the woman, and moved away from him.

The reality of what the woman had said did not immediately hit Ken, but when it did, he sunk into the pits of depression. What had happened to him while he'd been away? Normally, he'd have had no trouble picking up a slapper like her. In his drunken state, he approached another, obviously single woman at the bar.

"Hello darlin'. Fancy another?"

"No thank you. I want a toy boy not a pensioner," the woman also turned and walked away.

This time, Ken took it really badly and went outside and hailed a taxi to take him home. Not understanding why his life had suddenly taken a turn for the worse, he picked up one of his girlie magazines and took himself off to the bathroom.

Twelve months later, Ken was alone in his apartment, remembering that this time last year he and his love life were doing just fine. He'd enjoyed his time with Mandy on Paradise Island, and had been really disappointed when she wouldn't take their holiday romance further. Then coming home to find he'd lost Ruby as well had set him on the path he was now on, one of loneliness and depression. He had tried his luck with a few more women for a couple of weeks but without success. His strong sexual appetite suddenly disappeared and he had to go and see his Doctor who recommended ante depressants. He could hardly stay awake during the day and had had to give up his job. He soon became a shell of his former self. His divorce from Anna was due to come through soon and he tried to get back in touch with her to see if she'd have him back again, only to find that she'd changed her number and his daughter refused to give him her mother's new one. His daughter had also told her dad that Anna had moved in with a new man and were talking about marriage. Ken realised what an idiot he had been letting Anna go. Sure, their sex life hadn't been good for years, but at least she was some sort of company and she looked after him. Now he was all alone. He didn't know what the future held for him. All he knew was that he was not the man he used to be. And he blamed it all on his week at Paradise Island!

Three months after returning from Paradise Island, Anna had secured herself a great part time job at her local Library. She had been voluntary at first, but soon, a vacancy for a paid position had come up and Anna had had no trouble being accepted for it. She loved her work. One aspect of it was when she had to sort and take a selection of books around to a local Retirement Home. The Manager there was Paul Jacobs who was roughly the same age as Anna. They had hit it off from the start. Paul was funny and made Anna laugh, something that Ken never did. He also loved books, all sorts of different genres, as did she, and the music of the 60s was a firm favourite with both of them. Soon Anna and Paul were spending much longer chatting together than Anna's allotted half hour time at the Retirement Home. Anna had told Paul about Ken, and his lying, cheating ways, and of their upcoming divorce, and Paul had told Anna that his wife of over thirty years had left him for another man three years ago. Anna had recounted her experience with Marcello on Paradise Island and Paul was horrified.

"I hope you and the other lady reported the bastard. He should be sacked."

"Yes, we did report him and he was sacked the same week." Anna had by now got over Marcello and almost over her anger at him.

She'd been a fool to let him do what he did. She was old enough to realise that a younger man like Marcello wouldn't be interested in women like her and Sue. When she had told Pat, her boss at the Library, about Paul, Pat had positively encouraged Anna to take things with him further. Anna hadn't flirted, or dated, anyone for about fourty years and, although she really liked Paul, the prospect of a relationship with him was difficult for her to take in. However, later that week, the matter was taken out of her hands when Paul, having already gained Anna's phone number, rang her asking her if she'd like to go for a meal with him. Anna had said yes, without hesitation. They'd gone to a lovely little Italian place on the North Shore and it was here that Anna felt the first fluttering's of physical attraction for him.

"You know what, Paul", she'd said. "You are the first man in about fourty years that has made me laugh. I just want to say thank you for that. I've had a wonderful night."

Paul gazed into Anna's eyes. "Anna, over the last few months that we've known each other, I have been the happiest I've been in a long time. When my wife left me, I thought that was it for me. I'd never trust another woman again for as long as I live. But you're different. I feel as though I've known you for years and I would trust you with my life."

Anna was flattered. "That's a lovely thing to say Paul. Thank you. The feeling's mutual, I can assure you."

Afterwards, Paul drove Anna back to her apartment and gave her a warm kiss on the cheek as she was getting out of the car. Although embarrassed by it, Anna thought it was very welcome, and they arranged to see each other on the following Saturday.

"Why don't we go into the City, do a Museum or two and have some lunch, then go on the Manley Ferry? We can leave the car at home."

"I'd love that," said Anna. "How about I meet you at the ferry terminal at Circular Quay? Say around ten?"

"Yep, that would suit me. I'll look forward to it. And Anna, thanks for tonight. I've had a really good time."

Life for Anna and Paul went on this way for a few months, visiting interesting places and eating in nice restaurants. After each meeting, Paul would take Anna back to her apartment and give her the same warm kiss on the cheek. Then, one night, after they'd been to a particularly nice Thai restaurant, and perhaps both had drunk a little bit more than usual, Anna invited Paul in for coffee. They both knew what it meant. The sexual tension between them had been building up for weeks and they were now both ready to take their relationship to the next level. However, Anna was mortified to think of what she was about to do. She had only ever had three lovers in her entire life, one of them being Marcello, and it had been a long, long time since anybody other than him and Ken had seen her body, never mind make love to her. With Marcello, she hadn't got to know him, she was on holiday and had something to prove to Ken. It had all seemed so easy. However, she need not have worried as Paul was gentle with her, and didn't mind when Anna wanted the lights switched off. The sex itself was over very quickly and they spent a lot of time just lying there, Anna's head on Paul's shoulders, talking about things in their lives, their children and grandchildren, holidays they'd been on and their marriages. But she was content, and the happiest she'd been in a long time.

Within the next two months, Anna had moved her belongings into Paul's house. They both knew that they loved each other and that, at their age, life was short. When Paul asked Anna to marry him once her divorce from Ken had gone through, she had no hesitation in saying yes. She had her 'happy ever after', her daughter and grandson, a lovely new home and a man who loved her and who she could rely on a hundred per cent not to cheat on her or lie to her. Paul asked her where she'd like to go for their honeymoon.

"What about that Island you went to last year up in Queensland? How about we go there? It sounds idyllic, and I'll make sure I keep the lothario's away from you."

"No thank you," Anna almost shouted. "I couldn't face that place again. Let's go on a cruise." And six months later, they did, as happy as any couple could ever have been.

RACHAEL

"Daddy, daddy," Lily cried out as Harry came through the door.

Harry scooped his youngest child into his arms and swung her round.

"Hello baby girl. How are you? Been a good girl for mummy?"

"Yes daddy. I'm starting at Kindy next week daddy."

"Yes, I know honey. Have you got your uniform all ready?"

Before Lilly could answer, the two older children had come running in and threw their arms around their dad. They only saw him every other Saturday and today was their day. Jake, who had to be first at everything, pushed the other two away and pulled his dad over to the lounge.

"Hey dad, wait till I tell you…" and he was off, on a tale that would probably take half an hour.

Jake's behaviour had improved very little in the last twelve months and spending a day with his son every second Saturday was enough for Harry. A year ago, after leaving Paradise Island, he'd driven through the night from Mackay and had arrived home the following morning. He'd sat outside the still house in his car, dreading the thought that this was what he was coming back to. Back to the 'real life', one where Cassie didn't feature, and where work and his difficult children, along with a wife who he didn't know if he loved anymore, were waiting for him. He no longer wanted that life, but Cassie had made it very clear to him that he owed it to his family to give it a three-month trial before making any major decisions about his life. He knew she loved him but her determination not to come between a man and his family could not be argued with. Before they'd left Paradise Island, Cassie had made him promise that he wouldn't contact her for at least three months. That way, she said, he could put all his focus on his family. Finally, he got out of the car and made his way to the house. All three children and Rachael were in the kitchen eating breakfast. Even though it had only been a week, Harry thought that all his children somehow looked older. They all jumped up when they heard him come in.

"Daddy, daddy," all three shouted, and pushed and shoved to get their arms round him first. Rachael was standing behind them. After greeting the children, he made his way over to her.

"Before you say anything Harry, I admit I was in the wrong leaving you there on your own. I should have listened to you. Mum and dad would have had to manage. I should have stayed."

Rachael staying was the last thing that Harry had wanted. Her going home early had left the way open for him and Cassie to act like any other normal couple, and he was grateful for that. But here was Rachael apologising for it, so he thought he may as well take advantage of it.

"Have you any idea of the misery I've gone through on my own these last few days? Stuck on that Island by myself? I didn't want to do anything or go anywhere. Never again Rach. I'm going to unpack!"

Might as well make her suffer, he thought as he put his clothes back in the drawers.

And so life back home for Harry and Rachael had gotten back to sort of normality, although the tension of the next few weeks between them never really went away. Harry went back to work and came home at the end of the day to help Rachael look after a particularly naughty Jake. He'd gone out and bought a bed for Lily, and Rachael had started to try and wean her off the bottle, but it was proving difficult. She still refused to go to bed, even in her new 'big girl' bed, and they were often up until gone midnight with her. This was exactly what Harry had expected would happen, this life, and he was so very frustrated by it. And with every passing day, he hated it more. More than ever, he wanted a new life with Cassie. He couldn't just dismiss what they'd had on Paradise Island. They both knew it was something special. Why couldn't Cassie see that. Why did she have to insist he give his life with Rachael and his kids another go?

Three months after they had arrived home, Harry and Rachael had left the two youngest children with Rachael's mum and travelled to Parramatta in Sydney with Jake to see Dr Phillip Heachy. Dr Heachy specialised in treating children with behavioural disorders and their appointment that day was for 3pm. Jake, as usual, had been a nightmare on the six-hour journey there. Wanting to stop all the time, crying for chocolate bars and fizzy drinks, things that were sure to make him even more hyper, and when Harry and Rachael refused him, he'd put up an almighty tantrum. For Harry especially, the journey was a nightmare. He had promised Cassie that he would give it at least three months before contacting her again and it had been almost like a physical torture not being able to speak to her. Now, however, the three months were up, and life for Harry and Rachael was no better. While they waited in Dr Heachy's Waiting Room, Harry told Rachael he was nipping out to the toilet down the corridor. Once inside with the door locked, he had taken out his mobile phone and dialled Cassie's number. She had answered on the third ring.

"Cassie?"

"Hello. Who is this?" Cassie's voice sounded like music to Harry's ears.

"Sweetheart it's me, Harry," he was so emotional, that tears sprung to his eyes. "Look Cass. Can we meet up? Soon? I've done what you asked. I've tried hard for three months. Rachael and I are barely speaking to each other, never mind anything else. Jake's a bloody nightmare and I'm not getting to sleep till after midnight almost every night because of Lily. It seems to be exactly like it was before the Island and I can't take any more of it. Please say you'll see me Cass. I really want to see you. I can't wait any longer."

There was a silence at the other end of the phone, then Harry heard a sob.

"Oh Harry. You don't know how good it is to hear your voice. I've missed you so much. I think about you and what you're doing every day. You've kept to your part of the bargain. I'm sure you've tried with Rachael and the kids. Of course, I'll see you. When can you come up?"

"What about next weekend? I can tell Rachael that I've got to go to Sydney with work. I had to go once before so she won't be suspicious."

"Have you got something to write with?" asked Cassie. "I'll give you my address."

Harry opened his screen Notes, on his iPhone. "Yep, fire away."

"I'm at Unit 3, 18 Calwell Drive, Byron Bay. Do you want directions?"

"No sweetheart. I've got a Sat Nav. I'll find you easy enough. Let's say I'll be there next Saturday, sometime around lunchtime. It will take me about three hours' drive from home."

"I can't wait to see you Harry," Cassie whispered.

"Me neither. I've got to go now, but I'll see you on Saturday. Bye Cass. Oh, and by the way, I Love you."

"And I love you too Harry. Bye."

Rachel thought Dr Heachy was wonderful. He

was in his mid 50s and really good with Jake. He first took a full family history, then a background of Jake from when he'd been born. When he spoke to Jake, he spoke to him at an adult level, and Jake seemed to respond well to that.

"Jake, why do you think you behave the way you do?" he asked.

"Dunno," replied Jake. "They're always having a go at me and won't let me have the things I want."

Rachael interrupted, "But Jake, the things you want aren't always good for you, you know that. Then when you don't get what you want you throw a massive tantrum like a two-year-old."

"No I don't you fucking fat pig," Rachael was pleased that Dr Heachy was now seeing Jake's real side.

But the doctor remained calm. "That's not a very nice way to speak to your mum, Jake, is it? She and your dad are only ever trying to do their best for you. That's why they've brought you here today. How do you think I might be able to help you Jake?"

Jake was sulking now. "Dunno."

"Well, what we're going to do is to get you to do some breathing exercises at home for me Jake. Do you think you could do that, just for me?"

"Suppose so," Jake answered.

Dr Heachy turned to Harry and Rachael. "I'm also going to give him a medication called Risperidone. I want him to take one at night when he goes to bed. It might make him a bit sleepy during the day until his body gets used to it, but hopefully it will calm him down a bit. Even with this medication, a lot of Jake's behaviour is what we call 'Learnt Behaviour', it's habit now for him to turn on you both and call you names, and act out the way he does. It's not going to be a simple fix. I think next time I see you in, say, a month, we might work on rewards and consequences."

The doctor ruffled Jake's hair and handed him a sheet of paper.

"Ok young man. You do these breathing exercises when you get up in the morning and before you go to bed at night. Then I want you to do them again every time you start to feel yourself getting angry. Ok?"

Jake nodded and Rachael and Harry shook Dr Heachy's hand and he escorted them out of the room.

The following Saturday, Harry had no problem making Rachael believe that he was going to Sydney for the weekend with work. He'd packed an overnight bag and told the kids to be good for their mum. Driving the three hours to Byron Bay, he had his favourite AC/DC music on at full blast and his voice was becoming hoarse from singing along. Arriving at Cassie's, he immediately saw that her block of apartments overlooked the sea. This was such a beautiful spot. I could get used to this, he thought. Suddenly, he had butterflies in his stomach. He hadn't seen Cassie in three months, and he wondered if the same spark, the same depth of feeling, would still be there. Knocking on her door, he noticed he'd started to shake slightly, but then all of a sudden, there she was, dressed in short denim shorts and a snow-white top that showed off her flat belly. They fell into each other's arms, both almost in tears. Still holding on to each other and kissing deeply, they stumbled into

Cassie's bedroom and fell onto her bed in a heap, each trying to take the other's clothes off at the same time. Soon they were both completely naked and fast and furious sex followed. Afterwards, they lay side by side panting, trying to catch their breath.

"You still got it, girl," Harry quipped.

"You ain't so bad yerself big boy," Cassie came back with her own compliment. Soon afterwards, they made love again, only this time, gently and passionately. They spent the weekend going to see the Craft Shop Cassie worked in, strolling hand in hand around the Sunday Markets, Cassie commenting that she saw this crafty kind of stuff every day at work, walking along the water's edge on the beautiful beach opposite Cassie's apartment and eating in the local eateries, before going back to the apartment to make love once again. It was 3pm on Sunday and time for Harry to make the return journey home. Naturally, he didn't want to go. Sitting out on the verandah, drinking a last cup of coffee, Harry decided to say what was on his mind.

"Cass, I truly believe that me and Rachael are over. I just don't love her anymore. It's you I want to be with. I can still go down and see the kids regularly. I know I'll have to find a job and pay maintenance and all that, but is there any way you and I could give it a go? I know we haven't ever lived with each other, but I think we'd get along well together. And, well, I really do love you, you know."

Cassie took a deep breath. "Harry, I want nothing else than to be with you all the time. But what if you can't find a job up here? How will you manage to pay Rachael maintenance if you can't?"

"Darling, let's deal with that if it happens. All's I need is for you to say yes. The rest will take care of itself. Please say yes, that we can be together."

Cassie took Harry's face between her hands and kissed him deeply on the lips. "Ok then," she smiled. "But on one condition."

"Anything, my darling Cassie. You just say the word!"

"I want you to bring me tea in bed every morning, then I'll be happy!"

Cassie squealed as Harry chased her round the

apartment and finally caught up with her and threw her on the bed!

Harry was undecided whether to just take off and leave Rachael a note (the coward's way, his mind told him) or to tell her face to face that it was over for them. He decided face to face and two days after returning from seeing Cassie, he waited until the two older children had gone to bed, and Lily was falling asleep, still with a bottle, on the lounge. He poured both himself and Rachael a glass of wine and told her he had something he needed to say to her. At first, Rachael was unbelieving. She had no idea of Cassie's existence. She became incredibly angry when Harry told her that the affair had actually started on Paradise Island, and that Harry had said he had been lonely and stuck in the chalet while he was there, supposedly on his own. She was furious that he was prepared to give up on their ten years of marriage and their three children, as well as his well-paid job, for someone who he hardly knew. But Harry realised he would get nowhere arguing with Rachael. He went into their bedroom and packed as much of his clothes and toiletries as he could and walked out without another word, leaving Rachael distraught but angry. Harry drove back up to Cassie's and unpacked his things, which Cassie had made space for. She had a bottle of champagne on ice, and poured them both a glass.

"Here's to us sweetheart. Here's to our new life together. A week later, Harry had found another job and he felt as though he and Cassie had been together all their lives. He knew he'd made the right choice.

It had taken three months for Rachael to finally realise that Harry wasn't coming home and she decided to file for a divorce. Harry's maintenance money was being put into her bank every fortnight, without fail, and eventually, Rachael decided that Harry had a right to see his children. He started to come down every Saturday, when he took them out, either bowling or to the cinema, or just for a burger. For Rachael, still angry at Harry, it worked out Ok. The hurt had been so bad for her in the beginning, that she'd lain in bed sobbing for weeks after he'd left. The medication and the breathing exercises that Dr Heachy had given Jake had improved his behaviour slightly, but he was still a handful for Rachael, now a single mum. But something amazing had happened, Rachael's mum had stepped in, and now came around twice a week to help her with the housework and to look after Jake and the other two children when they came in from school. One day, when Rachael was particularly down, her mother had said "Rach, one day you are going to meet another man. One who will care for you and the children like you yourself care for them. I just know it."

"I doubt it mum," said Rachael. "Who'd want to take me and these three on?"

"Oh, you never know darling. You never know. You're a lovely looking girl and I'm sure some man will one day appreciate you.

Within 12 months, Rachel had found love again, this time with an older man, but one who she could trust herself and her children with. She had a part time job in a local café, and it was here that she had met Rory. He was fantastic with the children, especially with Jake. It hadn't taken them long to fall in love and form a relationship and they were soon inseparable. For Rachael, love had finally blossomed. The Island hadn't worked its magic for her, but in some respects, she was actually thankful that she and Harry had gone there last year. It had given her a new love and a man who could truly help her with her family. Life for Rachael and her children looked rosy at last.

SUE

As Sue reflected on all she had achieved since coming back off her disastrous holiday to Paradise Island a year ago, she felt very proud that she'd found the courage to change her life. She was still in her apartment overlooking the beach in Wollongong, but she had bought new Shabby Chic furniture and ornaments and made the whole place look fresh and bright and modern. The two biggest changes in her life though were Steve and Serenity, their new coffee shop with its cosy book corner. All thoughts of Marcello (she could never call him Mark) had now vanished but she had realised that, like he'd done to her good friend,

Anna, she had been made to feel that she could be loved, that they could think of themselves as attractive and desirable women, and they had both gained a confidence they never would have had but for the man they had both despised a year ago.

When she had returned from Paradise Island, Sue, still nursing her wounds of pride, rejection and hurt, had set about continuing with her life back at school, reading her books, drinking a glass of wine on the balcony, and just getting back to the boring life that she knew. One day, during school, about three months later, Sue had found that she was getting sick and tired of teaching the same curriculum year after year. Her new found confidence had made her stop and rethink what her life was all about and how, if at all, she could change it. After a particularly gruelling day, where a class of Year 9s were totally uninterested in what had caused the Boer War, and had let her know it, Sue went home feeling deflated and, for the first time in her teaching life, felt a failure as a teacher. It was as though something in her had changed, and the students had picked up on it and were not treating her with the respect they always had done. She sat on her verandah, sipping her wine and nibbling on some macadamia nuts, while watching the waves crash onto the sand in the distance. Suddenly, her phone rang.

"Hello."

"Hello. Is that Sue? It's me, Steve Oldham. We met on Paradise Island"

"Hello Steve. How lovely to hear from you. I've had a bummer of a day so it's great to hear a friendly voice." Sue was genuinely pleased to hear from him.

"So, have you settled back down to your old 'school Ma'am' life. How's it going?"

"Oh, I don't know Steve. I always thought I'd found my vocation in life but now I'm not so sure. Even I'm finding the Boer War as boring as hell, never mind my poor Year 9s. What about you?"

"Funnily enough," said Steve, "I'm feeling a bit the same. I feel like a change. Suddenly everything doesn't seem to fit, you know, like a jig saw puzzle. The reason why I rang was to say 'hi' and to see if you fancied driving up to mine on Sunday. There's a Jazz Festival playing in town here and I thought you'd like to come. It would give us a chance to catch up again. What do you say?"

"Oh Steve. I'd love to. I've nothing planned for Sunday, not that I ever have. What time should I get there?"

Steve suggested she arrive around 11am and gave her his address, then told her he was looking forward to seeing her again. Were those little butterflies I felt in my tummy, thought Sue, when she and Steve had hung up? Because she'd been so blown over by Marcello on the Island, she had never really had a chance to give any thought to how she really felt about Steve, other than she had liked him. He'd been there when she had needed him and she'd been grateful for that, but beyond that, she hadn't thought about him really in that way.

Sunday came, and Sue took an effort with her appearance before driving to Steve's at Bankstown. It was lovely to see him again, and this time, Sue really did appreciate his good looks, his intelligence, and the way in which they both seemed to like the same things. The Jazz Festival was a huge success and she and Steve once again hit it off, just as they had back on the

Island. As she was leaving later that evening to drive back to Wollongong, Steve said "I've had a wonderful day, Sue. It's been so lovely to see you again. Can we meet up again some time?"

"I've had a lovely day too, Steve. I'd love to meet up again. Are you free to come down to Wollongong next weekend? I've got a spare room so you could stay over. I could show you the sites, not that there's many to see. Maybe we could go and see a movie and have dinner in a lovely little restaurant I know on the beach?"

"I'd love to Sue, but can we make it for the following weekend. I've got my girls next weekend. It's my turn and I don't like letting them down."

"Of course, you mustn't let them down. We can easily make it the following weekend. Get me a pen and a piece of paper and I'll write my address down."

Sue got into bed that night, tired after the long drive and a wonderful day. She really liked Steve and hoped he liked her. I'll soon know if he bothers to come down and see me in a fortnight, she thought. She fell asleep happy.

For the next few months, Sue and Steve had taken it in turns to go and visit each other. They both felt their love for each other grow with every visit. One evening, when they were sitting on her verandah, Steve, sipping his wine, and talking about what he had done that week, let Sue feel that he definitely wasn't happy. He needed a change, he said. A new challenge from the boring job he currently had, and a new change of scenery. Before she could stop herself, Sue had said,

"I've got an idea Steve. Please feel free to say no if it's not what you want, but why don't you move in here with me. You can have the spare room. We get on really well together and I really, well…" Sue could hardly get the words out, "I really like you. A lot. I'm sure we could rub along nicely together. I'm sure you'd have no trouble getting a job here with your qualifications."

Steve put his head in his hands. Shortly, he said "It's a big decision to make Sue but thank you so much for offering. I'd really love to. I've become very fond of you over the last few months, but I have the girls to think about, and will I really be able to get another job? Do you mind if I have a few days to work it all out in my head and think about it? I really like you as well, and I think we'd get on great. Let me think it over hey? It's a big step but I feel I'm ready for a change. I'll ring you in a few days."

By Wednesday, Sue was beginning to think that Steve had given up on her, but at 8.30pm, while she was watching TV, Sue's phone rang. It was Steve.

"Hello my sexy Sue," this was so unlike Steve, that Sue was taken aback to being called 'sexy'.

'Hello yourself. How are you? I've missed you. I didn't know if you'd contact me again or not."

"Oh Sue, no. Of course I would have done, whatever my decision would have been. Look, I've talked it all through with Melissa, my ex, and we can make it work. She's going to meet me with the girls at the top of Bulli Pass every second Saturday, sort of half way. I can't believe she's been so good about it. I think it's to do with the fact that she has another new man in her life. Anyway, the answer is yes, I'd love to come down there and be with you. That's if you still want me?"

"Of course I want you, you plonker. When can

you come?"

"Well I'll have to give them a couple of weeks' Notice at work then sell my bits and pieces. I'm lucky that my Apartment is furnished so I don't have much to sell or bring. I'll have to sell my classic car though. I don't think it will fit in with my new life!"

"Oh Steve. Are you sure. You can bring it if you want you know. I'm so happy. I'll be counting down the days now till you get here."

"Sue, can I just say one more thing?"

"Sure. Anything."

"Don't make up the spare room." Sue's butterflies in her tummy did summersaults.

It had been a year this week, since Sue and Steve had returned from Paradise Island, and four months since Steve had moved in with her. On his first night there, Sue had shyly asked Steve if he'd meant what he'd said about not making the spare room up. Steve had stood up and taken Sue into his arms.

"I think you know I love you, don't you, and I think you feel the same. Now that I've found you, I want to hold you in my arms and never let you go."

They had kissed passionately and soon were laying on the bed, Steve kissing Sue all over. For the first time ever, Sue felt passion. When Steve entered her, she gave out a genuine moan of pleasure. As his thrusts became faster, Sue felt a tightening in her stomach and a delicious feeling down below. She didn't know what hit her when her body exploded and convulsed in pleasure. It was her first ever orgasm in the 50 years of her life. So, this was what she'd been missing? What a waste, she thought. As they lay panting and catching their breath, Sue lying on Steve's shoulder, he laughingly said "And how was that for you darling? Did I do well?"

"Wonderful. Absolutely wonderful! And yes, the boy did well!"

They'd had to be very practical when Steve's girls came every second weekend and had bought a set of bunk beds for the spare room for them. Sue had grown quite attached to Holly and Jenna. They were real 'girlie girls' and Sue loved helping them with their nail polish and their hair. Steve and Sue talked often about getting a bigger place for them all and one day, whilst walking hand in hand around the small row of shops by the main beach, Sue noticed a Café for sale. It was called 'Café by The Sea' and it looked as though it had an apartment upstairs. As if meant to be, Sue and Steve, looked at each other and smiled. Steve had found a job, but it was only part time and the pay wasn't very good. Suddenly, Sue realised she was looking at her dream. A café of her very own. On impulse, they went in and asked to speak to the owner, who turned out to be a lovely lady in her 60s, who said she had had the café for ten years now and that she wanted a change. She took them upstairs to her living quarters and Sue and Steve couldn't believe it when they were shown three bedrooms, theirs with an en-suite. Downstairs there were a dozen tables, a counter and big coffee machine, and two display cabinets with sandwiches in one and cakes in the other. The café was going for a song and had only just gone on the market. The owner wanted a quick sale and another person was due to come and have a look at six that night. Without thinking, Sue looked over at Steve, who nodded his head.

"We'll take it. Full asking price," said Sue. They all shook hands and arrangements were made for solicitors and finance. Sue had quite a healthy savings account and Steve had the money from the sale of his classic car and his holiday pay from his last job. As they walked back to Sue's apartment, both of them couldn't stop talking, they were so excited. They hadn't even looked over the café's books, but s

Somehow Sue could tell that they would make a go of it.

Within a month, the café was theirs. Both Sue and Steve had decided to give the slightly run-down café a makeover. They would keep the coffee choices but would offer a range of exotic teas. They would offer baguettes with luxury fillings and bought-in fancy cakes and muffins. Sue decided to add a corner of the café, where Steve would build two floor to ceiling bookcases, which they would stock with a selection of different books, add a few bean bags and a comfy chair, or two if they would fit, and install a 'Book Corner' for customers to sit and read, which, Steve said, would be good Marketing for them, and something different for the area. Sue decided that the new café should have a new name, and, after much brain storming, late into the night, they decided on the name 'SERENITY' for their new venture. Within six months, 'Serenity' was proving to be a big hit with visitors and locals alike. Sue's welcoming ambience ably assisted by Steve at weekends and when he wasn't working, made it a huge success.

"In the winter, let's close up and go back to Paradise Island for a week," Steve suggested. "If I remember rightly, the Advert, when I first saw it, said 'Let love blossom' and it certainly has for us, my love."

And he kissed her passionately on the lips. For the first time in her life Sue finally felt like a real woman. Her time on Paradise Island had left her with mixed feelings, but never would she have thought that her week there could have changed her life into this haven of happiness.

"I'd like that Steve. Paradise Island again."

THE END

AUTHORS NOTE:

All characters in this book are fictional. The Island itself does not exist but is based on an Island that my husband and myself have visited in the past.

Look for the sequel to this book called Return To paradise Island, where we will see some of the characters from this book return to the Island again, looking for love maybe, or just renewing it.

I hope you have enjoyed Escape to Paradise Island.

www.trishollmanauthor.com

Printed in Poland
by Amazon Fulfillment
Poland Sp. z o.o., Wrocław